A

TOM McGREGOR

PE A K
PRACTICE

PAN BOOKS

LONDON, SYDNEY AND AUCKLAND

First published 1994 by Pan Books Ltd

a division of Pan Macmillan Publishers Limited
Cavaye Place London SW10 9PG
and Basingstoke

Associated companies throughout the world

ISBN 0-330-33492-1

1 3 5 7 9 8 6 4 2

A CIP catalogue record for this book is available from
the British Library

Typeset by CentraCet Limited, Cambridge
Printed and bound in Great Britain
by Cox & Wyman Ltd, Reading, Berkshire

To Steve and Heather Paterson

The author would also like to thank the following for all their kind support and helpful advice: Gina Cronk, Lynne Dallow, Julian Murphy, Maria Rejt, Tony Virgo and Deborah Waight.

CH**A**PTER 1

Dr Jack Kerruish looked up and smiled. 'Trevor! So you've come back to us.'

Trevor Sharpe sidled sheepishly into the surgery. The sheepish look came naturally to him and had been remarked upon, unkindly, by several Cardale residents – and by the banking powers that kept Trevor as manager of a village branch, three days a week, and probably for life.

Jack gestured towards the seat opposite him. 'Not happy with the treatment you got at the Health Centre, then?'

'No.' Trevor looked peeved. 'Dr Reginald, he's all style and no substance, that man, if you ask me.' He sat down. 'Anyway,' Trevor looked accusingly across the desk, 'it wasn't you I asked to see.'

Jack sighed. 'We fitted you in at short notice, Trevor. I'm the only one on duty this early.' He picked up his tourniquet. 'We'll quickly do your blood pressure and take it from there, OK?'

Trevor took off his jacket, rolled up his sleeve and grimaced as Jack bandaged his upper arm and started pumping the tourniquet. Trevor remained silent until the brief process was over. Jack, radiating excess energy even at that early hour, then smiled reassuringly.

'Well that's perfectly normal, so no problems there.' He looked cheerily across at Trevor. 'These symptoms you were talking about – did you mention them to Dr Reginald?'

Trevor shifted uneasily in his seat. 'He said I was going through the menopause. I didn't think it was very funny.'

1

Jack did, and tried to suppress a smirk. Trevor was a very menopausal man. Keeping a straight face, he glanced down at Trevor's medical card. 'Occasional achy back . . . well . . . your driving position; could be your bed's too soft . . .' Jack failed to notice Trevor wincing. 'Nothing abnormal in your urine.' He looked up again. 'Any other clues at all?'

Trevor, on his guard, stared back. 'Like what?'

Jack shrugged. 'Anything.'

'Well . . .' Trevor squirmed slightly. 'I've been feeling a bit tired perhaps. A bit . . . you know . . . some off days. Like you get,' he added aggressively.

Jack spread his hands on the desk in front of him and lowered his voice encouragingly. 'Is there something you want to tell me, Trevor?'

Trevor's expression was a mixture of antagonism and embarrassment. 'I'm only thirty-four, you know. You don't want to feel like this at my age.'

Jack sighed. 'No. Of course not.' He picked up his pen. 'When would you say you feel the worst?'

Trevor shifted uneasily in his seat. 'Evenings. Mostly. And mornings.'

'And how long since you first noticed it?'

'A couple of weeks.'

Jack stood up and smiled. 'Well, there you go. No time at all. It'll probably go of its own accord and, if it doesn't, we'll do some blood tests.' He made to open the door for Trevor. 'But I very much doubt if it's anything to worry about.'

Trevor stood up, reluctantly. 'Is that it? What if it's something serious?'

The kindness of Jack's tone belied the increasing irritation he was feeling. 'If it's something serious, come back and tell me.'

Trevor stalked past him, obviously miffed. 'Not exactly knee deep in caring doctors, am I?'

Jack rolled his eyes heavenwards and bit back an angry

retort. Trevor Sharpe might be a bit of a local joke but he was, after all, a bank manager – manager of the bank that had nearly forced the closure of The Beeches medical practice. But that threat, thought Jack as he closed his surgery door, was firmly dead and buried.

He sat down again and thought, briefly, about the past. Nearly two years since he had left Zimbabwe and come to the Derbyshire Dales. Nearly two years since Beth Glover had invited him to join her and Will Preston at The Beeches. Jack smiled at the memory. Will's objections, while not voiced to Jack, had been written all over his sleekly handsome, supercilious face. Beth, he remembered, hadn't exactly fallen over herself either. But at least he now knew the real reason . . .

The angry buzz of the intercom jerked Jack out of his reverie. Kim's caustic tone brought him firmly back to reality. 'Is it one patient at a time, or just one per day?'

Jack smiled ruefully and buzzed back. 'Trevor Sharpe's quite enough for one day, Kim. But no, send in the next one.'

Trevor Sharpe was still looking and feeling unwell as he sat opposite a doctor for the second time that morning. But this time he was discussing mortgages, not medicine, and across from him sat Will Preston, occasional golfing partner, business client, and personal – though impecunious – customer.

Will crossed his elegant legs and smiled. 'So. It's all completed and approved. I'm impressed.'

Trevor smiled back. 'Never pushed one through so quick, but we did it. All you have to do now is move in.'

Will grimaced. 'Mmm. Move down, you mean. Doctors are supposed to get wealthier, not—'

'Wiser, Will,' interrupted Trevor. 'It's a good move. Things'll get better again.'

Something in Trevor's tone made Will look closely at him. A little frown creased his forehead. 'I'd like to think the same for you. You *do* look rough, you know. What *is* wrong with you?'

Trevor shrugged dismissively. 'Not a lot. According to Doctors Reginald and Kerruish, bugger all.' He stood up. 'Thought I might go for a walk. Fresh air . . . you know . . . might help.'

Will grinned and got to his feet. 'Good idea. Next time I come across someone really ill, I'll send them off on a ten-mile route march. But seriously, you really shouldn't be at work in this state, you know.'

Trevor looked gloomy. 'No choice. They're making managers redundant left, right and centre. I can't afford to be ill.'

Will, like every GP throughout the country, disliked the whiff of burning martyr. 'Well, for heaven's sake get down to The Beeches again and get yourself sorted out.'

Trevor looked mutinous. 'You lot never listen. Never think maybe I've got my own worries, maybe I can't sleep with it all.' He lowered his head. 'I'm just a joke, I am.'

Will, on his way to the door, now had his back to Trevor and a huge grin spread across his face. Trevor *was* a bit of a joke – and all because the poor man had got himself caught doing the sort of thing a lot of people do in their private moments. But Trevor had had the bad luck to fall off a wardrobe and break his ankle while attempting to leap on his girlfriend, and all this while dressed as a cowboy. She, poor thing, had been unable to help Trevor as she was, at the time, happily manacled to the bedposts, eagerly anticipating the attentions of her airborne lover. The extension of The Beeches overdraft had not a little to do with the fact that their rescuers had been none other than Doctors Glover and Kerruish. Cardale gossips had been all of a twitter for weeks.

Will, wiping the grin off his face, turned back to Trevor

4

and asked, with genuine concern, 'Why can't you sleep? Redundancy worries?'

'Among other things.'

Will sighed. 'Doctors aren't mind readers, Trevor. What other things?'

Trevor looked hastily around his tiny office, as if to check for lurking eavesdroppers. He approached Will and began, conspiratorially, 'Well, you know how you put everything on computer?'

'Ye–es.'

'So, what if someone tells you something really personal . . .?'

'I might not even write it down, Trevor. Unless it were medical and crucial.'

'And if it were, it'd be there for ever and ever?' Trevor was beginning to sound like one of Will's small sons.

Will was getting exasperated. 'Just say you want to discuss something and you don't want a record made.'

Trevor snorted dismissively. 'My customers say that, and I still know every damn thing there is to know about them.' He gestured back towards his desk. 'It's all on that screen.'

Will took a deep breath. 'Look, if you want professional help, you have to be honest. Try saying "I'm embarrassed, or scared" – or whatever it is – "and I need help, here and now."'

'Oh, yeah.' Trevor was unimpressed. 'Thank you and goodnight, Patience Strong.'

'OK. Please yourself.' Will picked up his briefcase and walked to the door. 'We're all scared sometimes, Trev. We all need a hand from time to time.' He looked Trevor in the eye. 'You just have to cut the crap and admit it.'

Will smiled ruefully to himself as he strode down the village street towards his parked Range Rover. Cutting the crap and admitting it; he was a fine one to talk. Most of Cardale knew about Trevor Sharpe: very few of them knew exactly what had happened to Will Preston when he had succumbed – to the great indignation of his patients – to illness himself.

Nine months ago Will had suffered a severe bout of reactive depression – akin to a nervous breakdown. For Will, product of a classic public school background, of a family renowned for the stiffness of its upper lip, the shock of being reduced to a gibbering wreck had been as nothing compared to the shame of it.

Jack Kerruish would have been surprised to know that Will still held him partly responsible for the crumbling self-esteem that had culminated in a complete breakdown. When Jack had arrived in Cardale he had found The Beeches teetering on the brink of collapse. Beth, a brilliant doctor, had never fully realized – or never wanted to realize – that a doctor's practice was also a business, and as such needed a good dose of financial acumen. Beth didn't have any; Will didn't care. As long as he could prop up his life and his marriage by doing as little doctoring as possible, playing as much golf as possible, and throwing as much money at his wife as he possibly could, he reckoned he could build a flimsy façade called happiness. But Jack's arrival – and subsequent partnership in the practice – had knocked both Will and Beth for six. Beth had called him a breath of fresh air. Will had called him an uncaring bulldozer. The energetic Jack had turned the practice upside down in a year, thrown himself with relish into village life, bowled Beth over – and almost destroyed Will.

But Jack Kerruish hadn't been the real problem. He had been the excuse. The major difficulty in Will's life had been his marriage to Sarah. Over eleven years – and all too often over the sharp antennae of their two small sons – they had battled and bickered, redefining, in the process, the concept of 'normal ups and downs'. And the final down had surprised them both; taking them back down to earth, and back together. Not that things were easy: the catalyst for Will's breakdown had been the catastrophic state of the family finances, and that, thought Will as he drove in the direction of their new house, wouldn't change overnight. Yet he was optimistic about the future: a cheaper mortgage, a job for Sarah and the novel concept of budgeting would soon get them going. Life, thought Will, was going to be good again.

Negotiating his way through the unfamiliar streets of the new estate (*executive* estate, the agent had trumpeted) that was their new neighbourhood, Will pulled up in front of the new house to find Sarah and the boys standing in a little forlorn group in the 'drive'.

Sarah smiled in relief as he approached. Clearly, the boys' first sight of their new home had failed to provoke ecstasies of delight. Too busy staring in horror, they barely acknowledged Will's arrival.

'Hi, boys!' Will was determinedly cheerful. He kissed Sarah as she tried to extol the virtues of the view to Tony and Julian. They remained silent.

'There's room for your goalposts,' Will added. 'And we thought that when we have a barbecue—'

'I'm not bringing anyone home.' Tony was adamant. And mutinous.

Sarah looked as if she were about to lose her temper. Will checked her with a gentle hand on her arm and cheerfully replied to his eldest son. 'Great! Much less work for us!'

Finally, Tony turned to his father, his little hands jammed defensively in the pockets of his duffel coat. 'Are we really poor?' The words were uttered in the same tone of shattered disbelief that patients used when they asked if they were really dying.

Sarah's eyes filled with tears.

'Christian Friers,' piped up Julian, 'says we're nearly bankrupt.'

Will sighed. He hadn't fully realized that losing the

cushion – or rather the illusion – of wealth would affect the boys so badly. Weekly boarders at a prep school, they were already, at the ages of nine and eleven, well aware of the importance of where they 'came from'. They used to come from a five-bedroomed rectory in the Cardale countryside. Now they came from an estate – and by no stretch of the imagination was it the sort of estate that would pass muster at school. That sort was in the country, with only one house on it.

Sarah and Will exchanged a look as the boys, despite themselves, ambled over to gauge the footballing potential of the front lawn. Will smiled at Sarah's beautiful, troubled face. 'You're doing great, darling.' He stroked her luxuriant mane of chestnut hair. 'We've had a hellish year, but we're still together. You're not the only one putting on a brave face, you know. I'm just as scared as you.'

Sarah looked up in surprise. The 'new' Will, the Will who admitted his true feelings, was still a novelty to her. Sometimes it unsettled her.

'Are you really?'

Will grinned. 'Terrified. That's why I keep saying stupid things. I'm scared of us failing. Losing everything.'

Sarah looked glumly at the house, making a mental note to demolish the crisp little nameplate that announced it as 'The Pines'. There wasn't a pine tree in sight. 'So am I,' she whispered.

Will took her in his arms. 'But we won't lose each other, will we?'

Sarah gazed over her husband's shoulder. She was silent for a moment. Then she changed the subject. 'When I walked into the shops today, everyone stopped talking. And the parents look at me like I've got no right to get this new job.'

Will sighed. 'I know. Doctors aren't allowed to have money problems. And doctors' wives aren't supposed to be school secretaries.' He pulled away from their embrace and jauntily tucked his arm through hers. 'Come on,

Sarah, Oh working wife, we can do it. You and me against the world.' He looked up at The Pines. 'When the cash flow's healthier we'll convert the loft.'

Sarah looked amused. 'And put on an extension; build a conservatory, yes, I know. But that's a long way off.' She sighed as they walked together up the garden path. 'I know it's not a very exciting job, but it will make a difference . . .'

'If it pays for the school uniform I'll be happy.'

Sarah stiffened slightly. 'I don't just mean money. I'll have things to talk about at the end of the day, a life outside the house. And in a couple of years I'll have a work record and be able to look for something really exciting.'

Will gazed speculatively at her. 'Like a new husband?' He meant it as a joke but Sarah suddenly jerked her arm away from his, stopped for a moment, then stalked ahead.

'Stop saying things like that, Will,' she replied angrily. 'Just stop. You say this is a fresh start, but you just keep on dragging up the past.'

Behind her, Will gestured helplessly. 'I'm sorry!' he shouted, but Sarah had disappeared into the house. He stood alone in the soulless little garden. 'I'm sorry,' he said again, in a whisper.

Patients wait for no man – not even if that man takes a day off to move house. Back at The Beeches, Jack and Beth had struggled chaotically, but happily, through a day's surgery.

'I see Trevor's already made another appointment,' said Jack gloomily as they sipped coffee together. He eyed the appointment book with distaste. 'With me.' He looked up at Beth. 'Will's not back till Tuesday, is he?'

'Mmm. Yes. No. What?' Beth looked back at him and grinned. Beth's grins lit up her entire face, transforming, in a flash of blue eyes and gleaming teeth, the serious doctor into an animated young woman.

'You haven't been listening to a word I've been saying, have you?' Jack's face, a healthily weatherbeaten contrast to Beth's smooth and glowing complexion, was wreathed in smiles. 'No,' said Beth. 'I'm far too engrossed in this.' She waved a magazine at Jack. The article was called 'Keeping Fit After Forty'.

Jack was amused. 'Oh! Planning for the future – or have you been lying to me all this time?'

Beth yawned and threw the magazine to the floor. 'Planning for *decades* away,' she replied. Then she looked at the pile of magazines still in front of them. 'We're really not getting through this lot, are we? Come on!' She jumped to her feet. 'Most of them need burning anyway.' She leafed through the next magazine. '"The Practice Nurse and Computers – Friends or Foes?"' she read. 'Yuk! That can burn in hell.'

'"Pre-Disposition to Maturity-Onset Diabetes",' retorted Jack, looking at the next publication. It too ended up on the floor.

'"The Mad Woman in the Attic and Pharmaceuticals Today." Eh?' Beth looked at the next title again, puzzled. 'I don't get it . . .'

Jack raised his tousled head, smiling. 'Come into my attic any day and you'll get it.'

Beth playfully threw the magazine at him. 'So I'm mad, am I?'

'No, just dangerous to know.'

Beth looked thoughtful for a moment. Jack missed the moment. He was studying an article about hypothermia and the old. 'You know,' he said at last, 'when you look at the state of the world . . . here we are, together, warm, well fed, doing the jobs we love—'

Amused, Beth interjected. 'That's not a case of smugness I've just detected, is it?'

'No. Contentment.' He paused for a moment, in serious contemplation. With a small shrug, he added, with conviction, 'I'm a contented man.'

For some reason Beth felt slightly irritated by his complacency. She wondered if that was how she made him feel. Complacent. Will, she recalled, had recently accused her and Jack of being joined at the hip. Beth had been wildly indignant, protesting like fury. Protesting too much, perhaps. She sighed. 'Oh, let's put this lot on the bonfire tomorrow. I'm bushed. I want to go home.'

Jack looked up, surprised at her abrupt change of tack. 'Oh! OK, then. How about I stop off on the way home and pick up a bottle of red? I'll only be a few minutes behind you.'

Beth paused on her way to the door. 'Actually . . . actually, Jack . . . I could do with a bit of a break.' She turned and smiled uncertainly. 'I'm sorry. I just want . . . I don't know,' she shrugged as if disowning the words, 'a lazy evening.'

Jack looked at her, wide-eyed. Oh, don't give me that little-boy-lost look, thought Beth. I'll melt. But Jack didn't give her the opportunity. Slightly surprised, but respecting her decision, all he said was, 'Right. Fine.'

'You know how it is,' continued Beth in a rush. 'Do all the things you do on your own. Mooch around. Soak in the bath. Read the paper and get it wet. Shout at the radio. You know.'

'Good idea,' retorted Jack brightly. 'I could do with checking my mail anyway. And I've still got that tax form to try and make sense of . . . Yeah, we can both catch up with ourselves. Good idea.' Brushing past her, he pecked her on the cheek and was gone.

But the good idea didn't last very long. Two hours later Jack was standing on Beth's doorstep, clutching a bottle of claret, and looking slightly anxious.

Beth, surprised by a caller at this late hour, and wearing only a bathrobe, opened the door a chink.

Jack waved the bottle and grinned impishly. 'A celebration. I finally filled in that flaming form.'

Beth looked at him for a moment. Then she flung open the door and grabbed him. She kissed him fiercely, possessively and passionately.

'Hey! Wow!' said Jack as they broke away and headed indoors. 'Is this what always happens when you're left on your own? I thought you might send me off with a flea in my ear.'

Beth, on her way to fetch glasses, laughed over her shoulder. 'You deserve one. It's no wonder that house of yours is smelling damp. You're never there to air it.'

'Whereas your house—'

'Smells of bubble bath.' Beth clinked the glasses, smiled lasciviously, and made for the stairs. 'This way, doctor. My back's in desperate need of a scrub . . .'

But despite the wine, the bath – and the company in the bath – Beth didn't sleep well that night. She spent much of the night alternately listening to the contented little moans that Jack made in his sleep and to the night sounds of Derbyshire that she loved so much. Did she love Jack as much, or was she – again recalling Will's words – 'stringing him along'? As the dawn broke she looked fondly at her sleeping lover. Will – perhaps resenting easy happiness when he himself had to strive so hard for it – had reckoned that Jack was about to propose to her. Then he had immediately knocked the wind out of her sails by saying that 'a little wife' was the final item Jack needed in his agenda for becoming the perfect country GP. Beth had snorted derisively. Whatever Jack's faults, they did not include proclaiming love when he didn't mean it.

Beth sighed and turned over. Love. God knows she saw enough patients whose lack of a love-life gnawed away at them until it made them physically ill. *And* she wasn't getting any younger. She smiled at the memory of 'Keeping Fit After Forty'. It wasn't, after all, *that* far off. She closed her eyes, alone with her thoughts. And when she awoke, she was alone in her bed.

'Morning, Eve!' Jack was, as always, full of vim. Eve, resentful at having to man reception for Saturday morning emergency surgeries, smiled weakly back. 'Anything yet?' continued Jack as he made for the kettle.

'Quiet as the grave.'

'Too right. The oldies have probably all died after that shindig at the Manor last night. Hell of a racket as I drove past. Any idea what it was all about?'

'Yeah. Rob Clulow – you know, the quarryman. Wife ran off. His daughter's getting married next week. Rob thought he'd have a sort of dry run for the reception.'

Jack snorted. 'Huh. Bet there was nothing dry about it. That man does like a drop occasionally.'

Then the image of a happy, inebriated Rob Clulow vanished from his mind to be replaced by the sadder, all-too-real image of a hopeful Trevor Sharpe.

'Jack . . .?' Trevor was almost hopping from one foot to the other. 'I know it's emergency surgery . . . but I thought, you know . . . if you've got a minute . . .' He faltered, unsure and embarrassed.

Jack put a friendly arm round Trevor's shoulders. 'No problem, mate. Come this way.' As he closed the door of his surgery he caught Eve's eye. They exchanged an old-fashioned, knowing look.

The two men sat down. 'I don't want to rush you, Trevor, but as this isn't an emergency—'

'Sex.' Trevor, red-faced, blurted out the word. It seemed to take him as much by surprise as it did Jack.

'I beg your pardon?'

'Sex,' repeated Trevor. He paused and then lowered his voice. 'It's all tangled up with sex.'

'Oh. I see.' Jack, too, paused, at a loss for words. 'Is it?' he added feebly.

Trevor looked angrily at Jack's computer. 'I don't want this going on hard disc.'

Jack bit his lip and answered gravely. 'It won't.'

Trevor twisted his hands in his lap and shifted uncomfortably. 'I don't know what to do,' he wailed. 'I'm meant to be getting wed this year.'

'Are you saying', enquired Jack carefully, 'that you don't feel like making love as often as you did? Or are you saying you feel like it, but can't?'

'Both.' Deeply upset, Trevor made his final confession: 'I haven't . . . you know . . . for days.'

'*Days?*' This wasn't quite what Jack expected. 'We're talking days, are we? Not weeks or months?'

Trevor looked the picture of misery. Hanging his head, he whispered into his lap, 'Days.' He sniffed. 'Last Saturday.'

Across the table Jack sat, open-mouthed and wide-eyed. He coughed discreetly and rearranged his features. 'I see. And . . . usually . . . how often do you make love?'

Now it was Trevor's turn to look astonished. 'Morning and evening,' he said matter-of-factly.

'*Every* day?'

'Yes.'

'Perhaps,' Jack's voice was gentle and careful, 'perhaps you expect too much of yourself?'

Trevor hung his head again. 'I don't expect anything of myself any more. I did a management course last month. Came tenth out of ten.'

'Is that when you started feeling ill?'

Angry with himself, with the world, Trevor almost shouted, 'I don't feel *ill*! I feel useless. I'm always tired.'

Jack paused to let the man's rage subside. 'I'm not surprised,' he continued slowly. 'Management courses, jogging, golf . . .'

'But it's not getting me anywhere, is it? People who joined the bank after me are already at head office. I just want to prove myself . . .' He looked imploringly at Jack.

'There's more to life than success and sex, you know, Trevor.'

'Oh?' Trevor was surprised – and interested.

'Well . . . affection, for instance. Commitment. Do you and your fiancée ever just cuddle?'

'Before or after, you mean?'

Jack had to bite his lip so viciously it nearly bled. Then he smiled in what he hoped was a doctorly way. 'Trevor,' he said, standing up and looking at his watch. 'I really think we're going to need some time with this one. This really isn't the right moment. I'll see you on Tuesday.' He ushered Trevor towards the door. 'But do think about what I've said, OK?'

Trevor, looking bemused but not unhappy, smiled at Jack. 'I will, Jack. I will.'

Jack couldn't resist telling Beth about his session with Trevor. They were, as arranged that morning, tramping through the Dales up Bull Ridge to the Fox House and the 'mean plate of chips' that Jack had joked was his reward for accompanying Beth on her favourite walk. Beth, pensive until now, giggled guiltily. 'Oh dear. Those two. I wonder where they get the energy from?'

'Dunno.' Jack, hands in pockets, was striding along with the loping gait common to those who embrace life with overpowering enthusiasm. Then he put one arm round Beth's shoulder. Her dog Connal, yards ahead, and forewarned by the intuition of the possessive, looked back inquisitively. 'Poor sods,' continued Jack. 'Nudge nudge, wink wink everywhere they go.'

'Bit like us really.'

'Oh! Who nudges?'

'Well, Ellie and Kim for one.'

'For two,' corrected Jack. Then he laughed good-naturedly. 'They only do it because they know it gets right up your nose.'

'I know.' Beth sighed. 'It's so boring.' She stopped abruptly and surveyed the scene. They were near the top of the ridge, and a great swathe of Derbyshire undulated gloriously beneath them. Beth breathed deeply, looking at, but not seeing, the panorama before her. 'Don't *you* find it boring?' she asked.

But Jack hadn't heard her question. Standing beside her, he too breathed deeply, as if mustering all his strength. Then the words came out in a rush. 'It's never going to be easy to say this, Beth, so I may as well get it over with . . .'

But Beth had turned away. 'I'm really hungry,' she said, 'and if we leave it too late—'

Jack stopped her, looking gravely into her eyes. 'Beth, we work together, sleep together, we share the same principles . . .'

'Not really.' Beth's voice was bright – and forced.

'We do. OK,' he smiled, 'a few little political differences here and there . . . But so what – if we love each other . . .?'

Beth couldn't bear it. 'Please, don't.' She looked away from him, her eyes again unseeing. 'I knew this was coming . . .'

'If we do,' continued Jack, oblivious to her reaction, 'and I think we do' – he faltered – 'and I *know* we do, we should make it permanent. Formal. Get wed.' Each syllable sent a jolt through Beth's body. Jack ploughed on, his every word reinforcing his conviction. 'Getting married makes sense. The way we're living now doesn't.'

'It does to me,' said Beth quietly. 'I'm not ready to be settled.'

'But, *Beth*. You've lived in Cardale nearly all your life. You're already settled.'

'No, I'm not.'

Jack was both puzzled and exasperated. 'Oh, come on . . .'

'Don't tell me what I am.' Beth's voice sounded ominously sharp.

Jack ignored her and continued. 'And we just about live together. We must have slept together three weeks in the last four.'

'And on the fourth week I needed breathing space from you.'

Hearing his sharp intake of breath, realizing that her words had really stung, Beth turned to face him. 'Look, I didn't mean . . .'

'So tell me about this breathing space you need so much.' Jack's tone was challenging, his stance stubborn.

Beth shrugged, wearily and unwillingly entering into combat. 'OK. But you started this, not me.' She bent to stroke Connal, now protectively at her side. With a sigh, she began: 'I've had everything. Career, friends, enough money to get by and lots of plans. The feeling of *going* somewhere.' She hesitated, looking at the scenery with a new and critical eye. 'And then I came home, "just for a year", to help out Dad at The Beeches.' She paused. 'Dad died six years later, and I was still here.' Gesturing defiantly, she continued, 'But I still had plans. A sense of going somewhere. I still have, Jack . . . I'm still going somewhere. So don't', Beth was adamant, 'tell me I'm settled.'

Jack shrugged. 'Sorry.' It didn't sound like an apology. 'So where exactly *are* you going?'

This was too much for Beth. Angrily, she whirled round and snapped at him, 'You've got no right to cross-examine me in that patronizing bloody way of yours. "Where exactly *are* you going?"' she mimicked. 'I don't even know if I'd want you along.'

That really stung. Jack rounded on her. 'You don't know what you want' – it was his turn to mimic her tone – 'except that you don't want me. You don't know where you're going except that you don't want me beside you. Good life-plan, Beth.'

Beth sighed, determined not to lose her temper again. 'Look, you've travelled, seen the world and all that. Now you want the opposite and—'

'No!'

'And I *don't*. I don't *want* to marry anyone. I'm not ready to bow out.'

'Bow out? Aren't you mixing up marriage with cardiac arrest?'

'Oh . . . probably.' Beth sighed in exasperation; tired of the subject; tired of the little bits of hurt they were flinging at each other.

'I don't see getting wed as the end of anything,' Jack pointed out reasonably. Beth didn't respond. A sudden gust of wind made them both huddle, separately, into their jackets. And then the futility of the situation got to Jack. 'You talk like I want to own you,' he shouted above the wind, 'stop you, wreck your life. Well, thanks. Thanks a lot, Beth. You really think a lot of me, don't you?' Turning in fury, he began to stomp down the hill, his every step taking him away from Beth, away from companionship, away from the suddenly desolate hilltop and the heavy, brooding rain-clouds sweeping the sky.

Connal, still at Beth's side, whined and wagged his tail expectantly. She looked down at him and blinked. 'And you can bloody shut up, too,' she snapped as the tears began to course down her cheeks.

chAPTER 2

Colin Meadows, striding heavily in his work boots, burst through his front door. 'Ey up. I'm here, love.' Then he stopped, horrified, taking in the scene before him. Wide-eyed and angry, he turned to his wife, 'The foreman said it wasn't an emergency!'

Anne Meadows, as calm as her husband was agitated, looked placidly at him. 'It isn't. But I knew you'd create if I didn't ring the factory . . .'

'Not an emergency!' Colin looked again at the sofa in the little front room – at his daughter lying prone, under a quilt, struggling for every breath, dry wheezing. Her face was almost blue and her terrified eyes were fixed imploringly on the man kneeling at her side.

Colin too knelt, gazed lovingly at his daughter, and took her cold hand. 'Hello, love,' he whispered gently and then, angrily, he looked at the other man. 'Who's this?' he barked.

Anne, hovering behind him, spoke again. 'John, this is my husband Colin.'

'Never mind who I am!' shouted Colin. 'Who the hell is *he*?'

'He', until now mouthing silent words over the struggling Penny, offered his hand to Colin. 'I'm John Adams.' Colin just looked. 'From the Laybourne church.'

Colin, with renewed anger, rounded on his wife. 'The church? So you're bringing them home now, are you?'

Penny, upset, managed a weak 'Daddy, please . . .'

'There, there, that's my girl.' He patted her hand. 'You're doing fine.' Then, concern replacing anger, he addressed Anne. 'Did she take her puffer when she woke up?'

'She was all right first thing—'

'What odds does that make?' Colin shouted. 'She takes that every day, no matter what. What's got into you?'

Anne tried to calm her husband. 'You saw her eating breakfast,' she pleaded. 'She was fine. We were on the way to school and she got wheezy. So I called John and asked him to pray with us.'

Colin fought back a blasphemous response. 'Don't be daft, Anne,' he said levelly. 'She needs the doctor.'

'Daddy.' Penny spoke with great effort. 'I don't mind. Honest.'

Colin stood up abruptly. 'Where's her stuff? Penny, where's your medicine?'

'Stop getting her excited! Leave it, Colin—'

'Get him out!' Colin jabbed a furious finger in John's direction. 'Get him out and find her puffer.'

John Adams looked up. 'Just two or three minutes, Mr Meadows. Please.'

Colin hesitated in mid-stride as Penny added, 'He's nice, Dad.' She reached feebly for her father's hand. 'He's nice.'

'You're making her worse,' snapped Anne.

'Please. Just two quiet minutes.'

Colin, still hostile, still reluctant, gave in for the sake of his only child. 'OK,' he nodded. 'Two minutes. And no gobbledygook.' Then, able to bear neither his daughter's distress nor the sight of his wife and John Adams praying over her, he went into the kitchen to search for her inhalers.

Silence, apart from the agonized labouring of Penny's breathing, reigned in the sitting-room. And then the child's breath became easier, softer, gentler, and the warm glow of health returned to her face.

Anne went into the kitchen where her husband was crashing about, opening cupboards, rifling through Penny's schoolbag, frantically searching. He sensed, rather than saw, his wife approaching. 'I'll phone the doctor, then,' he said through tight lips, 'if you've finished playing silly buggers.'

Anne laid a gentle hand on his arm. 'No need. Oh, Colin, it's so . . .' She gazed dreamily towards the door. 'She's fine.'

Colin, now rummaging through a drawer, didn't hear her. 'It's not like her to lose them . . .'

Anne laughed. He looked sharply, crossly at her. 'Really, she's fine. Look.' Anne opened the door to the picture of the seven-year-old lying peacefully and happily under the quilt. 'You see? I told you.'

John Adams came into the kitchen, a little smile on his unlined face.

'Thank you *so* much.' Anne was nearly tearful in her gratitude.

'Please,' replied John piously, 'don't thank *me*.'

Closing the kitchen door, Anne dropped the contents of her left hand on the kitchen counter. A beatific smile played on her lips. 'We won't need these any more, then, will we?' she said as the inhalers clattered on to the formica.

'Bloody hell!' Colin watched her in disbelief. '*You* had them!'

Ignoring him, Anne addressed John again. 'If only we'd known about you before. All the times we've had to sit and watch her suffer.'

Colin was aghast. 'How could you? How *could* you stand there, watching her fight for air?'

Anne turned on him. 'I've watched her doing that for years. With every puffer and every spray they've ever made. She's had enough of that. She's sick of it all and so am I.'

'So you'd rather have some prat praying over her?'

John looked forgivingly at the floor as Anne continued, suddenly exhausted, yet quietly triumphant. 'She's

21

sleeping. You can see that for yourself. Without us pumping her full of drugs.'

John sat down and addressed Colin. 'She's healed.'

'*What?*'

'She's cured, Mr Meadows. No more asthma. Ever again.'

Anne's churchgoing was the only bone of contention in the Meadows's otherwise harmonious marriage. Originally it hadn't posed a problem: Colin wasn't a believer, Anne was, and they both reckoned their daughter ought to be given the opportunity to make her mind up for herself. So every Sunday, Anne had taken Penny to church, hoping that she would enjoy the experience, but careful not to force religion down her throat.

And then, one recent Sunday, the pastor had introduced John Adams from the Evangelical outreach group. Excitable and afire with enthusiasm, his preaching had startled the elderly Cardale worshippers – and galvanized the young. After every phrase of his delivery, the youth group choir with him yelled, 'Yes!' or 'Praise the Lord!' Penny had found it tremendously exciting. Anne wasn't so sure until she began to take in what he was saying.

'Are you tired, weary, heartbroken?' Then he would punch the air with the Bible he held in his left hand. 'Here's your answer! Are you ill? Here's your answer! Is there anyone suffering at this very moment from some weakness of the spirit or of the body? Here's your answer!' And then, eyes blazing with the passion of his delivery, he lowered his voice, pointed to the Bible and stared intently at the congregation. 'Here's your answer. Only have faith and these things will fall away. There is no need for any of you to suffer.' A pause. 'Only have faith, and all these things will be healed.'

In the stunned silence that followed, the pastor caught the eye of old Alice North in the front row. She was positively bristling with disapproving rage. The pastor smiled sympathetically at her, as if saying, 'This isn't exactly my thing either.' Alice glared back.

And then John Adams had introduced members of his own flock, youngsters who bore witness, he said, to the goodness and power of God. The God for whom absolutely nothing was impossible . . .

During an impassioned testimony from a young woman whose arthritis had been cured by prayer, Anne had looked thoughtfully down at her daughter. The girl was still breathing heavily, wheezing after the effort of rushing to church. Anne looked back at the woman at the lectern, now waving her arms, finishing with an impassioned '. . . and God *heard*!'

It was then that Anne made up her mind; she would no longer do battle with doctors – she would have faith and work wonders with God.

Sarah Preston, after two weeks, was still hating her job at the village school. She found it demeaning, boring, and she knew she was the subject of many a knowing glance. Parents who came to collect their children made no secret of the fact that they thought she was 'hoity toity'. When she first heard the phrase applied to her, Sarah had nearly laughed. Hoity toity? They ought to try telling that to Will's mother, she thought. The old bag had all but told Sarah, on her engagement to Will, that she hoped she would 'lose her regional accent'. Sarah had spent the last eleven years hoping that Will would lose his mother. Neither event had happened.

Sarah had confidently expected that being a school secretary would finally give her a life outside the rarefied world of medicine: a world in which she was so involved – yet so excluded. And now this. She smiled ruefully as she cradled the girl's head in her arms. At least now 'the doctor's wife' had become useful. Looking down at the girl's pained expression and pallid face, Sarah gently stroked the hair out of her eyes. 'Try and relax, Penny. Try not to panic. The doctor'll soon be here.' Sarah wondered if 'the doctor' on call would be her husband.

It wasn't. It was Jack Kerruish. At that moment he came running into the classroom with Ellie, The Beeches' nurse, in tow. The headmistress, puffing slightly, was behind them. 'We haven't been able to help her at all . . .' she trailed off, relieved that she no longer had to assume control in a situation which defeated her.

Jack smiled briefly, gratefully, at Sarah, and then at Penny. 'Penny. Hello. We'll soon have you right.' He turned back to Sarah. 'How long has she been like this?'

'It started about ten minutes ago but then it all got much worse.'

Ellie, busy at Jack's side, offered him the peak flow meter. 'No,' he said. 'Nebulizer, please. That can wait.' As Ellie unwound the tube from the nebulizer mask and handed the mask to him, he noticed the Ventolin puffer at Sarah's side. 'How much of that has she had?'

'None,' replied Sarah. 'She didn't bring her own and by the time we got her spare she was like this.' She looked at Penny, worried.

Jack, busy with his doctor's bag, muttered to Ellie, 'Salbutamol, 2.5 milligrams.' He took the mask from her, now ready for use. 'Now, Penny, the magic mask.'

They watched as Jack put the mask to Penny's face. 'Wait for the magic to work, Penny,' whispered Ellie.

Penny's agonized wheezing grew quieter. Jack sighed in relief. His jocular tone since his arrival had belied the desperate anxiety he had felt on seeing Penny. She had been close to death.

'Is that it?' asked Sarah. 'Will she be OK now?'

'It'll take a while to absorb the full dose but yes, she's out of the woods. Aren't you, Penny?'

Penny managed a weak smile, and raised her little thumb. Jack stood up, addressing Ellie, 'If you could use the peak flow now?' As he turned to the headmistress the smile disappeared from his face. 'May I use your phone?'

Ten minutes later an ambulance and a taxi drew simultaneously to a halt outside the school. In swift, practised movements, the ambulancemen alighted from their vehicle and moved towards Penny, now secure in a wheelchair being pushed by Jack. Anne Meadows beat them to it. 'Where do you think you're taking her?' she snapped.

Penny, knowing what was about to happen, lifted her mask. 'I got ill again, Mum,' she said quietly.

Jack smiled. Reassuringly, he thought. 'It's OK, Mrs Meadows. She'll be fine now . . .'

'She's not going to hospital!'

'Anne—' began Ellie.

'No!' Anne turned to the bemused ambulancemen. 'You're not needed.'

Jack, gently laying a hand on her arm, tried to lead her out of her daughter's earshot. 'Mrs Meadows,' he said quietly, 'she hasn't recovered as well as we'd like. I'd like to admit her. Just to be sure . . .'

'What for?'

'Nothing, I hope. But her chest's so noisy, I can't be certain. She's best in hospital. Really. Just overnight.'

'No.' Anne returned to the wheelchair and stood protectively by her daughter. 'Why have you done this to her? She was better. She was well.'

The taller of the two ambulancemen, keen to be on his way, looked imploringly at Anne. 'If the doctor says she's ill, Mrs Meadows—'

'Her nails', interjected Jack, 'were going blue. It was bad.' He looked enquiringly at Mrs Meadows. 'She tells me she's had a couple of attacks this last week.'

'Has she been taking her medicine?' asked Ellie.

Anne, suddenly aggressive, put her hands on her hips. 'Medicine! Drugs! Soon as she was born, the first thing you did was shove her into an incubator.' With the pain of a doting mother, she added, 'She never had the chance to

25

be a normal child.' Then she made up her mind. Bending towards Penny, she helped her out of the wheelchair. 'Well, that's it – I'm taking her home.'

The ambulanceman sighed, raised his eyes, and looked at Jack. 'Are we taking her or aren't we?'

'Hang on. Yes, you are. Mrs Meadows! I strongly advise against this.'

But Anne was on her way to the waiting taxi, Penny at her side. 'Advise away,' she called over her shoulder. Jack ran after her. 'OK. OK, no ambulance, but let me take you to see her consultant.'

Anne turned on him, eyes blazing with fury. 'She's seen him every month for years! What's he going to do now he hasn't tried already . . .?'

'Mrs Meadows,' Jack was having difficulty in not raising his voice, 'Penny hasn't recovered fully. This is very unwise . . .'

Bundling her daughter into the taxi, she slammed the door with a last, defiant look at the little group outside the school. Anne Meadows had had enough.

As the taxi pulled away, Jack stamped his foot in frustration. 'Damn!'

Ellie sighed. 'These little things are sent to try us . . .' She trailed off, hit by a new and worrying thought. 'Did you start her on steroids?' she asked Jack.

Jack raised his eyes heavenwards. 'Oh, hell. No. I was so keen to get her to hospital.' Frustration and irritation were written all over his face. 'Great. Well, that's just great. Once the nebulizer wears off she'll be back to square one.'

Ellie considered the implications of this for a moment. 'When Anne's calmed down she'll let you finish the treatment properly.'

'Yeah. I suppose so.' He sighed. 'Come on. I'd better finish surgery and then visit them at home.'

*

But Anne Meadows was, if anything, even more defiant on her own doorstep than she had been outside Penny's school. Arms crossed, she stood on the threshold of her home, barring Jack entry.

'I *have* to speak to you and Mr Meadows.' Jack did nothing to keep the concern out of his voice.

'He's at work,' replied Anne shortly. Then she started closing the door.

'*Please* . . .' Jack stepped forward, as if to force his way indoors. 'I'm very concerned about Penny.' Seeing the expression on Anne's face, he added, 'Shall I try to get Dr Glover, would you prefer that?'

'I won't let any of you in, to make her ill all over again.'

Jack, feeling utterly helpless and defeated by Anne's logic, sighed in exasperation. '*How* are we making her sick?'

'We don't need you. All she needs is her church and our prayers.'

Jack groaned. Oh, God. So that was it. This wasn't just a desperate mother he was up against. This was the full force of two thousand years of dogmatic devotion. 'Her church? Is that what this is all about?' The door closed further. 'Mrs Meadows. *Please*. It's very important that I at least give her a tablet. Just something to get her over tonight. She must be exhausted . . .'

'No. All she needs is a bit of peace. Thank you for trying, but please leave us alone.'

Jack was left with one last, desperate card to play. As the door closed in his face he played it. 'Mrs Meadows, if you won't let me in I'll have to call the social services. I'll have no choice.'

That hit home. Anne Meadows's face reappeared, registering an appalled mixture of horror and disbelief. 'Social services? What, social workers?'

'What else can I do?' Jack opened his arms in almost religious supplication. 'I'm sorry. If Penny doesn't receive treatment, if you allow the effects of the salbutamol to wear off—'

'If. If. If!'

'—she might die!'

Anne was stunned into silence by the enormity of the thought. Jack seized the opportunity for another, gentler approach. 'Really.' He nodded. 'You're putting her life at risk.'

But the shock had worn off. Anne's lips settled back into a thin, defiant line. 'She's fine.'

'For now, yes.'

'She's fine and she's going to stay fine. She's cured.'

Exhausted and exasperated, Jack lost his temper. 'For God's sake, she's not "cured". Look, Mrs Meadows, your child is in grave danger. She's exhausted already. If I have to get an emergency order, I will.' He looked at her, pleading. 'But I'd prefer not to.'

Anne had had enough. Things like this didn't happen to people like her. Not to decent, caring mothers. 'Go away,' she snapped. 'She's my child and I'll not hand her over to any social worker.' With that, she slammed the door in Jack's face.

He stared impotently at it, at the barrier between life and death. 'Bugger,' he whispered. He turned and walked away, his shoulders slumped in defeat.

On the other side of the door, Anne looked worriedly at her daughter, again lying prone on the sitting-room sofa.

'What did the doctor say, Mum?' The voice was pained, each word an effort.

'Nothing.'

Penny looked at her mother and gestured in agony. 'My chest, I can't . . . I want my puffer . . .'

'We don't need it. Remember?' Anne smiled and held her daughter's hands. 'It's all right, love, I'm here.'

'My puffer . . . It's getting worse, Mum . . . call Daddy!'

Anne was already on her way to the phone. 'I will. Just as soon as I've called the church.'

'I don't want the church! I want Daddy!'

But Anne, oblivious to her daughter's pleas, had already dialled the familiar number.

John Adams was beginning to have doubts. Not about his faith – that was still intact – but about the faith others had in him and in the power of healing. Was he, as the pastor had intimated, getting a high out of what he preached? Was it – as the pastor had actually said – all about satisfying *his* needs more than the needs of others? He had been annoyed at the time, had taken the pastor's remarks as personal jealousy, as an example of the failure of older churchmen to move with the times. Yet, afterwards, he had admitted to himself that there was more than an element of truth in those remarks; that, yes, he got a tremendous rush of adrenalin from standing up in front of a congregation, enthusing them, having them *believe* in him. Anne Meadows had believed. More than that, she had embraced his words with an almost terrifying zeal. And he had let her believe.

But that belief (and his own arrogance?) hadn't, after all, healed her daughter. The last time he had set foot in the Meadows's house, he had been filled with hope. This time, as he entered the small sitting room, he was filled with fear. Penny was barely conscious. But Anne was relieved. The burden rested with him. Salvation was here.

'Everything's all right, Penny,' she was saying as she clasped her daughter's cold hands. 'Look who's arrived . . .'

'She can't even hear you, can she?' said John, terrified.

Anne looked at him – fiercely, imploringly, *believingly*. 'She just can't catch her breath to answer. Lay your hands on her. Heal her. Pray.'

Seeing his hesitation, refusing to acknowledge the doubt on his face, she grabbed his hand and put it to Penny's head.

'Heal her,' she commanded. 'You did it before.'

'I . . . I didn't do it. God did it . . .'

'Then tell him to do it again.'

It was true, thought John as he applied himself to his impossible task: the pastor had been right. He hadn't been doing this for Penny as much as he'd been doing it for himself. And now there was nothing he *could* do.

'I . . .'

Before Anne could round on him with further entreaties, they were interrupted by the loud, impatient knock on the door.

'Oh, God!' Anne flew to the window. Seeing the couple on the doorstep, she put her hand to her mouth in horror and, in near hysteria, wailed to John, 'It's the doctor again!'

John visibly relaxed. 'Oh, thank God. Let him in!'

'No! He wants to get the social.' Then she stared hard at the kneeling churchman and barked out a hysterical command. 'Pray!' Approaching him, almost threatening in her zeal, she started to shout. 'Come on. You said it was easy. Only have faith . . .'

John bent his head over Penny and closed his eyes. Marshalling his jumbled thoughts, he tried to pray. But Anne, beside him, was hysterical. 'She's not getting any better,' she screamed. '*Do* something!'

As the frantic knocks on the door increased with Anne's mounting rage, John prayed. Except it was for himself. 'Oh, God. Oh, God, oh, God,' he mouthed. 'Do something. Help us. Help her . . .'

Anne looked at him in contempt. 'You liar,' she screamed. 'You liar!'

'I've never seen anyone like this. I don't know what to do . . . you'll have to let the doctor in.'

'No! He's getting a court order! He wants her taken away . . .' Looking down at her daughter, realizing the full horror of the situation, she moaned, 'Oh, God, Penny, I'm sorry . . . I'll get Daddy.'

But John had already gone for help. Flinging open the

30

front door, he stared, wide-eyed and desperate, at Jack Kerruish. 'She's dying. Please, do something, she's dying.'

It had been Ellie's idea to try once more with Anne before calling an emergency social worker. Offering to accompany Jack, she had reckoned that she might be able to make Anne see reason. Now, following hard on Jack's heels as he rushed past John Adams, she wasn't so sure. Anne, still hysterical, was standing by her daughter. 'Leave her alone! Don't touch her!'

As Jack knelt beside the girl, Ellie tried to calm her mother. 'Anne, please . . .'

Mrs Meadows wrenched her arm from Ellie's. 'I don't want him touching her—'

'She needs help—'

'No! He wants to take her into care. Don't touch her!' she screamed at Jack as he gathered Penny into his arms.

Jack ignored her and turned to Ellie. 'Start the car, Ellie. We're going to hospital.'

Jack rubbed his eyes and looked imploringly at Beth. It was now seven-thirty, three hours after Penny's dramatic arrival at the children's hospital. Penny, thanks to the ministrations of the paediatrician, was now safely in the admissions room, in a bed, and looking more stable. Her mother, however, was not. The raw nerve that Jack had touched by mentioning every parent's nightmare, the social worker, was still exposed. And with Colin Meadows now adding to his wife's hysterical invective, accusing him of kidnapping their daughter, Jack had been left with only one option – to call Beth.

Asking her for professional help had not come easily to him. Relations between them, since their disastrous confrontation up on Bull Ridge, had been more than mildly

31

strained. Beth had tried her best to ensure that their relationship continued as it had done before, and Jack, because he loved her, had tried to comply. Yet now there was a chasm between them. Accustomed to getting his own way, not used to being spurned, Jack couldn't help but feel he was being taken for a ride. And he couldn't help feeling that Beth had made a fool of him. Still partners, still lovers, Jack was beginning to wonder if they were still friends. Beth, who was almost revered in Cardale, carried on as before: confident, secure, knowing her place in the community. Jack, on the other hand, was beginning to feel that everything had happened too quickly – that he had elbowed his way into the community and into Beth's life, that he had pushed too hard for the security and sense of belonging that he craved. And now, with the Meadowses treating him as if he were from an alien planet, he had a distinct and unpleasant sensation of being elbowed out on every front.

Sitting beside Anne Meadows, Beth was sympathetic, but firm. 'I'm sorry, Anne, but I'd have done exactly the same as Dr Kerruish.' She smiled reassuringly at Anne.

'Well, you would say that, wouldn't you,' interjected Colin. Nodding at Jack, he continued, '*He* pushed his way in like some bloody pied piper. Wouldn't listen to Anne . . . oh, no . . . just barged in and kidnapped our Penny.'

'I was *asked* to go in,' corrected Jack. He looked imploringly at Beth. 'Someone came to the door and said she was dying . . .'

'Who?' asked Beth, puzzled.

'John Adams,' said Anne reverentially. 'From the church . . .'

But her husband, sensing that this was no way to get Beth on their side, interrupted her. 'You said', he told Beth, 'that she should be kept calm when she was poorly.' He looked accusingly at Jack. 'He upset her. He was too hasty.'

'In my medical opinion, the child was in danger . . .'

Anne glared contemptuously at Jack. 'You don't even know Penny.'

'I had to make a decision on what I saw at the time. I was concerned about her heart.'

'Oh, it's her *heart* now, is it?' Anne's tone was scathing. 'There's never been anything wrong with her heart.'

'If the oxygen level falls too far she's at risk of a cardiac arrest.'

Colin snorted derisively. 'You're all talk, you. You acted too hasty and you know it and now you're fishing around for—'

But before he could finish they were interrupted by a commotion behind the swing doors. Suddenly and violently, they were pushed open by two nurses, wheeling a trolley at speed. Running behind them, his face taut with anxiety, was the paediatrician.

Anne Meadows shot to her feet. Her hand flew to her mouth. 'Oh, no! Oh, my *God*!' Colin, Jack and Beth looked in horror at the trolley. Under a crisp sheet, immobile and deathly pale, lay Penny Meadows. She looked peaceful and happy – as if she had finally given up the painful and impossible struggle to stay alive.

Seeing them all standing there, the paediatrician paused briefly. 'I'm sorry . . . bit of a rush,' he said distractedly. 'You can come up with us.'

'Where?' asked Colin, his eyes fixed on the departing trolley. The paediatrician looked at him in surprise. 'Intensive Care Unit. We're putting her on a ventilator.'

A little moan escaped Anne Meadows's lips and then her feet gave way beneath her.

'You handled it well, Jack, bringing her in.' Jack, Beth and David Ashmore – the only man who had ever caused Anne Meadows to faint – were standing by the door of the Intensive Care Unit. They were all looking at Penny, now surrounded by tubes, monitors and all the paraphernalia of emergency hospital care. But the emergency was over. The girl now had some colour in her face and her parents, still shaken but visibly relieved, sat at either side of her bed.

Jack shook his head. 'I didn't handle it very well at all. Believe me.'

David, now aware of the discord between Jack and the Meadowses, was reassuring. 'If she'd been left any longer she'd have died. I've told the parents, for what it's worth.' Then he looked quizzically at Jack. 'Did I hear the words "social workers"?'

Jack smiled with regret. 'You did.'

'Ouch.' David sucked in his breath. 'Fifty pence in the swear box.'

'I know, I know.' Jack sighed and added, 'It really shouldn't be like that.'

'Some words are more terrifying than your average shark attack, Jack. Top of the list these days is "social worker". Anyway,' he nodded towards the Meadows family, 'it's OK now. She's over the worst.' He looked at his watch. 'I've got to grab a bite to eat now.' With a friendly smile at Beth and a sympathetic nod to Jack, he was gone.

Beth, indicating to Jack that they ought to leave Penny with her parents, called over to Anne. 'We'll pop back in the morning, Anne.'

But Penny's mother remained bent over her child. It was Colin who replied, 'Thanks, doctor.' Then he took in Jack's presence. 'But don't bring him.'

Beth couldn't let that one lie. 'Mr Meadows . . .'

'We'll only be seeing you or Dr Preston from now on.' He paused, now openly hostile, and addressed Jack directly. 'There's some things you just don't do to people, decent people.' His contemptuous glare indicated that Jack was the last person in the world to be considered decent.

Jack opened his mouth to reply. Then he shrugged, turned away, and left the room.

Beth caught up with him in the car park. Both too dispirited even to mention the events of the evening, they walked in silence to their cars. Then Beth noticed the upright figure walking briskly towards the hospital entrance.

'Neil!'

'Hello, Beth!' The pastor, ever cheerful in times of adversity, smiled at both doctors. 'How's she doing?'

'She's in ICU. Holding her own.'

Jack, now recognizing Neil, addressed him curtly. 'I don't think they need any more church intervention.'

Neil paused. 'Er . . . John Adams—'

Jack snorted. 'Oh, yes, the faith healer. Mumbling more mumbo-jumbo amongst the terminally ill, I suppose?'

Beth laid a restraining hand on Jack's arm. 'Jack . . .'

The pastor addressed them both, almost apologetically. 'Em . . . no. John Adams has . . . he's left.'

'Left?'

'Yes. Left.'

'The church?'

'He doesn't know yet. He's left Cardale. The bishop . . . well, he and the bishop decided he should take some time out. Sort things out, you know.' Embarrassed, not wishing to elaborate further, he smiled warmly at Beth and continued into the hospital.

Beth broke the ensuing, pensive silence. 'What is it with you and the church?'

Jack shrugged. 'We don't mix ever so well.'

'I had noticed.' Looking towards the hospital, Beth added, 'Neil's OK. He'll talk more sense into Anne than all your badgering will.'

Jack looked at her, stricken. 'Badgering?'

Beth sighed and fished in her handbag for her keys. 'No. I'm sorry. Not badgering. Your impulsive, speak-now-think-later approach.' She looked up at him and smiled wearily. 'We need some rest. Goodnight, Jack.'

This was not what Jack needed. Already feeling excluded, he now felt rejected. 'You don't . . . er . . . fancy coming over to my place?' It was the closest to pleading he had ever got.

But Beth was already opening her car door. 'No. Not tonight, Jack.'

'Or . . .?'

'See you tomorrow.' With that she ducked into the car, gunned the engine, and was gone.

ch**A**pter 3

The Prestons had settled into their new house with ease rather than enthusiasm. Even Tony and Julian, after their initial, horrified reactions, rarely mentioned it – and never at school. But there remained one big bone of contention – their parents' ban on their going to the recreation ground near the estate.

'Why can't we go to the rec?' complained Tony as he struggled with his football boots. 'It's got a proper goal and everything.'

Will sighed and looked at his eldest son. 'Because', he said, 'it's also got yobs and bikes and dog droppings. You know the rule, Tony, it's the garden or nothing.'

Tony glared moodily at this father. 'Everyone else goes there.'

Will, feeling sorry for the boy, yet with no intention of giving in to him, cuffed him playfully on the shoulder. 'Well, you're not "everyone else". Now shoo, and I'll be out in a minute.'

Heading out of the kitchen, the boys nearly collided with Sarah and the large basket of dirty washing she was carrying. Will grinned as he watched his wife struggling with the precarious load. Sarah could never look like a washerwoman, let alone a housewife. As always, she was immaculately made-up and casually, though elegantly dressed. She was also looking harassed.

'You can have first turn at goalie,' Will said to her.

'You certainly know how to sweet-talk a girl.' Sarah wrenched open the door of the washing machine. But she was smiling as she turned to Will. 'Maybe later,' she added. 'I've got to clear up a bit first.' She surveyed the less-than-immaculate kitchen and sighed. 'Every time you turn round the place gets in a state.'

Will gently put his hands on her shoulders. 'It's fine. The house is fine. Really.' He smiled into her eyes.

'But you're still a doctor, Will.' Sarah's voice had risen, taking on a note of petulance. 'You're still a professional man. Suppose someone called in now?'

Will looked at the tiny kitchen. It looked all right to him. Not what he was used to. Not what Sarah had become used to. But not exactly a slum. Except, possibly, for the sad, dead house plant on the window sill. He picked it up, earmarking it for the bin. 'I think we'll pass muster, Sarah, so long as it's not the Prince of Wales.' He looked gravely at his wife. 'We're not the only ones in some financial embarrassment.'

Sarah looked back at him. She could feel the tension rising in her shoulders, could feel the flash of anger ready to burst. She fought both – and won. Smiling at Will, all she said was, 'I know.'

Sarah had made a pact with herself that after Will's breakdown she, too, would change. Always prone to wild mood swings, rarely stopping to think before she vented her anger, she had not, she conceded to herself, been the easiest person to live with. And she had fought so hard to try to change Will, to make him more successful, more ambitious, more ready to fight for what she saw as his due. And then, after his ghastly 'episode', as they called it, after her complete inability to cope with it, she had taken stock and realized that she couldn't change her husband – she could only change her attitude towards him. If Will and Jack Kerruish – chalk and cheese personified – could now rub along together as partners and even as friends, then she ought to be able to do the same.

After all, she thought as she watched him rather ineptly drying dishes, she had *chosen* him – and there was a lot to be said for her choice. She looked at his blond head, now bent over the sink. He was good-looking, an extremely good father, his patients seemed to like him and both Beth and Jack had fought incredibly hard to keep him when he had nearly thrown his entire career down the tubes. Sarah, obviously, had been the only one to think he was weak. But then she was incredibly strong.

'D'you really think', she asked, anxious to change the subject, 'that we'll get an invitation to the captain's dinner?'

'We have for the last three years.' He smiled reassuringly at her. 'They'll be sending the invitations out in alphabetical order. Probably get ours tomorrow.'

Sarah nodded. She wasn't so sure. News travelled fast in Cardale, and the news of their change of circumstances had travelled swiftly through the Dales and was talked about, she was sure, at the golf club. And the club, that bastion of the business community, was also the social barometer of Cardale. The lack of an invitation to the captain's dinner would be more effective than a public slap in the face. Antonia Preston, Will's mother, had once made a point of telling Sarah that the ability to play both golf and bridge made one socially acceptable anywhere in the world. Antonia had known full well that Sarah could play neither. Sarah shuddered at the memory. What had made it so hurtful was that, in her heart of hearts, Sarah knew that it was true: now more than ever.

And then she looked around her, at her new home, and smiled ruefully. A new and not pleasant thought occurred to her. 'When you sell the car,' she mused, 'we could say it was too big for the new garage. There's no reason to tell everyone we can't afford to run it.' She looked quizzically at Will. He was silent for a moment. Selling the Range Rover, Will had reluctantly agreed, was to be his big sacrifice. He looked at Sarah.

'I'm still not convinced we should sell . . .' he started.

'You've changed your mind!'

'We won't make anything on the deal. I'll still have to get a reliable, respectable—'

'Petrol and insurance!' Sarah wasn't going to let him get away with this one. 'It's hardly light on either!'

Will shrugged and looked at his watch. But Sarah wasn't going to drop the subject; wasn't going to let him walk away, as he used to do so expertly, from a difficult situation. 'This is so typical of you, Will! I get a job.' She drummed her fingers on the work surface. 'We move house. But oh no, when it comes to your precious vehicle . . .'

'OK. OK.' Will made a gesture of defeat. 'You've made your point . . .'

And she'd also lost her temper. Flouncing out of the kitchen, she retorted with an exasperated 'Oh, go and play with the boys.' Then, remembering, she added, 'And get them to clean the car. We won't get a decent price for a pig sty on wheels.'

Will raised his eyes heavenwards. 'Yes, ma'am,' he whispered to himself. Loping off to join the boys in the garden, he wondered why he and Sarah were so good at starting conversations – and so bad at ending them.

Beth Glover was thinking similar thoughts about Jack as she prepared for morning surgery at The Beeches. Was she being incredibly naive? Was it unrealistic to expect that their relationship could continue on exactly the same footing as before? Immediately after the event she felt she had rejected Jack's proposal rather tactfully. Now she conceded that, however delicately you turned down an offer of marriage, it was still a rejection – and it hurt. And a man like Jack, she reflected ruefully, wasn't very good at taking rejection. Beneath his raffish, boyish Peter Pan image, he was, after all, a very proud man – and proud men don't like being spurned. Beth sighed. She had been going over the problem of their relationship again and again, wondering how it could continue. She *wanted* it to continue; she wanted them to be friends, lovers, companions, yet still with their separate lives and identities. But that wasn't enough for Jack – as was patently obvious by his new attitude towards her. 'Cool', Kim had called it, adding an unspoken question mark. Kim was always trying to quiz Beth about her and Jack. Well, she wasn't going to get any answers. How could she when Beth couldn't work out any answers herself?

Dismissing her troubled personal life from her mind, she smiled as the door opened after a gentle knock and Rob Clulow walked in. Her first appointment of the day. She liked Rob. A jolly, bearded chap, always the life and soul of any party, he hid, beneath the bluff exterior, a multitude of personal problems far greater than her own. And now he had another, potentially deadly one.

'So, what can I do for you?' she asked cheerfully.

Rob Clulow, puffing slightly, sat down and smiled across the table. He put his hand to his chest. With the 'It's nothing really' expression so typical of patients who were in real pain, he joked, 'Think I must've swallowed a needle, doctor. Bit of an odd pain now and again.'

Beth smiled. 'Sewing, eh? Funny hobby for a lorry driver.' But there was sympathy, not humour in her voice as she added, 'So what else have you been doing? Still at the quarry? Still partying? Still running a family single-handed?'

Rob winced slightly. It was a source of great pain and anger that his wife of nearly twenty years had run off with, as Rob succinctly put it, 'a bloke with brass', leaving her husband with two teenagers and an eleven-year-old. And it was Harry, the eleven-year-old, who worried him most. Most of Cardale knew that the boy, suddenly shy and sullen after his mother's departure, was having trouble settling down at school – and being bullied into the bargain.

Beth, feeling that her anger over his situation in life had made her sound sharp rather than sympathetic, smiled warmly and gestured to the examination couch behind her. 'Let's have a little prod, Mr Clulow. Just to make sure it isn't a needle.' When Rob had his back to her, she frowned and looked at his medical notes. His arduous job and difficult home circumstances were not a good recipe for health; especially considering his medical history and stressful life.

A few minutes later, with Rob again sitting opposite her, she examined her notes. 'Well, you had the angioplasty just over two years ago. Bit disappointing if it's angina again so soon.' She looked questioningly at him.

Rob, on the defensive, knew what was coming. 'I try to watch what I eat and everything . . .'

'Yes, but the real question is—'

Before she could finish asking Rob answered the question by spreading his hands helplessly in front of him and sighing sheepishly.

'Oh, Mr Clulow.' Beth sighed in frustration.

Rob looked at her, eager for reassurance. 'I gave up for a bit. Honest.' Beth was silent. 'Terrible it was,' he continued. 'Then I went on them little cigars but they just sort of led me back to the fags . . .' He trailed off, realizing the futility of his argument. 'Hopeless, aren't I?' he said to a spot on the wall behind Beth's head.

'Yes.' Sympathetic as she was to his plight, Beth wasn't going to hold him entirely blameless. She referred again to her notes. 'Well, you won't get away with angioplasty this time – we can't keep on unclogging a damaged blood vessel indefinitely.'

Rob looked alarmed. 'So what'll it be, then? A heart bypass?'

'I'm sure that's what the consultant will say, yes.' She smiled reassuringly. 'Put in a nice healthy blood vessel to replace the old clapped-out one.'

'Oh. Well, if it has to be, it has to be.' Rob was nothing if not philosophical.

'I'll try to get you a hospital appointment next week. The sooner the better.' Looking up again from her notes she added, 'You'll have to stop driving that monster of yours for a while.'

This, for Rob, was worse news than the heart by-pass. No lorry driving meant no money. But he wasn't going to tell the doctor that. 'Oh, well,' he shrugged. 'I'll get them to put me on light duties.'

Something in his tone made Beth reply, rather sharply, '*Are* there any light duties in a quarry?'

Rob waved his hand dismissively. 'They'll put me in the office or on maintenance or summat.'

Beth, now writing a note for the consultant, smiled up at him. 'And you'll have to get those children of yours to spoil you for a bit.'

This was the wrong thing to say. Beth knew it as soon as she saw the worried frown that greeted her well-intentioned remark. 'Easier said than done, doctor . . .'

'I know, I'm sorry, Rob. I know you've been having a difficult time.'

'It's not that. It's just that our Amanda got married last week. . .'

'Oh, yes! Of course. Reception at The Manor. Chloe told me all about it.' Beth suddenly recalled Amanda's age. Eighteen, wasn't she? And here *she* was, Dr Beth Glover, pillar of the community, a good fifteen years older than Amanda, tying herself in knots at the prospect of rushing into marriage with Jack.

'Aye. Grand do that was.' Rob grinned in recollection of his dancing, drinking and smoking the night away at his daughter's wedding. 'Thing is,' he added, unused to confiding but suddenly eager for the opportunity, 'our David isn't doing his share of looking after young Harry. Getting into trouble, poor lad. Playing truant and all that.'

Beth looked at him with genuine feeling. This was what she hated – the only thing she hated – about her job. Will had told her on more than one occasion, quite gently, that she would have to harden her heart; that she was a doctor – not a counsellor, therapist, bank manager and magician

43

rolled into one. Beth knew Will was right, she knew she could only offer limited help to people whose problems weren't only medical, but she couldn't help herself getting involved sometimes. And she still viewed general practice, especially in a small community, as a sort of binding that helped keep that community together. She certainly didn't see it as a business, concerned only with margins, profits and losses. She grimaced as she thought of the way GPs were being encouraged to become businessmen; fundholders controlling their own budgets, looking for the best financial deals for drugs and operations, overlooking, as she saw it, the fact that patients were real people, not figures on a balance sheet. She involuntarily stiffened her shoulders. Well, she was still senior partner at The Beeches – and they would only become fundholders over her dead body.

Realizing that Rob Clulow was waiting for her to reply, she nodded sympathetically. 'I'm sure it's just a phase, Mr Clulow. Dr Preston's boy is going through the same sort of thing.' She knew she shouldn't gossip about Will's problems with Tony, but she only wanted to reassure the man. 'And he's about the same age as your Harry, isn't he? Eleven?'

Rob nodded. 'Aye, that's right. They're by way of being mates as well. Bunking off together of an evening.'

'Oh?' Beth was genuinely surprised. She knew Harry Clulow to be a nice, well-mannered boy, but some of his contemporaries in Cardale were, for want of a better word, little thugs.

Then she smiled at Rob. 'Well, there you are then. It's not Harry: it's his age.'

'Bit young to be a terror and a tearaway, isn't it?' Then, with a grateful nod and a rueful smile, Rob Clulow took his leave. Beth, lost in thought, stared unseeingly at the closed door. She was hating herself for what was uppermost in her mind after listening to Rob Clulow's problems. It wasn't his heart, his traumas with single parenthood or his concern over Harry. It was his daughter Amanda. The teenager with the wedding ring.

By the time of his appointment with Nick Jenkins, 'the heart man', Rob Clulow's worries had increased. Only the previous day, he had been back at The Beeches – not with his heart, as he had joked to Dr Kerruish – but with Harry. The boy had been badly beaten up, yet with the stubbornness of youth and the terror of being branded a 'sneak', he had refused to say who had attacked him. That in itself was enough for Rob to know that his son's assailants had not been village kids, but children from the North End, the rough housing estate that would have made Tony Preston regard his parents' new home as palatial. Despite the fact that Harry's wounds had been bad enough to need dressing, and despite the brilliant rapport that Jack Kerruish had with kids, Harry had remained stubbornly silent about who had attacked him. Now, sighing with weariness and worry, Rob had no energy left to battle for his own health with the suave, sophisticated and rather disapproving consultant seated opposite him.

Jenkins was studying the angiogram in front of him. Wanting to be kind, yet mildly exasperated, he addressed Rob curtly. 'Barely three years ago we restored the blood supply to the cardiac muscle. In effect, you have a good heart. You were all set up.' He looked challengingly at Rob. 'How many cigarettes a day do you smoke?'

Rob hesitated. 'Twenty.' Jenkins looked at him with an 'I've been a doctor for twenty years' expression. Rob reddened slightly and shifted in his chair. 'Well . . . maybe more.'

Jenkins sighed. 'I told you; we all told you . . .' Looking Rob directly in the eye, he added, 'Don't you care?'

Rob bridled. 'I've got kids, an eleven-year-old boy . . . Of course I care! Say you do the op and I try again—'

But Jenkins, abruptly pushing his chair back and crossing

his arms, interrupted him. 'I'm sorry. It doesn't work like that. You have to give up smoking right now and after the operation you have to stay off. For ever.' Seeing the look of horror on Rob Clulow's face, he decided to seize the opportunity to get through to the man once and for all. 'If not, we can't operate' – Rob opened his mouth in silent protest – 'and I give you a couple of years at the most. The choice is yours.'

Rob was shattered. 'Wait a minute . . . are you refusing to give me the by-pass?'

Jenkins wheeled his chair forward again. 'Mr Clulow, with every puff you take you're creating the very condition we're trying to cure. Can't you see how pointless it all is?'

Rob stared miserably at the consultant. 'I'm all my family's got,' he pleaded. 'The wife's run off with some flashy sod. I have to do her job and mine . . .'

'We'll get you on nicotine patches.' Jenkins was determined not to be sidetracked. 'I'll also recommend you to attend The Beeches' stop-smoking clinic.'

Rob scratched his beard in exasperation. 'I've tried all that! I've smoked since I was fourteen. Nearly forty years.' He glared at Jenkins. 'You don't know what it's like.'

Recognizing the man's genuine distress, Jenkins was kind – but firm. 'I'm sorry. I'm sure it's very difficult, but my resources are finite. I have to find a fine balance between your physical needs and plain common sense.' Indicating the finality of the situation, he stood up. 'I want to help you. I want your son to grow up with a father, but I can't give up this poison for you. Only you can do that.'

CH**A**PTER 4

'Thought you'd be here again,' said Tony Preston as he approached the small figure huddled broodingly by the broken window.

Harry Clulow looked up. He was glad to see Tony: he had been getting lonely, sitting all by himself in the huge, deserted cotton mill with only his troubles to think about and the great undulating sweep of the Derbyshire countryside to look at. From this vantage point the Dales looked both magnificent and intimidating; a landscape that changed dramatically even as you looked at it, with great grey rock faces in the distance and pocket-like fields, nestling where they could in the difficult terrain. The mill itself, also magnificent, was a relic of a bygone age – a monument to the Industrial Revolution that had started almost on the streets of Cardale itself. Neglected for many years and derelict, it now served no purpose – save that of providing a safe haven for the troubled Harry Clulow.

Harry didn't smile at Tony, but mumbled a greeting. As Tony sat beside him, he acknowledged his friend's remark. 'Only place I can get away from our David. Getting on at me all the time.'

Tony nodded wisely. 'Like my mum. Yelling at me and Dad.'

Harry thought for a moment. 'Your dad should get rid of that yuppie car. Get some money.' He looked down at Tony's feet in disapproval. 'You could have proper trainers then.' Tony, too, looked critically.

'*She* won't let us have proper ones.' He seethed with bitterness at the memory of his conversation – no, fight – with his mother. Then it had escalated into a full-scale battle with both his parents when Will had brought up the subject of his letter from the school. 'Disruptive', it had said. Huh. Tony would show them disruptive. Well, perhaps when he was older. Now he would make do with running away on the night of their precious golf club dinner. That would show them.

'Your dad wants to sort her out,' said Harry with the alarming insight of the young. 'Soft sod.'

'He's not soft!' Tony wasn't going to listen to his father being criticized. 'Mum wanted him to sell the car but he fixed it so's the man at the garage wouldn't give a decent price.' Tony wasn't sure if this was right, but that was what Sarah had screamed at Will when the sale had fallen through the other day. He shuddered at the memory. Another fight. Another screaming match. And they'd said that things were going to be better in the new house. His lip trembled slightly. He bit it, and then enquired of Harry, 'Did your mum and dad row all the time?'

But Harry didn't want to be reminded of his mother. He shrugged his shoulders dismissively and looked over at the horizon. The evening sun was hovering tentatively over a distant peak, soon to plunge beneath it and transform the Dales into a murky gloom. He wondered why grown-ups liked the area so much. He wanted to live in Nottingham. It had arcades, someone had said.

Tony was silently practising his accent. Maybe if he could always speak like Harry none of the local kids would call him a poncey git. 'You told your dad about them kids yet?' he asked gruffly.

'Can't.' Harry shrugged. 'He's sick with his heart. And they won't give him an operation 'cos of the fags.' It was Harry's turn to bite his lip.

'Oh.' Tony wasn't quite sure what to say about this.

'An' it's partly my fault,' continued Harry. 'I was running away from our David yesterday so Dad chased after me and had an attack of an . . . ang . . .' he struggled with the unfamiliar word.

'Angina,' corrected Tony, who had been familiar with the word stethoscope since the age of three.

'Yeah. Doctor had to come round.'

'Who? My dad?'

'No. Her.'

'Oh.' Both Tony and Harry liked Beth Glover, but women, they felt, weren't much of a topic of conversation. 'So's he all right now?' asked Tony.

'Dunno. The doctor went bananas when she heard that they weren't giving him an operation. She thought they was.'

'Bananas' was an understatement for the towering rage Beth had worked herself into by the time she'd driven from the Clulows' house back to The Beeches. And it was just as well that neither Tony nor Harry knew the context of her subsequent conversation with Jack and Will. Jack had been on her side, claiming that Rob Clulow, smoker or no, had as much right as anyone to a life-saving operation. And he had added, quite sensibly, that it was a bit rich for society in general, after positively encouraging smoking for so many years, to brand smokers as social pariahs – as people who deserved to die.

Will had snorted dismissively and said that as far as he was concerned, Rob Clulow's angina was self-inflicted. Beth and Jack had rounded on him anew, asking him who else he thought it correct to refuse treatment to; people who drink too much, eat too much or take drugs? People who climb mountains and break their legs? Beth, her colour high – and looking incredibly sexy, Jack had thought – had stormed out of the room, unable to trust herself even to speak. Will, sarcastic as always when he was under pressure, had remarked that it was no wonder so many doctors keeled over from stress. That had been the wrong thing to say. Jack had suggested that, as doctors' heart attacks were probably self-induced, then perhaps Will's pal Nick

Jenkins could extend his ban on operations to every medic in the country and, while he was at it, to everyone who had a stressful job. That would keep the cardiac unit happy – and in the money.

It hadn't, as arguments went, been a very constructive one. Will, left alone in The Beeches' meeting room, had started to think about his colleagues' attitude. Perhaps they were right and perhaps, he had guiltily admitted to himself, he had sprung so quickly to Nick Jenkins's defence because the man was a golfing pal. And perhaps the system itself was wrong – there *had* to be a way for GPs to ensure that their patients got the operations they needed. Then Will had smiled to himself. There *was* a way – but he was sure they could only get agreement on that over Beth's dead body.

Seeing that his friend was concerned about his father's plight, Tony sought to bolster his ego. Turning to Harry, he smiled encouragingly. 'But they don't scare you, do they?'

'Who?' asked Harry, startled out of his reverie.

'Them kids. Wayne's gang.'

Harry unconsciously squared his shoulders. 'Nah. Not them.' But it didn't sound convincing.

Nothing, not even the absence of her eldest son, was going to stop Sarah from going to the golf club dinner. She wasn't – contrary to Will's unvoiced but evident opinion – being hard-hearted. She just knew, with that instinctive understanding of mothers, that Tony had chosen his moment with great deliberation, that he was trying to see how far he could frighten and manipulate his parents. She knew perfectly well he was in no danger, that he was only trying to exercise his power over them, to make them worried enough to abandon the golf club dinner. 'Well, tough, my lad,' she said to herself as she scrutinized the mirror for any flaws in her perfectly made-up face. 'In this battle of wills, I win.'

At that moment her husband walked into the room, anxiety written all over his face. 'No sign?' he asked.

Sarah bit back the obvious retort. Will, she felt, was being needlessly irritating about all this. It wasn't as if it was the first time. She smiled at his reflection in the mirror. 'He'll be back when he's hungry.' Then she swivelled round from her dressing-table, pleased with her stunning appearance. Will didn't appear to notice. Sighing, she smiled brightly and, as she reached forwards for her evening bag, she stroked her husband's cheek and smiled. 'And then you can ground the little tearaway for the rest of his life.'

Two minutes later, downstairs in the sitting-room, Will tried to give his mobile phone number to the baby-sitter. Sarah, laughing but determined, took the phone out of Will's hand and placed it firmly on the side-table. 'You will *not* give Michelle the number and you will *not* take that wretched thing with you!' She raised her eyes conspiratorially at Michelle, comfortably settled beside Julian in front of the TV. 'Men!' she added. 'Always fussing.'

Michelle smiled uncertainly at the glamorous vision in front of her. Men, in her experience, did very little fussing when they were around her. Perhaps if she looked like Sarah Preston they would try a little harder.

Will, still looking worried, turned to Michelle. 'If he's not back in half an hour—'

'He'll be back,' interrupted Sarah with utmost certainty. Putting her hands on his shoulders, she steered him gently but firmly towards the door. 'Don't be silly. He's just jerking our strings.'

With that, and a cheerful 'Have a nice evening!' from Michelle, they went to their dinner.

*

Harry and Tony looked uncertainly at each other. 'You can't make us come down!' yelled Tony out of the broken window.

'Yew carn't make us come dine,' mimicked Wayne from below. 'Who's the poncey friend, Harry?' Standing in the shadow of the mill with Terry, Daz and six other members of his gang, Wayne was positively basking in bravado. Finally they'd tracked down that little wimp Harry Clulow – and got the doctor's kid into the bargain. And Wayne had made sure that they were blocking the only remaining exit from the mill.

Terry, taking his lead from Wayne, shouted up to the two frightened boys. 'Hey! Doctor's kid. Bet you lot are dead rich. Bet you've got wads of money.'

'Yeah, snob,' added Wayne. 'Chuck us down some money!'

The other boys took the cue. Individually and privately, they weren't too keen on beating up Harry – but the prospect of hounding him and his friend for money seemed altogether more attractive. 'Yeah! Chuck us some money! Chuck us some money!' they chanted. And at a nod from Wayne, they entered the mill at a run.

Tony and Harry looked at each other. They had two options – to try and run for it, or to stay and fight. Silently, in sudden mutual understanding, they turned into the mill and began to pick up the loose stones that littered the abandoned factory floor.

Ten minutes later, bruised, dirty and out of breath, they realized they were running out of ammunition. Wayne's gang had split into two and, although Harry and Tony knew the terrain of the mill and had been able to maintain the element of surprise as they chucked everything they could find at their assailants, they were now cornered. Trapped on a part of the roof that jutted out behind the mill, dodging the missiles that Terry and some of the others were hurling from above, they looked down. Through the thick glass of the factory roof beneath them, they could see Wayne and three other boys advancing towards the staircase, brandishing metal pipes and heading towards them. What had begun as mere taunting had escalated into a terrifying, very real fight.

Harry looked helplessly at Tony. 'Nothing left!'

Tony, momentarily frozen with fear, looked at the debris around them. There was nothing they could throw back at the boys above them; no way to stop the boys below. Then he noticed the ancient, rusty fire extinguisher lying on the parapet. Strengthened by the adrenalin pumping through him, he picked it up, wincing at the weight of it. As Harry stared, wide-eyed, Tony staggered towards the glass roof beneath them and hurled the extinguisher over the edge. There was a brief silence, followed by the deafening sound of splintering glass. And then came the piercing, agonized scream that ended as abruptly as it had begun. And afterwards an eerie, deathly calm that enveloped the entire mill and echoed more ominously than any scream.

Sarah was enjoying herself immensely. The Wharfdale, an old and grand former country house commanding majestic views over the countryside, was a suitably smart venue for the golf club dinner, and most of the guests were attired in fitting elegance. The effort Sarah had put into her appearance had, gratifyingly, not gone unnoticed. Sitting beside Nick Jenkins, listening attentively to his wife Sue, she was on sparkling form. And she had also used the opportunity to invite people she liked – and some, admittedly, that she didn't – to their housewarming party. The idea of the party, at least when she had mooted it, had brought a smile to Will's face. It had told him that she was no longer embarrassed about their new house; no longer trying to pretend that their change in circumstances was but a minor blip in their lives. But tonight Will was being as entertaining as a damp squib. Looking repeatedly at his watch, he had hardly spoken all evening.

Sighing, Sarah looked across the table at him. It really wasn't fair, she thought. Will knew as well as she did that Tony would be at home by now, curled up in front of the television, happily munching the hamburgers that Michelle was cooking the boys as a treat. Yet he was insisting on making a drama out of the boy's disappearance. If he continued like this, thought Sarah, then next year they probably *wouldn't* get an invitation and not just – as had been the case this year – one sent to the wrong address.

Leaning over to Will, she smiled encouragingly, her expression belying her irritation. 'Do stop worrying, Will. He'll be fine.'

Will looked distractedly back at her. 'I think I'll make that call before they start serving dinner.'

It was Sarah's turn to look at her watch. 'But it's not even eight-thirty yet.' Then, catching Nick's flicker of attention out of the corner of her eye, she turned to him and explained, 'Our eldest was late coming home this evening.'

Nick smiled in mock horror. 'Start of the terrible teens, Sarah. Soon you'll be lucky if they're home by eight-thirty in the morning.'

Sarah laughed. 'But he's only eleven! Bit early for all those adolescent hormones to start charging about, isn't it?' Nick and Sue Jenkins laughed, and then they all turned to Emma Gabbertas, who had started to regale them with tales of her own boys who, as everyone in Cardale knew, had hit manhood rather earlier than was good for them. Will, under cover of Emma's loud and wittily diverting voice, slipped away to the phone.

But just as he was trying to weave between the tables towards the exit, John Reginald, captain of the golf club and host for the evening, stood up from the high table and called for silence. 'My lords, ladies and gentlemen,' he began. 'Tonight it is my pleasure to introduce to you a man . . . oh!'

Knocked off his stride by the sudden, noisy arrival of the head waiter and an accompanying policeman, he looked disapprovingly in their direction. All eyes in the room followed his and for a moment a silent tension enveloped the room. Then someone shouted, 'It's no use, John! They've got you now. Told you broke the rules of golf with that putt last week!' Everyone burst out laughing. Laughing with them and regaining his composure, John Reginald began his speech again. But the excitement of the policeman's arrival had captured more interest than any speech that John Reginald could make. Pretending to listen to him, most people watched the unfolding drama out of the corner of their eyes. But when the head waiter pointed out Will to the policeman, they began to lose interest. 'Must've been an accident outside or something. Poor old Will. And he's not even on call.'

'Dr Preston?' The policeman came up to Will.

'Yes.'

'If we could go outside, sir . . .'

Sarah, sitting just a few feet away, was livid. 'But he's not even on call!' she wailed.

With that the policeman approached her. 'Are you Mrs Preston?'

A flicker of alarm crossed Sarah's face. 'Yes. Tell me what the hell's going on.'

Refusing to be hurried, the policeman consulted the notepad in his hand. 'You have a son, Tony, is that right?'

A little moan escaped Sarah. By now John Reginald had again fallen silent, and every eye in the room was on Sarah and Will. 'Oh, God!' Will had gone white with fear. 'What is it?'

The policeman turned to him, reassuring. 'He's fine, sir, not hurt. But I wonder if you could just come down to the police station?'

'Yes, of course, but what—'

Lowering his voice, the policeman interrupted him. 'We've detained your son and several other boys.'

Will looked back blankly, not understanding. Sarah, now on her feet, shouted, more in fear than in anger, at the policeman. '*Detained* him? This is ridiculous! He's only eleven years old!'

A murmur ran through the room as the policeman, in an even quieter voice, bent closer to Sarah. 'I really think you'd better come along, madam.' Grimly, he ushered both Will and Sarah out of the room. At the other end, John Reginald groaned. He had spent weeks perfecting his entertaining words of introduction. Now they echoed unheard by the gathered crowd.

Two hours later and rigid with shock, Sarah was sitting bolt upright on the sofa at home. Staring straight ahead, with glazed, unseeing eyes, she was repeating, again and again, 'Our son. Our son. Our son's killed another boy.'

Beth Glover, beside her on the sofa, patted her arm. They had been sitting like this for nearly ten minutes and still she wasn't getting through. Wearily, she sighed and drew a hand through her tousled hair. 'A brandy, Sarah. I'll get you a brandy.' Standing up, making her way to the drinks cupboard, she wondered, for the umpteenth time, why every time she made a decision in life, it was overtaken by a disaster. Earlier that evening, she and Jack had been drinking wine, eagerly anticipating the dinner that she had spent so long preparing – she was intent on rebuilding some bridges. It had been fun. And Beth had been determined that before the night was out, she would tell Jack.

And then he had been called out to Beldon Mill and that was the last she had seen of him that night. They had spoken on the phone fifteen minutes ago – but it had been anything but a lovers' conversation.

As Beth sloshed a generous amount of brandy into a glass for Sarah, Will entered the room. His finely chiselled features looked drawn, his floppy blond hair ruffled into an untidy fringe. He glanced at Sarah, and stepped towards Beth.

Beth put her arms round him. 'Oh, Will,' she said with feeling. 'I'm so sorry.' Resting his head on her shoulders for a moment, he then drew reluctantly away from her comforting embrace. It was strange, he thought, that the deep and genuine affection they felt for each other could only express itself in moments of crisis. They could spend days on end bickering with each other, yet beneath it all there was a strong, even loving bond. Will would never be able to forget how Beth had reacted to his nervous break-down. From the word go, she had been a tower of strength, sympathy and support.

'How's Tony?' asked Beth.

Will gestured above him. 'In bed. Wide awake and stiff as a board with shock.'

Beth nodded and gestured towards Sarah. Will stepped towards the sofa, sat on an arm and put his own arm round her shoulders. Beth handed the brandy to her. Mechanically, she accepted it without a word.

'He'll be OK,' said Will without conviction.

'A murderer,' replied Sarah, still miles away.

A thought suddenly occurring to him, Will turned to Beth. 'They've not phoned, have they?'

Beth shook her head.

'There were lots of them,' said Will to Sarah. 'All older than Tony and Harry. They were throwing bricks. Stones. They even had metal pipes . . .'

'A gang of bloody yobs.'

'Yeah.'

'And our son's one of them. The worst of them.' Sarah's voice was flat, unemotional. Will raised his eyes. Exasperated, he got up from the sofa.

'Will.' Beth's voice was authoritative. 'Sit down. I'll get you a drink. You've looked after everyone else, now let me look after you.'

At this Sarah suddenly looked up. 'Yes,' she said, spitting out the words with venom, 'let's look after Will! Let's give poor Will all our loving care and attention as we lurch from one family disaster to the next!'

'With a little help from you!' shouted Will.

Beth groaned silently. 'Sarah, Will. Go to bed. You're both shattered. Go to bed and I'll bring your drinks up.'

Meekly, with the docile acceptance of people in shock, they obeyed her.

With both of them out of earshot, Beth picked up the phone and dialled the familiar number of the hospital. Eventually she got through to Jack.

'Jack. It's me. How is he?'

At the other end of the line, Jack Kerruish sighed wearily into the mouthpiece. But his words carried hope. 'They've just finished running through the blood.'

'So he'll be OK?'

'He won't be leading any gangs for a few weeks but apart from that . . .'

'Oh, thank God! Maybe Will and Sarah'll believe me. They were sure he was going to die.'

There was a brief silence at the other end. 'So was I, Beth. So was I. I thought he *was* dead when I first saw him. I've never seen so much blood in my life.'

Sensing the horrors that Jack had witnessed, Beth replied gently, 'His artery was severed, Jack. I saw one myself once. It's like oil gushing out of a well.'

'Yeah. Christ, Beth! I'm a doctor and I never knew the human body contained so much blood.'

'It's OK. It's OK, Jack.' Beth paused for a moment and then added, 'What about the parents?'

'Whose parents?'

'Wayne's parents.'

'Oh. You know, shocked, disbelieving. Can't believe their precious lamb's really a bloody hooligan.'

'Jack . . .'

'And they're braying for Tony's blood. Want to get him convicted for attempted manslaughter.'

'But that's ridiculous! He's only eleven!' Beth had to let that appalling thought sink in for a moment. Then she remembered. 'What about Rob Clulow?'

Jack groaned. Rob Clulow had been the evening's final disaster. Called to the police station at the same time as Will and Sarah, he had collapsed on hearing the news and had been rushed to hospital. 'He's OK,' replied Jack. 'On a cardiac monitor. Sleepy but out of pain.'

Beth had plans for Rob Clulow, but she could sense that Jack was all in. 'Not the only one who's sleepy, by the sound of you. Why don't you go home, Jack? You must be exhausted. And by the sound of it there's not much more you can do there.'

'Nah. You're right. I've had enough.' He paused. 'Pity about our evening, eh?'

Beth, too, was briefly silent. 'It's a bit late now, Jack . . .'

'I know, I know. Anyway,' he yawned down the line, 'I've got to look in on Harry Clulow. Reassure him about his dad.'

'Oh, Lord.' Beth had forgotten about Tony's supposed partner in crime. 'Who's looking after him?'

'Chloe.'

'Chloe?' Chloe White, who ran the Manor Pub and Inn with her husband James, had enough on her plate. After years of trying to conceive, she had eventually given birth to a daughter nine months ago. And Beth, although she hadn't voiced her concern to anyone, was worried that Chloe was taking forever to get over what Beth suspected was post natal depression. 'Oh, well, send her my love, will you?'

'And me?' Jack was cryptic.

'What about you?'

'Don't I get any of that love?'

'Oh, Jack . . . oh, Jack.' Beth paused and added, 'You know you've got it all . . .'

'But only on your terms.'

Physically tired, emotionally exhausted, Beth ran her hand wearily through her hair. 'Oh, Jack . . . not now. Not on the telephone . . .'

'No. It's never the right time, is it?'

And then the phone went dead.

CH**A**PTER 5

'Oh, Isabel . . . I just don't know what to do.'

'About what? Jack? Will and fundholding? Your life?'

Beth cradled her cup of coffee in both hands and laughed. 'You really know how to put things in perspective, don't you? Why have just one problem when you can have twenty all at once?'

'Well, Beth, the more problems you have, the more chance you have of solving them. Anyway,' Isabel jumped to her feet, 'nobody ever solved anything by sitting around chatting idly. Are you going to help me hang those pictures or not?'

'Depends what's in it for me.'

Isabel looked at her watch. 'A thumping great sherry? It'll be twelve o'clock by the time we've finished. And if it isn't,' she added with a mischievous grin, 'we can always pretend . . .'

Beth grinned back. 'Done.'

Some people did try to solve their problems by sitting around chatting idly – but not Isabel de Gines. She was congenitally incapable of sitting still for more than a few minutes at a time. Forever striding about the countryside organizing anything and everything, she led a full, active and happy life. Or at least that was the impression she liked to give. Beth, who had known her all her life, knew better. Isabel was lonely; and no amount of frenetic activity could replace the void left in her life by the death of her beloved husband five years previously.

For nearly thirty years Dominic and Isabel de Gines had been that modern rarity: a blissfully married couple who were everything to each other – lovers, companions and best friends. Rich, good-looking and popular, they had travelled widely, entertained lavishly and lived splendidly in the beautiful Georgian country house that Isabel still occupied. But there had been one sadness in their lives – their inability to have children.

And that, thought Beth as she followed Isabel's neat ankles up the stairs, was where she had come in. Isabel and Dominic, although younger than Beth's own parents, had become their best friends. And when Beth's mother had died so tragically and so young, Isabel had stepped into the breach and, ever since, had been Beth's surrogate mother, best friend and confidante. Beth was the closest Isabel had ever come to having a daughter – and the bond between the two women was stronger and more harmonious than most natural mother–daughter relationships. The only bone of contention was that Isabel always ran Beth off her feet. At sixty-three, it wasn't only Isabel's appearance that was immaculately preserved: her energy also showed not the slightest sign of withering.

Upstairs on the landing, her perfectly pressed Jean Muir suit notwithstanding, Isabel sprawled on the floor and started attaching picture-wire to her latest acquisitions. She had been delighted to get the set of six Lowry prints for what she called 'a snip'. Beth looked doubtfully at the matchstick figures. Isabel's version of a snip was markedly different from her own.

'So what's the problem?' Isabel asked the question with an almost casual indifference. She was concerned about Beth and had all the time in the world for her problems, yet she knew Beth too well to let her launch straight into the telling of them. Beth would almost immediately declare she was boring Isabel, before changing the subject. Much better to let her come out with it slowly. 'Hand me the screwdriver, will you?' added Isabel, deep in her task.

'Oh . . . well, you're right, of course. There seem to be so many problems I don't know where to begin.' She handed over the screwdriver.

'Made your peace with Will yet?'

'Mmm? Oh, yes, thank God. We appear to be friends again. My fault entirely, really. Silly of me to insult one of Will's guests in his own house.' She paused and looked at Isabel. 'Why weren't you there, anyway?' she asked, referring to the occasion of the insult – Will and Sarah's housewarming party.

'I . . . er, I thought it would be cancelled. You know, after Tony and all that. I assumed Sarah wouldn't be able to face a party.'

Beth looked at her friend, amused. 'You mean you didn't want to go in the first place. You know Sarah, Isabel. Takes more than that to make her cancel a party. Come on,' she teased, 'you thought it wouldn't be your sort of thing, didn't you? And in a housing estate, too!'

'Oh, Beth! Don't be so . . . Well, *was* it my sort of thing?'

Beth laughed. 'Actually, no. Wasn't really my sort of thing either.' She grimaced. 'Lots of loud music later on. Bit studenty, really.'

'Told you so.' Before Beth could reply to that blatant untruth, Isabel swept on. 'So what exactly did you say to that man, anyway? Ghastly little creep, isn't he? Smarmy, I seem to remember.' Isabel was not one to mince her words.

Beth laughed. 'I'm not sure the Family Health Services Authority would care to hear their general manager referred to as a ghastly smarmy little creep, but, yes, he's far too smooth for my liking.' She frowned, trying to remember how she had insulted Greg Miller at the party. 'I think I told him he should be more impartial in the advice he gave us. I accused him of being far more concerned about budgets than patients.'

'And is he?'

'Of course he is! Budgets and I daresay whatever mention in the Honours List he's hoping to get for pressurizing more and more GPs to become fundholders. Huh!'

'Oh dear. I really don't understand this fundholding business, Beth. All a bit complicated for me.' What Isabel really meant was that she really didn't want to hear about it again. Not only was it the current political hot potato within the health service, it was Beth's personal *bête noire*.

Beth, however, took Isabel at her word, took a deep breath and launched into a lengthy explanation. 'Well, in very simple terms . . .' She stopped and frowned at Isabel, now up the ladder and placing the first print against the wall. 'You *must* know about it. I'm sure I've explained before.'

'Have you? Oh.'

'Do I detect a glazed look in your eye, Isabel?'

'No, no. Go on. I really am interested.'

'Well, I just don't think it's *right* for a general practice to have to manage its own finite budget and to rummage around buying operations and whatnot in advance. It's just so . . . so *clinical*.' She paused and, realizing what she had said, started to laugh.

Isabel joined her. 'Nothing wrong with being clinical if you're a doctor.'

'No, I know. But the way I see it is that it creates far more dilemmas than it solves. I mean, if we can buy operations at private hospitals that will be both cheaper and more immediate than at NHS ones, then what hope for the NHS itself? They're not going to be generating any income from us, are they?'

'No. But . . . well, competition and all that. It might encourage the NHS to be more . . . more competitive,' she finished lamely, only one ear on the conversation and both eyes on the Lowrys.

'Competition! Free markets! For God's sake, Isabel, we're talking about ill people, not washing powder.' She sighed. 'Anyway, it's not going to benefit us either.'

'What? More work?'

'Yes, but it's not just that. I mean supposing we work out our first year's budget with the FHSA and then we underspend—'

'You'll have made a profit!'

Beth glared at Isabel's back. 'No, we wouldn't. We couldn't spend the money on ourselves. And anyway,' Beth bridled at the very thought, 'that really *would* be horribly unethical. No, the point is that in the next financial year our budget would be reduced by the saved amount. I mean, you do see where that's leading, don't you?' Working herself up into a rage, she shook the ladder so hard that Isabel nearly fell off.

'Beth!' Isabel looked down in alarm. Then she smiled. '*I* didn't invent fundholding. It was the government, not me. Honest. I swear. Brownies' honour.' She held up her hands in innocent protestation. 'Now will you stand over there and tell me if these are straight? And then', she said adamantly, 'you can tell me about Chloe. I really am concerned about that poor girl.'

Jack shared Beth's concern about Chloe White. She had looked dreadful at Will's party; tired, drawn and depressed. Jack, despite his having been in Cardale for less time than Beth and Will, knew the Whites better. Before buying his cottage, he had stayed at the Manor and had been looked after – or spoiled, as he remembered it – by James and Chloe. The three of them had cemented a deep friendship; a friendship that had strengthened as Jack looked after Chloe during her longed-for pregnancy. The lack of joy on Chloe's face was not unusual for a new – and exhausted – mother. Only Chloe was no longer a new mother. Sarah Jane was now nine months old and Chloe was looking worse.

Jack's consultation with her the day after the party had been strained. Chloe had been thirty-four when she had given birth for the first time, after ten years of trying. Eventually, as a last resort, she and James had tried in vitro fertilization and Sarah Jane had been the happy result. Except Chloe was no longer happy. Jack had tried to make her voice the fear that he knew was on her mind – the fear that she, who had only ever wanted to be a mother, was not cut out for the job. It was not an uncommon fear – and usually a groundless one. Yet if the feelings of hopelessness, shame and guilt went unchecked, the results could, as he knew from experience, be tragic.

But Chloe had alternated between being tight-lipped and determinedly cheerful. The slight swelling in her neck, she claimed, was probably a minor recurrence of the glandular fever she had had years ago. Nothing to worry about. Brought on by stress. Jack, wanting to believe her, had done a blood test. And the results were back. No glandular fever.

Chloe, again looking cheerful, marched into Jack's surgery. 'Thought I'd finished with doctors after Sarah Jane.' At Jack's invitation, she sat down opposite him.

Jack, taking in her shape, frowned slightly. Even before her pregnancy, Chloe had been what her husband had jokingly referred to as 'pleasantly rounded'. Jack waved the piece of paper in his hand.

'Blood test results. No glandular fever.'

'Oh.'

Jack paused for a moment. 'Have you been dieting, Chloe?'

Chloe grinned. Her? Dieting? 'No. You know me. I like my food.'

'You've lost a fair bit of weight.'

'Course I have. Seven pounds, ten ounces of crying machine called Sarah Jane.'

Jack didn't return her impish look. 'Have you been getting any night sweats? Y'know, waking up like you're in a pool of water.'

Chloe frowned. 'I think so, yeah . . . a couple of times.' Then she brightened. 'But only 'cos James gets too hot and pushes the whole duvet on top of me.' Seeing Jack's expression, she added with a smile, 'Come on, Dr Kerruish, you're worried, aren't you? What about?'

'No, not worried,' lied Jack, 'but I do want you to have a couple of tests, Chloe. Just to be on the safe side. A chest X-ray and—'

'Chest X-ray? I haven't had a fag in five years, three months and about a week. Not that I'm counting.'

Jack grinned. 'No, not for that! But I want you to have a small biopsy as well. All that means is that they take out some cells from—'

'I know what a biopsy is, Jack.' Chloe's tone was calm, ominous. 'Where do you want it from?'

'I want to find out exactly what the lump is.'

Instinctively, Chloe touched her neck, feeling for the barely perceptible, painless lump. All traces of her previous, bantering tone now gone, she replied tonelessly, 'You're talking about cancer, aren't you?'

Jack shifted in his chair. 'We're ruling things out, Chloe, that's what tests are for. And in any case, you came to me good and early so if there's anything going on, we can deal with it. OK?'

But Chloe was already miles away, in a place called shock.

'Do you think,' asked Isabel, 'if it's what Jack thinks it is, that I could be of some help?'

'You?' Beth, now cradling her second thumping sherry, was aghast.

Isabel looked piqued. 'Yes, me. As a soon-to-be Samaritan.'

'Oh.'

Isabel, Beth knew from experience, was the very soul of kindness, but her recent decision to become a Samaritan had given rise to some prickly conversations between them. Privately, Beth thought that Isabel would frighten people away with her forthright, sometimes intimidating manner. Yet that was none of her concern. What did directly concern her was the possibility that Isabel, in her new role, would impinge, with the best intentions but not necessarily results, on Beth's territory.

Beth cursed herself for the indiscretions brought on by the sherry. She should never have told Isabel about Jack's fears for Chloe. 'Isabel,' she said carefully. 'I know you only want to help, but we're treading on shaky ground here.' She looked at her friend. As always, Isabel's ash-blonde hair was perfectly coiffed, her face beautifully made-up. But her expression, usually warm and full of laughter, was threatening. Undaunted, Beth ploughed on. 'I shouldn't have told you about Chloe, I don't even *know* about Chloe – this is pure conjecture – but if she really is ill and if she insists on keeping everything to herself, there's nothing you can do.' She paused. 'There's nothing *Jack* can do without Chloe's consent. And if she did want the help of the Samaritans, she would have to contact them herself.'

'But—'

'Yes, I know doctors can give the Samaritans their patients' phone numbers . . .'

'Which you wouldn't do for me . . .?'

'Which I *can't* do for you without asking my patients first! Anyway,' Beth tried to drop the subject, 'Chloe isn't even my patient, so that's the end of it.'

Isabel took a sip of sherry. 'I know, I'm sorry, Beth. It's just me charging ahead as usual. It's terrifying, though, the statistics about people in isolated areas . . .'

'I wouldn't exactly call Cardale isolated. Derby, Nottingham . . . good God, this is practically the birthplace of British industry, you know. The Industrial Revolution—'

'Started on our doorstep. Tell me about it.' Isabel raised her eyes. The Industrial Revolution had been Dominic's pet subject – and the only subject upon which she had declared her husband a bore. 'But', she continued, 'the Samaritans' outreach programme – the one I'm on – is targeted specifically at isolated . . . well, rural areas. Just think', she gestured grandiloquently, 'how many farmers there are on the hills around us, living in near poverty. Lonely. Isolated. In financial trouble. Needing someone to talk to . . . There's a very high incidence of suicide amongst farmers, you know.'

'And amongst GPs.'

'Don't be flippant, Beth . . . All right! . . . sorry, yes, you're absolutely right, but I'm afraid you don't fall into the category covered by our rural initiative.' Isabel, although still on her training course, was already possessive about the Samaritans.

'But how do you reach these people? There's also a very high proportion of farmers who don't even go to see their GPs from one year to the next, you know.'

'Yes, I know. Farmers tend to be macho traditionalists. You can imagine the sort . . . huge stigmas attached to even admitting to any emotional problems, however minor.' Isabel, Beth realized in some amusement, was quoting from a pamphlet.

'So,' she swept on, 'our outreach initiative is raising the profile of the Samaritans in rural areas. We've got specially designed publicity material and there are talks and lectures and—'

'And you're formalizing links with a number of organizations like the National Farmers Union and the Citizens Advice Bureau.'

'How did you know that?' Isabel was highly offended.

'I'm a doctor, Isabel. The Samaritans cite GPs as their major partners. And', she grinned mischievously, 'I've read the pamphlet too.'

Two days later, Chloe White had decided that she wouldn't ever tell her husband about her illness. Jack had told her the results of the biopsy and the X-rays, and now, at last, Chloe knew what to do. She would carry on as normal; looking after Sarah Jane, joking and laughing with James, and serving the punters, as she had always done, with a smile on her face and a cheeky glint in her eye. And then she would die.

Entering the Manor Hotel by the back entrance, deep in thought, Chloe made her way towards the staircase behind the bar that led up to their flat. James, serving at the bar, caught a glimpse of her. 'Chloe!' he shouted. Paying him no attention, Chloe continued upstairs. James shrugged and went back to pulling a pint. He looked at his watch and smiled. It was time for Sarah Jane's lunch. No doubt that was why Chloe was so preoccupied.

Upstairs, Chloe shrugged out of her coat and went into the room where her daughter lay. Sarah Jane was sound asleep, her little face puckered against the pillow, breathing gently. Occasionally a little gurgle escaped her lips and a tiny frown would cross her broad forehead. And then she would smile, her worries resolved, and sleep contentedly once more. Chloe stood motionless for several minutes, watching her little baby dream her way through life. Then she walked towards the bookshelves in the corner of the room, took a cassette out of her pocket, and inserted it into the stereo.

She sat down as the cassette crackled into life. Jack's voice, radiating his positive attitude to life, filled the room. Chloe closed her eyes and began to relive the conversation she had just had with Jack – the worst of her life.

'I've put the tape on so that you'll be able to listen to it later . . . when you want to. To remember what we've chatted about, y'know. Because it's not particularly good news, love, I'm afraid. What the tests have shown is that you actually have a very unusual condition . . .' There was a brief pause. 'It's called Hodgkin's disease.'

Chloe, motionless in her chair, shuddered as she relived the moment of Jack's ghastly revelation.

On the tape, Jack coughed and continued. 'You have some malignant cells in your lymphatic system. Those are the small glands – lymph glands – that live in various parts of your body as part of your immune system . . . Now, the good news is that the glands in your chest aren't affected. But those in your neck on one side look as if they are. Before we work out exactly what the best treatment for you is, we're going to have to do one more test. Completely painless, of course. As for treatment, Chloe, as things stand we're looking at a combination of some drugs and a course of radiation therapy, done over five or six weeks. It isn't painful and it has no real side effects, except that it will make you tired and listless. But we won't begin any treatment at all until we've seen what the scan has to tell us . . .'

'Hodgkin's disease. Who was he, then? Did he have this?' Chloe's own voice, playing back to her, sounded like that of a small girl, baffled by something, yet also bored by it.

'He was the doctor who first diagnosed it back in the nineteenth century.'

'Oh.' Then, after a brief pause, 'Am I going to die?'

'No, Chloe, you're not going to die.' Hearing the words, even for the second time, Chloe still didn't believe them. 'This type of cancer is very, very treatable . . . Can I suggest that we both have a chat with James together? Y'know, because he'll be alarmed and—'

Chloe nearly jumped at the ferocity of her own words as she butted in, 'I'm not telling James. He just couldn't take it.'

'Chloe, I really think—'

'James?' Her voice was scornful now, almost angry. 'You're joking, aren't you? You know what he's like, he's a baby.'

'But he'll want to know what the results of your tests are, won't he?' Jack's voice was gentle. 'And what we've talked about today.'

'He doesn't know I'm here. And I told him I went to the hospital to get tested for glandular fever. What does he know?'

'Y'know, I really think . . .'

But there was no time for Chloe to replay what Jack really thought. Hearing her husband's heavy tread outside she switched off the cassette recorder just in time and turned away from the door.

'Chloe?' James entered the room. 'What you listening to? Sounds like Jack.'

'Radio play.'

'Ah. You all right?'

'Fine.' Chloe turned to face him and smiled.

'Well, come on, then, there's punters down there dying of thirst. No time to be enjoying *Listen With Mother*.'

Jack Kerruish was pissed off. He'd had a bad day at The Beeches, his neighbour was irritating the hell out of him, he was having a bad time with Beth, and the news about Chloe was just plain bad. Savagely chopping a red pepper, he realized that he was doing what he was always warning his patients not to do. He was blaming himself – for not having spotted Chloe's illness sooner. He threw the pepper into the frying pan where it sizzled with the onions, garlic and chilli. Sighing, he went to turn the music up. Jack was doing what he always did when he was upset: cooking himself a hot, spicy meal, drinking red wine and listening to Eric Clapton.

But before his hand reached the volume control there was a sharp, firm knock on the door. He paused. Thanks to Eric Clapton he couldn't pretend he wasn't in, yet he was loath to answer the door for fear it might be Richard, the immensely charming but incredibly irritating neighbour. A few weeks previously, Richard, an ardent ecologist, had informed Jack that he was going to put his three acres of land on the outskirts of Cardale to good use. Jack's immediate response had been positive. And then, after Richard had installed twenty pigs next door, he had begun to think again. But worse was to come. Returning from work one day, he had been alarmed to see a strange, makeshift building erected about thirty yards from his kitchen window. This, Richard had proudly explained, was his new generating plant. No more overpriced electricity for him – his household was going to be run on pig manure. Jack felt he couldn't really say anything. He had, after all, bought a cottage outside Cardale because he wanted to be closer to nature. And what could be closer to nature than pig-shit?

Jack shook his head, silenced Eric Clapton, and went to answer the door. He was sure he knew what was coming. Although the smell of the pig manure was getting alarmingly close, the pigs themselves were getting even closer. And one pig in particular. Alberta, the largest and – so claimed Richard – sweetest of his brood had taken a shine to Jack. He fully expected to see Richard's endearingly apologetic face at the door, wondering if Alberta had escaped to Jack's garden.

But it was Beth, looking neither apologetic nor particularly endearing.

'Oh! It's you,' said Jack.

'Yes, I know. Expecting someone else, were you?'

Jack looked apprehensively behind Beth. No lurking pig. No anxious Richard. 'No, no, I just thought it might be about Alberta.'

'Alberta?'

Jack grinned. 'Yes, Alberta. She's got rather a thing for me . . .' Then the smell of frying peppers reached them. 'Oh, God! Look, you'd better come in.' He marched over to the cooker.

'I'm cooking. Want some?'

'No, thanks.' If Beth had been a little tight-lipped beforehand, now she was positively brusque. She had had to steel herself to come here in the first place to talk about their relationship. And now she was being casually told by her lover that he had another girlfriend.

73

'This . . . this Alberta. Is she a patient?'

Jack roared with laughter. 'I s'pose she could be if I were James Herriot. No, she's a pig.'

'A pig?'

'Yes. A pig.' He nodded in the direction of his only neighbour. 'One of Richard's.'

Smiling with relief, and then feeling foolish for doing so, Beth giggled and looked out of the window. 'So that's what this smell is. Yuk!'

Jack had turned back to the cooker. While not exactly ignoring her, he wasn't being over-welcoming either.

'You couldn't stretch to a drink, could you, Jack?'

'Glass of red do you?'

'Mmm.' She took a sip from the proffered glass. 'So what was Chloe's diagnosis?'

'Nodular sclerotic Hodgkin's disease. Very aggressive lymphomas. I just pray to God we've caught it early enough.'

Beth grimaced. 'Poor lamb. How did she take it?'

'I don't think it's sunk in yet. Doesn't surprise me. But what does worry me is that she's adamant about James not knowing.'

'That's ridiculous!'

Jack gave her a warning look. 'I know it's ridiculous, Beth.'

'D'you want me to talk to him?' Beth obviously hadn't taken the hint.

'She's my patient, Beth. If I need your help I'll ask for it.'

Beth flinched imperceptibly. She took a slug of her wine. 'Sorry,' she said. 'Sure.'

Jack turned back to the cooker. 'Look,' he said after an ominous, uneasy silence, 'I'm really pissed off you gave Brian Drake that medical without checking with me.'

'Oh.' So he really had been upset about that. Sighing, Beth remembered the unpleasant meeting all three partners had had that morning. Will, uptight because Beth was scathing about his wanting to go to a seminar on fundholding, had accused her of only doing what she wanted to do, regardless of the issue – and regardless of whom she might offend. While the accusation had been rather too brutal, he did have a point. And the point, in this instance, had been Brian Drake. Due for a routine, non-urgent medical as a condition for a mortgage on his ailing business, Jack had booked him on the third Saturday of the month – as was usual in these cases. Beth, by chance discovering that the need for the mortgage was urgent, had squeezed him in between her own appointments and done the medical early – and without clearing it with Jack. Yet he had, of course, found out.

'I'm sorry if I invaded your space, Jack, but the man needed that check-up done in a hurry.'

'Not for medical reasons he didn't.'

'Each patient has different requirements, Jack, and—'

'But we're *doctors*, Beth! Nobody's arguing about the fact that all patients are different, but we need our "protected time", as we call it.' He looked challengingly at her. 'That's why non-urgent, routine check-ups are allocated to the third Saturday of every month. I mean, for God's sake, it benefits no one if we're at everyone's beck and call all the time.'

'To be at everyone's beck and call is exactly what I consider our job. If I wanted nine to five, I'd have gone to work in a bank.'

'Some of us have a life outside The Beeches, Beth.'

Beth looked at him, an unfathomable expression on her face. 'Yes, that's what I came here to talk about.'

CH**A**PTER 6

Will grabbed Jack's arm as they walked into The Beeches together. 'Look, Jack, I really want to go to this fundholding seminar in London. Greg Miller's arranged a place for me . . . it's pretty high-powered and getting me on it was a pretty big favour, you know.'

Jack looked up at Will, impressed by his forthright confidence. Gone was the man who had once cowered in a corner, trying to hide from life, yet being constantly battered by it. Now, Will carried with him an air of authority that matched his film star looks and, Jack thought incongruously, the Range Rover. Will still used it every day. Funny, he thought, he was supposed to be getting rid of it.

Will interpreted Jack's momentary silence as uncertainty. 'Can I count on you to back me,' he continued, 'if Beth tries to block me?'

'Yeah, sure, Will,' Jack reassured him. 'I really am with you on this, but to be quite honest I'm not in the market for a fight with Beth about Beeches policy at the moment.' Wearily, he ran a hand through his hair. He looked exhausted.

Will grinned in sympathy. 'Broken heart keeping you awake?'

Jack ignored that one. He and Beth were still 'seeing' each other. But Beth, still terrified of anything that might smack of losing her independence, had inserted a 'less of' after the seeing.

'Broken arm, as it happens. Attached to an insomniac ecologist who's moved in over the road. Along with twenty pigs and a methane generator.'

'What?'

'Pig-power. Waste not, want not. He's using the pig waste to generate his own electricity.'

Will wrinkled his nose. Even Sarah, still harping on about economizing, hadn't thought of that one. Thank God. 'So how come the broken arm?'

'Fell off the shed into a pile of pig-shit.'

Will laughed. 'Oh, well, now that he's injured perhaps he'll leave you in peace.'

'If I thought a broken arm could stop him I'd have broken it myself.'

'Jack!' Both Jack and Will, on the point of closing the door behind them, turned to see James White, slightly red in the face from the chill of the morning and his brisk walk to The Beeches. And, it transpired, from anger. 'Jack,' he repeated as he approached them, 'what the bloody hell's going on? Where's Chloe gone off to this morning?' He glared defiantly at Jack. 'She won't tell me, so I want you to tell me.'

As Will tactfully headed for his own office, Jack sighed, put an arm round James's shoulders and steered him into the building. 'I think you'd better come in, James.'

In Jack's surgery, James refused either to sit down or to take his coat off. 'Just tell me, Jack.'

'She's gone to the hospital for a CT scan. For some tests.'

'Why? What for?'

Jack took a deep breath. 'Chloe's ill, James. She didn't want you to know because she didn't want you to worry.'

'What's she got, then?' James was still hostile, not wanting to believe that Jack had just confirmed his worst suspicions.

'It's quite serious, but . . . but I'm not supposed to tell you because of "patient confidentiality", y'know? And—'

'Don't give me that bullshit, Jack! This is *me*.' James prodded his chest. 'I'm supposed to be your friend! Christ, you've lived in our bloody house yet you're not even going to tell me what's wrong with my wife!'

'James, calm down! I'll talk to Chloe and—'

'Don't bloody bother!' With a last, angry glare, James stormed out of the room, nearly bowling Beth over in the process.

'Ouch!' said Beth as he left the building without even a backward glance. 'What was all that about?'

'Chloe's still not telling. Oh, Beth!' Jack turned to her, almost pleading. 'I feel I've made a real mess of this. Perhaps you should take the case over.'

Beth stared at him for a moment. What had Will said about 'protected time'? God, she really needed protecting at the moment – but taking over Jack's patients was not the way to do it. She knew where that would lead. 'No, Jack,' she said quietly, 'they're your patients. You don't need my help, you're more than capable. One of the best doctors I know.' But this last observation Beth decided to leave unspoken.

Jack met Chloe off the bus on her return from the hospital. Surprised to see him, Chloe gave him a cheery wave.

'Someone stolen your car?'

'No.' If someone really had stolen Jack's beloved 1955 handmade Bristol, he wouldn't be hanging around at bus stops, that was for sure. He shrugged and replied uncertainly, 'I'm waiting for you.'

'Oh.'

'Shall we go for a walk, Chloe?'

'Don't have much choice, do I? You've obviously got something to tell me.'

'Yes, I have.'

Taking Chloe's arm, Jack led her towards the footpath that took the 'scenic route' to Cardale. Tourists loved this walk. It incorporated the Derbyshire Dales in all their dramatic splendour. While it didn't involve any exertion, the path meandered beside a stream and gave stunning views of the hills on either side, the little farmhouses clinging to the hillsides, the emerald green fields and, in the distance, the huge, majestic chimneys of the now-redundant mills that had brought wealth – and the Industrial Revolution – to Derbyshire. But none of these things were on Jack's mind as he walked arm in arm, in uneasy silence, with Chloe.

'James threw a wobbly in my room this morning,' he said eventually.

'Oh.'

Jack looked at Chloe. 'You can't blame him. I'd be upset if the woman I loved left me completely in the dark about something so serious.'

'Did you tell him?' Chloe'e tone of voice left Jack in no doubt as to what she would do to him if he *had* told James.

'No, of course not. I can't tell him . . . not without your permission. But I don't want to tell him, Chloe. I want *you* to tell him.'

Chloe was silent for a moment, battling with her inner turmoil. 'He'll break up if he knows what's the matter with me,' she said. Then she turned to Jack, all the rage, fear and frustration suddenly boiling over. 'Why me, Jack?' she shouted through her tears. 'Why does it have to be me? What have I done to deserve cancer?'

Jack took her in his arms, relieved that she was at last finding an outlet for her emotion. 'There's no blame, Chloe.' He looked into her tearful eyes, usually so impish under the dark fringe. 'You did nothing wrong. Not ever.'

'I shouldn't have had the baby.'

'Don't say that. It's the best thing you've ever done. Take strength from her, Chloe. Encouragement. Her love for you will help you fight the illness.'

But Chloe just stared vacantly around her. Then she swiped savagely at a healthy-looking sprig of cow-parsley. 'I feel alone, so bloody helpless.'

Jack nudged her and they resumed their walk in contemplative silence. 'When I first told you about it, you told me that I was in charge.' He looked fondly down at Chloe. 'Well, I'm not in charge. You are. Take charge of your illness. Fight it. But don't fight it alone, there's no prizes for that. I can help you, Chloe, but James can help you more. Demand our support. And from others who love you.'

'I feel dirty,' said Chloe quietly.

'That's very usual. Try to remember that cancer isn't a dirty little illness that you should be ashamed of. It's an arbitrary, cruel condition that doesn't discriminate. Learn about Hodgkin's disease, Chloe. Read about it. Talk to others who have it . . . I'll help you with that, of course.' Jack's words were strong, vibrant, confident as he added, 'Give yourself weapons, Chloe. So you can win.'

'Am I going to be sterile and lose all my hair?'

Despite the seriousness of the situation, Jack smiled. The words were Chloe's first, tentative admission that she was prepared to fight her disease. 'No, love, you won't. The treatments are very sophisticated these days.'

Then Chloe looked up at Jack. 'D'you think that stupid husband of mine can take it?'

James did take it – much better than Chloe had expected. Having known something was terribly wrong, yet having been deliberately left in the dark, he had been suffering at the mercy of his own imagination. An imagination that had run riot. So when Chloe had eventually told him, his immediate reaction had been one of relief. Relief because at last he *knew*. He knew his wife wasn't going to die tomorrow, wasn't going to become mentally incapacitated, wasn't going to be crippled for life.

But then the reality of the situation sunk in. Chloe had cancer. A word that, despite the enormous advances made in medicine, despite huge success rates at treating it, was still the most terrifying in the English language.

And so, three days later, as Chloe and James entered The Beeches together to find out the results of Chloe's CT scan, it was James who appeared most ill at ease, more terrified than his wife.

Chloe nudged him in the ribs. 'Don't be so nervous, you prannock. You know what Jack said. Stage two Hodgkin's disease, that's what he reckons. Other folks have this much worse than me, you know. Some even have to have bone marrow transplants.'

James shuddered. Chloe was right. They would beat this together.

Beth, in reception with Jack, saw them approaching. While she still had Jack's attention, she said quietly, 'I would very much like to come round this evening. We need to talk.'

'Sure,' he said. 'But right now I have the most difficult consultation of my life.' He waved the letter in his hand. 'It's grim. The scan revealed stage four Hodgkin's, not stage two as we'd hoped. The cancer's reached her abdomen.'

James and Chloe greeted Jack's bombshell with stunned silence. Then, while Chloe still sat mutely, James started to become agitated. 'But you *said*! You *told* her she'd only need the – the radiotherapy . . .'

Jack, feeling utterly wretched, leaned forward to explain. 'I didn't, James. I was hoping the CT scan would confirm our best prognosis, but it hasn't worked out that way.' He turned from James's belligerent glare. 'Chloe, this is bad news, I'm not going to try to hide it from you. But everything I said to you before is still true. You have a more difficult fight, yes, but it's still a winnable fight. Chemotherapy will help you – of course it will – but *you* have to help *it*. Your will to survive is your strongest medicine.'

Chloe's reply was cold, almost chilling in its remoteness. 'I won't be able to have babies, will I? And my hair'll fall out.' Beside her, James buried his head in his hands. 'You didn't warn me I might have it this bad.' Still with a complete absence of emotion, she added, 'What are the odds?'

Jack paused for the briefest moment before replying. 'We don't talk about odds, love, they tell us nothing. All I know is that for the next five or six months you're going to think about nothing but life. Draw strength from all of us around you and fight like hell. Any time you want me, day or night . . .'

'I won't have the chemotherapy.'

'Chloe . . .'

'I'm going to die anyway. I don't want my body poisoned.'

'But, Chloe. Think who else is going to lose. James . . . Sarah Jane . . .'

'She's all right, isn't she? Bouncing with health. And she's too young to know. She'll get over it.'

And with that Chloe stood up and left the room without a backward glance. James, still hiding his face, clumsily shoved his own chair back and stumbled after her.

Beth didn't go to Jack's that evening. He came to her. Although he would never admit it, he preferred her house to his own. Her beautiful house on Cardale High Street, tucked away in a courtyard behind a large, wrought-iron gate, exuded quiet good taste and an air of permanence. Jack's own house was a base – Beth's was a home.

When he had proposed to her, Jack had envisaged selling his place and moving into hers. Beth, after all, had grown up in that house and wouldn't want to leave. It held too many memories for her, and contained too many mementoes of her life. While she had replaced her parents' heavy, Victorian furniture with more delicate yet unfussy pieces of her own, her family's enduring importance in her life was reflected in the numerous photographs dotted all over the place. Her beautiful mother, cruelly dead at fifty, her bluff, hearty father whose zest for life had allowed him another thirty years. A succession of healthy, loving Labradors and retrievers. Isabel and Dominic de Gines, smiling happily, protectively. And Beth herself, younger, more carefree and quite astonishingly beautiful.

Jack had been tactlessly surprised the first time he had seen the small photograph Beth kept discreetly behind a vase. She must have been about twenty. Her hair, now immaculately coiffed in a short yet slightly formal elegance, was long then. It tumbled around her face and matched her joyous expression. The photograph was of someone eager to accept everything life had in store. It was on seeing that photograph that Jack had decided he loved and wanted Beth. He wanted to share his life with her; to give her the things she had missed out on; to stop her becoming middle-aged before her time; to love someone who loved *him*.

But somehow it hadn't turned out like that. As he sat in front of the open fire in Beth's chintzy, yellow and blue sitting-room, Jack reflected that not only was he losing Beth, but he was losing his touch as a doctor. He sat in moody silence, while Beth, almost like a mother with her little boy, stroked his hair.

'Nothing I can say will persuade you you're wrong, will it?'

'I let her down,' replied Jack. 'I led her to believe it wasn't life-threatening. I failed her because I'm too close to her.'

'Oh, Jack, don't punish yourself like this. Breaking bad news is the hardest part, especially to someone you love.'

'I'm a crap doctor. And a crap lover.' Jack's voice began to waver. 'I don't know what I'm doing with my life.'

Beth put her arms round him. She could almost feel

something breaking inside her. Then Jack sniffed loudly and looked at her through brimming eyes. 'Anyway,' he said brusquely, 'enough of all this. You . . . erm . . . you wanted to talk to me. Fire away.'

Beth returned his look. Then she planted an affectionate kiss on the top of his head. 'It can wait.'

But Jack had obviously underestimated his abilities as a doctor. While Beth, claiming pressure of paperwork, had bundled him off home before he could disprove his notion of himself as a 'crap lover', his visitor the next morning restored his faith in his career. Just as he was reaching for his doctor's bag, cramming a slice of toast into his mouth and searching for his car keys, there was a knock on the door. 'Oh, God,' he said under his breath. Alberta on the loose again.

But it was Chloe, carrying a large casserole dish. She beamed at him. 'Hot-pot,' she announced.

'Chloe . . .'

'If you're going to be treating me, I'm not having you undernourished.' She marched to the kitchen table, deposited the casserole and turned to Jack. Where yesterday there had been despair, her face now bore a different expression.

'How are you today?' asked Jack tentatively.

'Well . . . not bad, y'know. And I've been thinking . . . I've always wanted to wear one of those brightly coloured nylon wigs. Y'know, bright pink or blue. I mean, there's no point in trying to hide the fact that all my hair's going to fall out so I might as well have a bit of fun while it happens, don't you reckon?'

Jack felt like crying. 'I reckon.' He smiled at Chloe: she smiled back in tacit understanding. The first hurdle had been crossed. Chloe was going to tackle her disease head-on and undergo chemotherapy. Jack went to hug her but was stopped in his tracks by her change of expression.

Suddenly she was looking as if she had swallowed something repellent.

'Jack . . .?'

Alarm bells rang in his head. 'What is it, Chloe?'

But Chloe was now looking at her hot-pot. 'I've been making this for years. It's never smelled anything but delicious.' She bent to the dish and sniffed. 'No, it's not that. It's . . . it's *you*, Jack. You . . . you *stink*!'

'Me?'

'Yeah, well, p'raps not you but,' she was like a bloodhound now, sniffing all around her, 'your *house*. You haven't got a dead granny in the attic, have you?'

Jack laughed, comprehension dawning. 'No, she's in the cellar. You're smelling pig-shit. I'm sorry, I must've got used to it . . .'

'Pig-shit?'

'Yeah.' Jack nodded in the direction of his neighbour. 'Richard. He's using pig-shit to fuel his methane burner. Cheap electricity, you see.' He took a deep breath. 'It *is* disgusting, isn't it? I keep meaning to call the environmental health people but—'

Suddenly he was stopped in his tracks by the sound of a massive explosion. Aghast, Jack and Chloe stared at each other as the sound reverberated through the little kitchen. Then, still wordless, they rushed outside.

They were in time to see what remained of the methane gas burner floating down from the sky. What had been the corrugated iron shed containing Richard's revolutionary fuel supply had been flattened. Bits of metal were lying around the field and a pall of smoke hung over the evil-smelling source of supply. In the corner of the field, the pig sty was a squealing mass of distressed animals. Yelping and snorting, the pigs appeared nonetheless unhurt. But Jack was looking around in desperation. Where the hell, he wondered, was Richard?

Just as Jack was debating whether or not to rush back to his house to telephone for help, a figure emerged from behind the dry stone dyke that marked the boundary of Richard's land. It wasn't, at first, a recognizably human figure. Jack heard Chloe's sharp intake of breath as she saw it stumbling towards them. Like a comic-strip character, Richard was almost completely black from the explosion. Yet there was nothing comic about the blackness. He was burned from head to foot, and hobbling in agony towards them.

Jack rushed to his aid. Then he stopped abruptly as a huge grin replaced his expression of anxious horror. The black bits were falling off with each step Richard took and Richard himself was grinning sheepishly – and smelling to high heaven. He stood in front of Jack and wiped ineffectually at the remains of the pig-shit that had been blasted all over him.

'Another mishap?' grinned Jack.

''Fraid so.' Richard looked sadly at the remains of his shed. 'I wonder . . . I wonder if it wouldn't be an altogether better idea to build a windmill?' Then, doubt crossing his features, he looked back towards the pig sty. 'But then I'd have to sell the pigs.'

For the first time in days Jack looked ecstatically happy. Then his face darkened as Richard continued. 'Hey, Jack! I know, you could have Alberta if you want. I know how fond she is of you. Look, see?'

Jack didn't have to look. He could feel. Alberta, true to form, had escaped the confines of her sty and, as if by instinct, had rushed to safety. And safety, for her, was at Jack's side. Richard looked at her in fond admiration as she nuzzled contentedly at Jack's feet. Jack looked down in disgust.

And then, the sound piercing the cool morning air, Chloe started laughing uncontrollably. Helpless with mirth, she nearly lost her balance but instead collapsed happily into Jack's arms. Jack, now laughing with her, stroked the glossy hair blowing gently into his face. The hair, he thought, may go: but Chloe's will to live was here to stay.

At The Beeches, Will and Beth greeted Jack's news with unconcealed delight. Beth's relief at Chloe's decision had betrayed not a trace of self-congratulation – although she had every right to congratulate herself. Her real reason for sending Jack home the previous night had been a sudden and secret desire to visit Chloe for herself. What had passed between the two women was something she hoped Jack would never find out. Without a doubt Beth had overstepped the mark on two counts: she had muscled in on one of Jack's patients – again – and she had given Chloe a lot more than impartial medical advice. She had bullied, cajoled and finally used emotional blackmail to renew Chloe's will to live. And she had succeeded.

'Oh, Jack, I'm *so* pleased. You deserve a break.'

Jack looked surprised. '*I* don't deserve anything. It's Chloe. She deserves to live.'

But Beth had now turned her attention to Will. 'So at least we'll be holding a happier fort while you're away on that fundholding seminar.'

Will nearly jumped out of his skin. 'What?'

'You are going, aren't you?' A wicked little smile played on Beth's lips.

'Well . . . yes . . . of course.'

'Good. You're right. I need to know more than I do about fundholding.'

Will and Jack looked at each other in amazement as Beth walked out of the room.

'Beth?' Kim stopped her at the doorway. 'It's Brian Drake on the phone. Can you have a word with him?' Unseen by Beth, Jack's expression darkened.

Ten minutes later Beth was back. 'That was Brian Drake,' she said unnecessarily, her tone casual. 'He was wondering if we would care to carry out occupational health services at his factory. Screenings, medicals. He says he could make it worth our while.' She looked up at the two men. 'Financially speaking.'

'Which he would never have offered, of course, if you hadn't brought forward his medical,' said Jack.

'Oh, I shouldn't think that's the case. I guess it's just that we're his doctors; first people he thought of, I s'pose.'

Just as, thought Jack, our patients should have first place in our thoughts. Point taken.

As he left the room, Beth allowed herself a tiny smile of triumph. Perhaps, she mused, interfering did bring benefits after all. Then she looked at Jack's retreating back. Tonight, she thought. Tonight I'll tell him.

Jack was surprised – not unpleasantly – to see her.

'Hi!' He grinned, remembering the last time she had called unexpectedly. 'Tonight I may even offer you a drink before you ask for one.' He ushered her in. 'Hang on a mo and I'll open that bottle of Gran Reserva.'

Beth hesitated. 'I don't, to be honest, feel much like drinking.'

'Oh? What's the matter? Not poorly, are you?'

'No, doctor, I'm not poorly.'

Jack frowned. 'Mmm. Something's on your mind. You wanted to talk to me last night, before I selfishly mentioned my problems.'

Beth took a deep breath. 'You're right, Jack. You're absolutely right. You deserve more. You deserve commitment. I've been stringing you along these past months . . .'

'You haven't been "stringing me along"—'

Beth stopped him with a gentle hand. 'Hear me out, please.' Again she took a deep breath. 'I've wanted to be your lover and you to be my lover – but only at my own convenience. Only on the condition that it didn't interrupt

88

the rest of my life. And that's ridiculous.' She looked Jack straight in the eye. 'Immature and selfish.'

'Beth, come on . . .'

'So, I've made a decision.'

Jack, despite Beth's pleas, began opening the bottle of wine in his hand. Pity he had no champagne. 'No one's pushing you, Beth. I'm sorry I gave you a kind of ultimatum, that wasn't fair of me . . .'

'Please, I've made a decision—'

'About bloody time!' Jack was all smiles.

'It's over.'

'*What!*'

'I'm finishing this. Us. It's over.' She saw Jack's expression. Bewildered. Hurt. Dumbfounded. Trying to soften the blow, she continued. 'I'm not ready to make a commitment. Not totally. I'm not ready to . . . to grow up yet.'

Anger now flashed through Jack's eyes. 'Maybe you never will be.'

'Maybe not.'

'You can't just walk out of my life!'

Beth's reply was gentle. 'I'm hardly doing that, am I?'

'If I knew this was going to happen, I'd never have asked you to marry me.'

'Oh, Jack! Relationships can't stand still. They flourish or wither. You said that once. And you were right.'

'No, Beth, listen—'

'But it doesn't mean I don't love you.' Quickly, she kissed him on the forehead and turned towards the door. 'I'll always love you.'

CH**A**PTER 7

Douglas Hart and Alice North were of the old school. Both widowed, both elderly, they had struck up a friendship some years ago. It was a friendship that had led several Cardale residents – including the doctors at The Beeches – to suspect that the couple were sweet on each other. Alice, had she known, would have greeted the news with her habitual scoff and replied that Mr Hart was a 'silly old bugger' who couldn't look after himself and was more trouble than he was worth. Douglas Hart, for his part, would have offered his treasured old wartime medals to anyone who could stop Alice from fussing over him all the time. In other words, they were sweet on each other.

Shortly after Jack Kerruish's arrival in Cardale, Mr Hart had tried to take his own life – for no other reason than his being a casualty of the ailing health service. Douglas, plagued by cataracts in both eyes, was going blind. The condition was reversible by a simple operation, yet the consultant at the hospital had seen no grounds for urgency. And so Mr Hart had been at the end of a waiting list that topped two years. Beth Glover, while saddened by the situation, had felt there was nothing she could do about it. Jack had seen differently. Even before the suicide attempt, he had badgered the consultant to bring forward the operation. The consultant had replied that there was neither the money nor the medical grounds to take such an action. Jack had pointed out that, one way or another, money from the state was going to be spent on Mr Hart: either the cheaper option of the operation or the traumatic and hugely expensive alternative of placing an elderly, blind man in a home. The consultant had been unmoved – and then Mr Hart had attempted suicide. After that, the combined efforts of Jack and Ian Hart, Douglas's son, had finally got the old man into hospital within two weeks.

Alice was another story – although one that The Beeches' doctors had kept to themselves. Her life had been put in danger by the actions of one of them – Will Preston. It had been a year ago, when Will, beset by financial and marital problems, was, unknown to anyone, teetering on the edge of a nervous breakdown. In a last-ditch attempt to earn easy money and – so he thought – placate Sarah, he had got himself involved in drugs testing. A highly sophisti-cated and extremely safe practice, it was nonetheless regarded by some doctors as unethical. They didn't see why they should use their patients as guinea-pigs for no other reason than the greater good and profit of the drug companies. Will, knowing full well that Beth, his senior partner, was one of those doctors, had kept quiet about the fact that he was privately using a new anti-inflamma-tory drug on those of his elderly patients who could benefit from it. There was nothing wrong with what he was doing, apart from the fact he noted those patients' symptoms on a separate file, and not on their medical cards.

And then the worst had happened. Alice North had fallen seriously ill and it had been Jack, not Will, who had been on call that night. Unaware of the drugs with which Will was treating her, Jack had not been able to consider any side effects they may have had. He could have seriously endangered her life by prescribing treatment directly at odds with Will's. Luckily, he hadn't. And, also luckily, Alice's illness had turned out to be an inflamed gall bladder due (although she still didn't believe it) to seventy years of enthusiastic over-indulgence in fried food. Alice's life had been saved, and so, after his mental state was discovered, was Will's career.

Both these experiences had drawn Alice and Mr Hart

even closer. And it was Alice, on a cool, clear morning, who had just been to the Cardale General Stores to do Mr Hart's shopping. Men, she knew, hadn't a clue.

She entered the house in her own inimitable fashion – at a brisk trot and as if she owned the place. Mr Hart, who had spent the last ten minutes carefully arranging cups and saucers, a little jug of milk and a plate of biscuits, glared at her.

'More stodge and Brussels sprouts, I suppose.'

Alice was unperturbed. 'Needn't eat it if you don't want to.' She laid the shopping on the kitchen table with a thud. 'You owe me three pounds forty-two.'

'Humph.' Getting his money out, he proffered the plate of biscuits. 'Have a custard cream.' He might as well have been offering her rat poison. 'Getting that huge packet when you know I hate them.'

'They were on offer.' Alice was indignant.

'Good job they weren't selling off roller skates, eh?'

Glaring at each other in companionable silence, they sipped their tea.

'You're having a day out,' said Mr Hart suddenly. 'Sunday the twenty-seventh.'

'Oh. Who says?'

'We're going to watch a Spitfire fly-past . . .'

'A what? They still flying, then?'

'Of course they are, woman! Nearest thing to engineering perfection there's ever been!' Then, seeing her expression, he asked with undisguised concern, 'You'll enjoy it, won't you?'

'Can't wait.'

'Not many of us left to pay our respects. Every year a few less.'

Alice, sensing how much this event meant to him, relented. 'Oh, well if it keeps you happy. Better than dragging me down a coal mine, I suppose.' Then, after a final sip of tea and another custard cream, she got to her feet. 'Better be off, then. No rest for the idle.'

'Wicked.'

'What?'

'There's no rest for the wicked, Alice.' He chuckled. 'You're a wicked woman.'

'Aye, and you're a daft old bugger,' she replied, reaching for her coat.

The next ritual in Mr Hart's life, after carefully washing up the tea crockery and taking a leisurely constitutional, was the small sherry before lunch. Mr Hart held no truck with modern namby-pamby views about alcohol. You had a sherry before lunch, a whisky before dinner, and if you had company you had wine with your meal. The last time Ellie from The Beeches had visited him – imposed herself upon him – she had left a leaflet entitled 'Alcohol and the Elderly'. Mr Hart had used it to polish his best brogues, gleefully watching the newsprint leaving a final sheen on the already glossy leather.

He frowned slightly as he sipped his sherry. The thought of the leaflet brought another ritual to mind. His muddy boots from yesterday were still on the window-sill above the draining-board, waiting for a good clean. Humming merrily to the military march playing on the radio, he entered the kitchen and decided – since there was no rest for the wicked – to cook his lunch and clean his boots at the same time. Alcohol and the Elderly, he thought scornfully. Pah! He downed the remains of his sherry and reached for a can of baked beans.

The next moment he nearly overbalanced as a blinding, searing pain shot through his head. Wincing, he put a hand to his forehead – and then, as suddenly as it had come, the pain disappeared. Blinking, he shook his head in exasperation. Sometimes, although he would only admit it to himself, old age did give you funny aches and pains. Then he dismissed the little episode from his mind and set about his tasks anew. But again he was distracted; not by pain but by disbelief. In front of him, the contents of the can of baked beans were heaped, not in the saucepan, but in the muddy boots. He stared, aghast, for a full minute. This was not the action of a healthy, capable man. Something had happened, something he didn't want to think about. Then, angrily, he tried to clean up the mess. In his haste he dropped one of the boots on the floor and the beans slopped out. He shook his head in frustration. Later. He would clear it up later. Absently, he reached for his sherry glass. Only after the first fortifying sip did he realize that he couldn't remember pouring a second glass.

'Dad? Where are you?' The voice startled Mr Hart out of his reverie. Quickly, before his son started looking for him, he yelled, 'Coming. Just coming,' and rushed out of the kitchen, shutting the door firmly behind him.

Father and son met in the hall. Ian, a sales rep based in Birmingham, was always in a perpetual rush. Now he was looking agitated.

'You should be on your way to the airport,' barked his father.

'I am. I am. Taxi's waiting outside.' Ian smiled fondly. He hated leaving the old man for this long. Normally he tried to look in every two days, but this trip to Germany was going to take a full week. 'Just thought I'd better put the central heating timer on.' He stepped towards the kitchen, adding, 'The nurse is going to keep an eye on you . . .'

'I don't need a nurse!' With surprising agility, Mr Hart stepped in and barred his son's way. 'And I don't want the heating on all day long!'

Ian paused. 'Yes, but if there's a really cold snap and we don't set the timer—'

'Don't treat me like a senile old fool, Ian. I don't want the damn heating on. It gives me a thumping head. Leave it.'

Ian, seeing his father's ferocious glare, nodded – unwillingly – in acquiescence. 'OK. OK, Dad. But you'll have to stop this.'

'Stop what?'

'Pretending to be a bad-tempered stubborn old sod.'

Relieved that Ian wasn't going to press the issue of the heating, Mr Hart smiled. 'I am a bad-tempered stubborn old sod. Now,' he pushed Ian back towards the front door, 'get going or you'll miss your plane.'

As Ian climbed into the taxi with a last, resigned wave, Mr Hart turned back into the house. He looked at the kitchen door and the smile disappeared from his face.

Will was feeling on top of the world. The fundholding seminar in London had been a huge success. Jack and Beth had rechristened it a 'funholding seminar' and teased him about wanting a 'jolly' with fifty other GPs, an excuse to drink as much as possible, behave like irresponsible schoolboys, and sleep off the hangover in the lecture hall the next day. Yet Will – while anything but averse to having a good time – had behaved impeccably and surprised himself by his enthusiasm for his self-appointed task of becoming The Beeches' authority on fundholding. He had worked hard, learned a lot and even Beth, on his return, had shown a surprising willingness to read with interest the brochures he had returned with. It was funny, he thought. Now that Jack and Beth were no longer 'an item' and were skirting warily round each other, they were both looking to Will to provide enthusiasm and new ideas. Things had changed.

Whistling to himself as he walked down Cardale High Street, Will reflected that things had not, sadly, changed at home. Sarah was enjoying neither the house nor her job. But far worse than that, she seemed unable to forgive Tony for the appalling episode at the old mill. On the surface, it had been forgotten. Tony and Harry Clulow, as first offenders, had merely been cautioned. The ghastly Wayne had made a full recovery and his gang, shocked by what had happened, had disbanded. And Rob Clulow had had his heart by-pass operation.

Strictly speaking, Rob's by-pass had been helped along by the old boy network. Will, playing golf with Nick Jenkins, had finally succeeded where both Jack and Beth had failed. He had persuaded the consultant to take Rob on as an urgent priority. Dominic, sweetened by his victory (Will, the better golfer, had been playing for ulterior motives), had sworn this would be a 'one and only' favour. If only things could be so simply sorted out at home.

Will had been prepared to dismiss the whole unhappy episode. Tony, shocked to the core by what he had done, had become quieter, better-behaved – and closer to his father. Will had waived Sarah's rules about the rec and regularly took Tony and Julian – and Harry Clulow – to play football there. It had certainly brought father and sons together. But Sarah felt alienated. Will had tried to reason with her, but to no avail. It was their sadness that they were still unable to communicate properly with each other, and it was Sarah in particular who was prevented by her pride from admitting what was uppermost on her mind: namely, that she thought she was a failure as a mother; that any problems with her sons were because of her, her compulsion to improve her lot; her shame at failing to do so.

Lost in thought, Will nearly collided with Douglas Hart outside the old man's house. 'Oh, Lord, I'm sorry, Mr Hart. Didn't see you. Miles away.'

'Thought you were supposed to cure me, not kill me.'

Will grinned and then looked closely at Mr Hart. 'Well, you're certainly looking better. No more attacks?'

'No.' He patted his pocket. 'Got my pills. Not that I need them, I'm sure, but that old busybody won't let me out of the house without them.'

'So Alice has moved in then?'

Mr Hart looked mutinous. 'Yes. *Temporarily*, mind.' He grimaced with distaste. 'Hardly lets me out of her sight, the old witch.'

Will laughed. He was glad to see Douglas Hart out and

about – and doubly glad that Alice North had moved in. She was hardly, he conceded, a spring chicken herself, but she was a good five years younger than Mr Hart and in considerably better health. And it was she, thank God, who had found the old man after what had turned out to have been the third minor stroke he had suffered – without telling anybody.

'Well,' replied Will, 'it's good to see you looking better, and I really can't see any reason why you can't go to the fly-past,' Mr Hart smiled triumphantly, 'as long as you take your aspirin in the morning and have someone with you.'

'Just don't tell Alice, eh, doctor? She's forbidden me to go since my "turn" – as if it's any of her business. I'll get there somehow, even if it's on her bloody broomstick.' Chortling at his own wit, he doffed his hat at Will and continued on his morning constitutional.

Will carried on walking down the street. It would be nice, he thought, if someone could drive Mr Hart to Ladybower Reservoir where the fly-past was taking place. Make sure he was warm and comfortable all day long. Then he grinned. He knew the very person. He reckoned she'd be good. And she was, after all, in training to be a Samaritan.

That evening, Isabel and Beth had dinner together. They had gone to the restaurant in Brompton and purposely avoided, by mutual and unspoken agreement, The Manor in Cardale. Chloe had started her chemotherapy that week and James, understandably, was distraught. For once, Beth was glad of the 'protected time' that the doctors gave themselves. Somehow she didn't feel like bolstering James tonight. She herself needed a good ego boost.

'So, how's that girl with RSJ?' asked Isabel as she put down the menu.

Beth giggled. 'It's RSI, Isabel. Repetitive Strain Injury.

RSJ's an architectural thing. Anyway,' she added, suddenly serious, 'how did you know about Carol Dart?'

'Ken Alton told me.' Ken Alton, sixtyish, gentlemanly and good-looking, was Carol's boss, owner of a local factory, and now the bewildered employer of a girl with a condition he'd never heard of. 'Said that you're establishing all these new rules about people who work with computers. Time off every ten minutes or some such nonsense.' Isabel's tone indicated that she thought the very idea of becoming ill from typing ridiculous.

'It's not that bad, Isabel. And it's not *us* implementing all these new rules. It's the government. Europe and all that.'

'Hmm. But what about that judge the other day? Said there was no such thing as RS . . . I. Only people with "eggshell personalities" got it, I seem to remember him saying.' The concept of an eggshell personality was also alien to Isabel.

'And I seem to remember *me* saying I'd like to throttle the old fart.' Beth leaned forward in her seat. 'He's a *judge*, Isabel, not a diagnostician. I think it was jolly irresponsible of him to say there was no such thing. Remember ME? Nobody used to believe in that until important people started getting it. Wait till that judge gets a sore bum from lounging about in a seat all day. Then he'll believe in your RSJ.'

They both laughed. Isabel beckoned the waiter and ordered a bottle of expensive burgundy. This dinner was her treat.

'Well, I can see you're in a fighting mood this evening, Elizabeth. Bad day at the office?'

Beth looked suddenly mournful. 'Oh, Isabel. I feel . . . I just feel I'm suddenly being left out of my own practice. Marginalized, somehow. Will's acting all cock-a-hoop and claiming to be the Delphic Oracle of Fundholding and Jack's rushing about being Dr Kildare and knowing better than anyone and . . .'

'And you're miffed because he ought to be pining for you.'

'No. Not a bit of it. I chucked *him*, after all.'

'Doesn't mean you don't still fancy him, does it?'

Beth was getting annoyed. 'Oh, for heaven's sake, Isabel! Stop talking like a teenager.'

'Sorry. Sorry.' They were silent as the waiter poured the wine. Isabel tasted it and nodded at him. She was easily old enough to be his mother, yet he blushed as he met her eyes. Isabel had that sort of effect on waiters.

'Actually,' Isabel leaned forward, 'I *feel* a bit like a teenager.'

'Oh.' This meant a man on the horizon. 'You've found a man?'

'Don't be vulgar, Beth. You make it sound like I go trawling the streets.' She did her best to look indignant. 'No, I met him on the counselling course. When we were doing our role-playing. I was a stroppy teenager and he was my irate father. I, of course, ran rings round him.' That was true. Isabel, the other trainees on the course had decided, had missed her true vocation as an actress. She had revelled in playing a teenage, shop-lifting truant. She'd had the 'audience' in silent stitches and Ken, her 'father', had finished by asking the tutor if he could belt her. Instead, on the way back, he had kissed her.

Beth grinned. She could well imagine Isabel being a very difficult, very volatile teenager. And she was pleased for her friend. Someone, after all, deserved to be lucky in love.

'So who is he, then?'

'Well, since you ask, it's . . . it's er . . . Ken Alton.'

'Isabel! You are a dark horse! So *that's* how you get your inside information on my patients.' She took a sip of wine. 'Mmm. Must say, I've always thought he was quite dishy myself.'

'Well, hands off. He's mine . . . or, at least,' a kiss

99

didn't, after all, constitute possession, 'at least we appear to be getting on quite well. And we're having a day out next week.'

'Oh, what fun! Where?'

'Ladybower Reservoir. To watch a Spitfire fly-past.'

'Good God, he can't be that old, surely?'

'What d'you mean "that old"?' Isabel was forever touchy on the subject of age.

'He can't be old enough to be a veteran pilot.'

'Oh, I see. No, no. That's not why we're going. We'll be there in our capacity as Good Samaritans.'

'Oh?'

'Will's idea. You know old Mr Hart? Well, the poor old thing has his heart set on going – all his old cronies'll be there. And, well, apart from the fact that I'd volunteer like a shot to take him anyway, I do feel rather guilty about him.'

'It wasn't your fault he had that stroke, Isabel.'

'I know, I know. But I did promise his son I'd look in on him that day and I . . . well, I didn't. Alice found him all bewildered. Poor old soul.' Isabel felt genuinely wretched about the whole business.

But Beth was smiling. 'She's not just Alice, Isabel. She's his lady-love.'

'What? At their age? Don't be ridiculous!' Then she saw the wicked gleam in Beth's eye and quickly changed the subject. 'Anyway, Will called me today and asked if I'd like to take him. Chauffeur him and pamper him . . .'

'And have a quick snog with Ken Alton in the bushes while he's not looking.'

'Beth! Now who's talking like a teenager? It should be very interesting,' she added primly. Then she grinned. 'And come to think of it, I was brought up on war films featuring *amazingly* handsome pilots . . .'

*

'Where I do or do not go is no business of yours.'

Alice bristled. 'It is when I'm meant to be looking after you.'

'I don't need looking after.'

'How come I'm living in, then?'

'That's soon sorted.' Mr Hart glared at her. This was not one of their usual, mock-serious arguments. This was a right royal row. With bells on. 'Go home.'

But Alice chose a new line of attack. 'The only place I'm going is to phone the doctor. Just you wait till he hears about this.'

'He already knows. And there was no argument from him. I'm going to the fly-past and that's that.'

Alice was now genuinely frightened for her friend. 'With some stranger of a taxi driver who won't know what to do if you have a turn . . .'

'With Isabel de Gines, actually. Not that it's any of your business.'

'*Her?* Isabel de Gines. That stuck up . . .' she paused. 'Your Ian asked me to look after you.'

'We're not married. I don't have to "cleave unto you forsaking all others". Thank God.' He sounded as if he really meant it.

'I won't be responsible. I'll call Ian and tell him . . .'

'If you do, you'll never set foot in my house again.'

'But he ought to know.'

'I flew those damn things in the war. It was *me* up there, not *you*.' Then, despite his rage, he lowered his voice. 'It was my friends killed, not yours. And I won't have you treating me like this.'

Alice had never seen him like this before. And she had never felt like this. Brusquely, she wiped a hand over her eyes. 'Isabel de Gines!' she snorted. 'All fur coat and no knickers!'

But Douglas Hart was now laying out his coat and scarf. 'Bugger off,' he said.

Fifteen minutes later Ken Alton's car drew up outside Mr Hart's house. Both Ken and Isabel alighted, the latter wearing, Alice would have been pleased to know, a waxed cotton coat with a fur lining and a fur hood. Her underwear could only be guessed at, but, as Ken had said when he'd picked her up, 'You'd be daft not to be wearing thermals in this weather.' It was a typical Cardale day: bitterly cold with a thin drizzle.

"Morning, Commander Hart! Lovely day for it!' Ken was in joking, looking-after-old-people mode.

Mr Hart missed the irony. 'Wonderful, wonderful,' he countered. Now muffled securely against the weather, he handed his binoculars to Isabel, sniffed the morning air and stepped into the car. Isabel, all concern, placed a travelling rug over his knees. With Isabel and Ken in the front, and Mr Hart sitting regally in the back, they made their stately progress down the High Street. None of them noticed Alice North, her face set in a firm, disapproving line, making her way to church. Alone.

'He's in his element,' said Isabel, looking fondly at Douglas Hart. He was sitting on a bench, looking out over the reservoir, and surrounded by faces from the past. On arrival at Ladybower, he had informed Ken and Isabel that he imagined they had better things to do than 'stand about with an old fool like him'. They had taken the hint. This was a highly emotional occasion for the old man, and if he was going to have tears in his eyes, he was damned if he would let Ken and Isabel see them.

So 'the young people', as he called them, were standing well apart from the little group on the bench, watching the proceedings with interest. A great many people, both young and old, had come to watch the fly-past. Small boys were rushing about, pretending to be aeroplanes; a hot-dog stall was doing a brisk trade and, in the midst of the activity, a team from Central TV was setting up cameras in preparation for the Spitfires. One of the organizers was dispensing coffee from a large urn. Most people had to help themselves – but not the veterans. This was a special day for them. She approached Mr Hart's bench and handed out the warming drinks. With a brief nod, Douglas Hart thanked her and then fished in his pocket. Along with his coat, gloves, scarf and hat, he had brought that other essential barrier against the cold – his hip-flask.

'Here we are, lads,' he said, passing it round. Amidst murmurs of approval, he added, 'I thought there'd be no one here. Fifty years on,' he raised his mug, 'and never forgotten.'

'Never forgotten,' they toasted. 'To absent friends.'

Mr Hart chuckled. 'Let's hope they're somewhere a bit warmer than this.'

Jim Samson, on his left, scratched his hearing aid. 'Denny Wilson will be, anyway. I said,' he raised his voice, 'Denny Wilson will be anyway!'

'We heard. It's you that's deaf, you daft old git, not us.' The others laughed. Douglas hadn't lost any of his dour, affectionate wit.

Brian Derbyshire, dressed in an identical charcoal-grey coat, huddled against a sudden gust of wind and wrapped his woollen scarf tighter. 'Bit different', he indicated the inelegant item, 'from your silk cravats.' Then, reminded of something, he turned to Douglas. 'I suppose you still get the women, do you?'

'Rotten with 'em. Sick of fighting them off.' Douglas Hart was, indeed, in his element.

Ken put his arm around Isabel. 'Come on, let's leave them to it. Mind you,' he added, as they walked back to the car, 'if they continue toasting each other with that stuff, they won't even be able to *see* the fly-past.'

'It *is* rather exciting, isn't it?' Isabel was feeling particularly mellow. And she had also brought a hip-flask which, back in the car, they proceeded to enjoy.

For a moment they were silent, both taking in the

sweeping panorama of the reservoir, the woodland on the other side and the craggy hills beyond. This, remembered Isabel, was a well-known tourist spot. It was also famous as a lovers' meeting-place.

'I don't think', said Ken suddenly, 'that I'm a natural counsellor. Not like you.'

Isabel, surprised, turned to him. 'Me? Beth calls me a moral bully.'

'You're very close, aren't you?'

'Nearest thing to a daughter I've ever had. And I suppose I became a sort of substitute mother . . .' She trailed off as memories caught up with her.

'I don't have anyone close. That's why I thought counselling . . . I have a lot of time and few calls on it, so I thought if I tried to give some service . . . y'know . . .'

'I'm the opposite. There aren't enough hours in my day or days in my week.'

'Perhaps that's why you're such a natural. Why I'm so stilted.'

'Come on, Ken! You're great!' Isabel laughed.

'No, really, I'm not,' he insisted. 'I don't think counselling's for me.'

'Oh.' A tiny frown creased Isabel's brow. Was this leading where she thought it was leading? 'I'm sorry,' she said quietly. 'I'll miss you on Wednesday afternoons. And who'll help me with my homework?'

Ken touched Isabel's shoulder. 'Why not me?'

Isabel turned to him. He was smiling broadly, invitingly. 'Oh, I am glad,' she said, and melted into his embrace.

There was silence in the car. And then Isabel, another thought occurring to her, broke free from Ken's arms. 'I'm not a counselling substitute, am I? Like counselling was a friendship substitute?'

Ken stroked her cheek and looked her in the eyes. 'You'll never be a substitute, Isabel. You'll always be a main player.'

A low growling in the distance indicated the imminent arrival of the Spitfires.

'Here we go,' said Douglas Hart. 'No sound like it.'

Brian Derbyshire scanned the horizon. 'Can't see a damn thing.'

'Always were as blind as a bat. Come on!' Douglas struggled to his feet as the rest of the spectators moved towards the edge of the reservoir. 'Don't want to be left behind.'

Fumbling excitedly for his binoculars, he led his little group forward. Scanning the horizon, he was silent for a moment and then gave a triumphant shout. 'Angels at three o'clock!'

All heads were angled up now, transfixed by the tiny plane heading straight for them. Flying low, suddenly deafening, it passed overhead, the colours and the noise taking the veteran pilots back fifty years, back to the time when they were the ones in the cockpit, battling for Britain.

Around them, children jabbered excitedly; behind them, Isabel and Ken watched, enchanted, from the car's open doors. Yet they were oblivious to all except the little fighter and the roar of its Merlin engine as it passed over again, this time with a victory roll. And then, dipping its wings in salute to the men who had made this possible, the Spitfire flew gracefully away over the reservoir.

A collective sigh broke the ensuing silence. Then the woman who had been handing out coffee announced to the veterans that there was to be a break for 'brandy all round'. But Douglas Hart didn't hear her. Walking away from his friends, he gazed, misty-eyed, into the distance. And then he moved quietly out of earshot of the others, wanting, just for a moment, to be alone with his treasured memories.

Nobody noticed he was absent. Nobody saw him nearing the muddy undergrowth that sloped towards the water. And nobody saw him suddenly clutching his head, dropping his hip-flask and falling heavily to the ground.

Isabel, in her best jolly, schoolmarmish manner, stepped briskly towards the group of veterans. Drinking and laughing, sharing old remembered stories, they could probably, as she said to Ken, stand there all day. But she had to get home.

'Now, gentlemen, if you've all had enough booze and memories . . .' Nobody paid her the blindest bit of attention. Unperturbed, she went up to Brian Derbyshire and tapped him on the back. 'Mr Hart?' He didn't turn round. 'Mr Hart,' she repeated, 'I think it's time . . . Oh!' She jumped back in alarm as Brian turned round. 'Oh, I thought you were Mr Hart.' All the old men were now looking at her, mildly, with polite interest. 'Where is he? Where's Mr Hart?' Suddenly Isabel was seized by panic as she realized that it had been Brian Derbyshire, not Douglas Hart, who had been in her sights for the past few minutes. They were wearing identical coats.

'He was here a minute ago,' said someone helpfully.

'Yes, but he's not here now!' Isabel shouted. 'Oh, God, oh, God! Where is he?' She looked around frantically, transferring her panic to all around her.

'Isabel?' It was Ken. 'Look, no need to panic. He's probably gone to the loo or something . . .'

'Oh, shut up, Ken!' Isabel's anxiety was making her increasingly aggressive. Brushing past Ken and approaching the organizer, she shouted at the bemused woman, 'Do you think you could leave that *bloody* tea for just one minute? We've got a missing person . . . Oh, God,' she added in an angry murmur, 'that stupid coat of his . . . I should have stayed with him.'

They found his hip-flask first. The silver cup, glinting in the hazy sunshine, beckoned at the water's edge. Douglas Hart lay a few feet away, almost hidden by the damp, muddy undergrowth. His eyes were closed, his face was a picture of contentment – and he was still breathing.

'Call an ambulance!' someone shouted.

'He's frozen!'

'Someone give him a coat!'

'Isabel, scrambling to her knees, shrugging off her coat, enveloped Douglas Hart in the luxuriant fur. She touched his cheek. 'Douglas? Douglas . . . can you hear me?'

There was not even a flicker of an eyelid in response. Isabel jumped to her feet and addressed the anxious faces clustered around her. 'I'll call his doctor. I know what's wrong . . . he was being treated . . .'

A minute later she was babbling frantically down Ken's car-phone.

Will, on the other end of the line, tried to calm her. 'Try to tell me what happened, Isabel . . . forget whose fault . . .'

Isabel took a deep breath, brushed the tears from her eyes, and started to explain.

After listening for a moment Will, calm and decisive, gave her instructions. 'It'll take the ambulance too long. Better for you to take him. I'll meet you at A and E . . . No. Go straight there.'

They made an incongruous group at the hospital. Will, casual but elegant in a Barbour and jeans; Ken, slightly dishevelled, and Isabel, completely distraught and trailing mud. The trio watched as the trolley, with doctors crawling round it, was rushed through casualty.

'They won't even try, will they?' said Isabel, tears coursing down her cheeks. 'He's in his eighties.'

Will put a comforting arm round her. 'They'll try, Issie. Give them a chance.'

'Did you get Ian?'

'No. No time to track him down. I called Beth and she's seeing to it.'

But it took Beth two hours to get hold of Ian Hart. And by that time his father was dead.

*

'I can't go through with this. I can't face him.'

'Yes, you can.' Ken looked over to Isabel, rigid in the passenger seat, staring straight ahead. In the past twenty-four hours she'd managed to tidy herself up, but sleep, by the look of her, had not visited her last night.

She shuddered visibly as Ken pulled up outside Mr Hart's house. 'Ken . . . I . . .'

'It's too easy to wallow in blame and what-ifs. You're made of sterner stuff.'

'I don't feel like it.'

'He'd have had the stroke wherever he'd been . . . you heard Beth. He was eighty-four, he'd had a couple of warnings and, for God's sake, he was ready to go.'

'Was he?' Isabel was unconvinced.

Ken sighed. 'You can't fix, organize and sort out every damn thing in the world, Issie.'

Alice North answered their knock. Isabel, ready with her condolences, was too shocked to utter them. Alice seemed to have aged ten years overnight. Wordlessly, she ushered them into the sitting-room.

Ian Hart made to stand up.

'Stay there, Ian,' said Isabel. 'Please.' Alice, still silent, gestured to a chair. Gingerly, Isabel perched on its edge. 'How are you both?'

Ian smiled. 'We're OK, aren't we, Alice?'

But Alice, arms crossed defensively across her chest, was not interested in small-talk. 'In the *Evening Telegraph* it said he was found after a search.'

'A brief search, yes,' replied Ken.

'He wandered off. He watched the fly-past and then he must have just—'

'"Wandered off"?' Alice glared at Isabel. 'And where were you two? Together?'

'We were talking in the car.'

'Very cosy, I'm sure.'

'We were watching him,' continued Isabel. 'He was only a couple of minutes away . . .'

108

'You weren't! How could you have been watching him when—'

'Please!' Ian Hart couldn't stand it any more. 'Please. He wouldn't want this.'

Ken turned to Alice. 'Alice, he told us that you'd argued. He asked us if we'd stop at the farm shop on the way home. Get your favourite fruit cake.'

Alice, close to tears, looked away.

Isabel smiled. 'He said you'd be waiting for him, still pretending to be cross.'

'Said he'd walk through the door and you'd tell him he was late, and a daft old sod to boot.' Ken's voice was very quiet as he added, 'He was very fond of you.'

'He told us what Ian called you both.'

'"Bert and Bertha",' laughed Ian. 'The nightmare double act. An insult in every line.'

A smile played tentatively on Alice's lips. 'He was better at it than me.' Then, angry again, she added, 'Dying like that. In some hospital bed. No one to hold his hand.'

'We're all alone when we die,' said Isabel. 'No matter who's with us.' She looked from Alice to Ian. 'Neither one of you was ever far away from his thoughts.'

Alice, lost in her own memories, stared unseeing into the fireplace. After a moment she turned to Ian. 'But we still came second place to a Spitfire, didn't we?'

CH**A**PTER 8

'Seen my car keys?'

Sarah didn't look up from her paper. 'Where you left them.'

'Great,' said Will through gritted teeth. 'Is that a yes or a no?'

But Sarah's interest, such as it was, in her husband getting to work on time had already waned. Still in her dressing gown, she was engrossed in a supplement of *The Times*.

Irritated, Will leaned over her shoulder and then snorted derisively.

'Don't laugh at me, Will!' Sarah looked up, eyes flashing in sudden anger. 'I want a proper job.'

'You've got a job!'

'No.' Sarah was emphatic. '*You*'ve got a job. I'm the part-time secretary at the local primary school and I'm bored with it.'

'You're bored,' replied Will, as if to himself. 'Great. What about the boys?'

'What about them?' Sarah got up and tightened the belt of her dressing gown. 'It's 1994, Will. We can get a nanny.'

Will raised his eyes. 'And when', he called to her retreating back, 'were you going to tell me you're looking for a new job?'

'When were you going to ask? Don't blame me if you're too busy to see what's happening right under your nose.' And with that Sarah stomped up the stairs. 'Your keys', she added, as Will began another frantic search, 'are in your coat pocket.'

'Oh.'

Oh, indeed, thought Will, as he drove to The Beeches. What exactly *was* happening under his nose? He supposed, now that he stopped to think about it, that he had noticed that Sarah was increasingly preoccupied of late. But not, he thought ruefully, with him and the boys. He had vaguely assumed that she was busy with her job, and pleased that Will was paying far more attention to the boys, enjoying their company as they so evidently enjoyed his.

Will had no experience of working wives and mothers. His own highly repressed childhood had not given him much insight into that sort of thing. His father went off every day to direct companies and his mother, like most of her contemporaries, 'did flowers and charities'. And that arrangement had always seemed to work perfectly satisfactorily, although it had occurred to him that his parents had little to say to each other and that his mother's 'work' was of vital necessity to preserve the façade of family unity. To stay together, his parents had to lead separate lives.

He had always thought that he and Sarah were different. They did things together, they had the same ambitions, they brought up the children together, and they talked to each other. Except nowadays – despite the new leaves supposedly turned over months ago – all they seemed to do was bicker together. Negotiating the sharp bend that led to The Beeches, Will frowned. Sarah, he felt, was being unfair. How was he supposed to notice what was 'happening under his nose' if Sarah refused to talk to him about it? How was he supposed to know what Sarah was feeling if she kept those feelings to herself? Well, now that he knew his wife was bored he would try to liven things up. Perhaps dinner out tomorrow night; just the two of them? He made a mental note to organize a baby-sitter himself. That would please Sarah.

Happy with his decision, Will parked his car and sauntered jauntily into The Beeches.

"Morning, Kim!'

'Hi, Will!' Kim looked up from her computer and smiled. 'I'm cracking this, y'know. Slowly but surely.'

Will also smiled. When he had suggested that Kim, as practice manager, might like to help him with his fund-holding proposals for The Beeches, he had privately assumed that he would be wasting his time. He had always thought of Kim as a jolly, friendly soul – but a dim one. Yet Kim had surprised him. She had embraced the project with enthusiasm – and a not inconsiderable display of brain-power. And, as a single mother of twenty-five, Will knew she must have little enough time to mug up on homework.

'Great!' Will grinned encouragingly at her – a grin that vanished as soon as he looked at the appointment book. 'Yuk!' he groaned. 'Peter Doland.'

Beth, preoccupied and hassled, spared a sympathetic look as she rushed past him. 'Rather you than me!'

Will glared at her. Peter Doland was a representative from a drugs company, not a patient. He was also – and all three doctors were unanimous on this – oily, smooth, supercilious and patronizing. And furthermore, Beth had also recently been able to confirm that he was a lecher. Hearing – no one knew from whom – of Beth's recent split from Jack, he had sought to cheer her up with his charms.

Five minutes later Doland marched into Will's room with his habitual air of breezy confidence, a dapper figure in the expensive three-piece suit. Will managed a thin smile. An impressive-looking individual, thought Will, but there's less to him than meets the eye.

Doland was thinking exactly the same thing about Will.

'Morning,' he said brightly. Depositing a routine consignment of drug samples on Will's desk, he added, 'Sorry to rush you, but could you sign for these now? I'm in a hurry.'

And I'm not, I suppose, thought Will as he nodded and picked up his pen.

'How's Sarah, by the way? Behaving herself, is she?'

Will looked up sharply. 'Thought you were in a hurry?'

'I am, I am. Only joking. But', he added earnestly, 'it would be nice to see you and your delightful wife when we're . . . when we're all in civvies, so to speak.'

Ignoring Will's resolute silence, he ploughed on. 'I'm organizing a do – the twenty-eighth. Chance to meet a few of the chaps, y'know. Should be a laugh. Can you both come?'

'The twenty-eighth?'

'Yeah.'

'Parents' evening.'

Doland smiled dismissively. 'Well, that shouldn't take too long. I'll smuggle you in later. We're paying . . .'

'No. Thanks.'

Doland, despite his earlier protestations, didn't look remotely concerned. 'Another time, then?'

'Yeah.' Will saved his look of genuine contempt for Doland's retreating back. Damn the man, he thought, he isn't even attempting to disguise the fact that he's after Sarah. He made his second mental note of the morning – to warn his wife about the predatory Peter.

But he was too late. Frowning at herself in the bedroom mirror, Sarah scrutinized her appearance. God knows, it ought to be good – she had spent half the morning trying to wash away all traces of hassled housewife. Make-up: discreet but perfect. Hair: nicely cascading over her shoulders. And the little black suit struck just the right note: businesslike and slightly sexy. After all, she thought as she reapplied her lipstick, Peter Doland couldn't even look at a skirt without thinking of sex. Sarah already knew a lot about Peter. And after their lunch date, she hoped to know more.

'This is just great, Peter.' She looked around the busy country restaurant and then back at her beaming companion. 'Very smart too. Thank you.' She twirled her elegant fingers round the stem of her wine glass. 'I just had to get out of the house before I died of boredom.'

'What about your job? Haven't they put you in charge of the Wendy house yet?'

Sarah flinched. Peter didn't notice – he was too busy smiling at his own wit. After a momentary hesitation, Sarah looked him straight in the eye. 'Actually, the Home Corner is my territory.'

Unaware of what he was doing, Peter licked his lips.

'I've got to get out, Peter. It's driving me mad. I'll be turning into a kid myself.' She looked him straight in the eye. 'You *were* serious, weren't you, about offering me a job?'

'Definitely.' Peter smiled smugly. 'You must be desperate, but if it's a job you want, you can do much worse than us.' He paused for reflection. 'In fact, we've a big conference coming up next month. I'll need someone to help organize . . .'

'You really think there's something I could do?' Sarah leaned forward, eyes shining. Now she knew she'd been right. Peter was definitely a bit of an oaf but once you got past the silly sexual banter there was, beneath it all, a decent – and serious – businessman.

And then Doland blew her hopes as quickly as he had raised them. There was an unmistakable glint in his eye as he replied, 'To be honest, Sarah, I can think of plenty you could do.'

'Sorry?'

'Well, come on. You're a good-looking girl, I'm offering you a job. I don't ask for any qualifications but . . . erm

114

. . . what I need to know is . . . how do you feel about a job directly under me?'

Sarah stared at him: surely the man couldn't be *that* crass?

He could. Peter leaned towards Sarah and tried to put his hand over hers. 'It would do you a lot of good. Be just the job, wouldn't it? In more ways than one . . .'

Sarah glared back contemptuously and snatched her hand away.

'Nice try, Peter,' she spat, grabbing her handbag, 'but no dice.'

Several heads turned as she stalked away from the table towards the exit. Peter, after a brief hesitation, ran after her. 'Sarah?'

'What?'

'I thought', he said, as they reached the door together, 'you said you were bored.'

'I've never been *that* bored!'

'What's that supposed to mean?' Peter looked the very picture of wounded innocence.

A flicker of doubt crossed Sarah's face. 'I thought you wanted to talk about a job.'

'I did.' Then Peter laughed half-heartedly, covering his embarrassment. 'All right! All right . . . so I was a bit—'

'No, it's *not* all right! All right? I didn't come here for fun. And I don't like being laughed at, so let's just forget it, shall we?'

'Sarah! I'm sorry. I was out of order.' Peter paused to collect his thoughts. 'Look, we do need someone. Seriously. Just tell me you're interested and I'll try and arrange something. Honest, I'm sorry. Will you think about it?'

Sarah, torn between distaste for the man and desire for the job, frowned at him. 'We are on the same wavelength, aren't we, Peter? I'm interested in the job – and nothing else.'

'Sure. The job – and nothing else.'

115

'Good. Let's discuss it further on the phone, shall we?'

And then they went their separate ways, both of them with a little victorious smile on their faces.

Chloe, sitting beside her husband in Jack's surgery, was looking pale, worried and wan. Absently, nervously, she put a hand to the headscarf, wound turban-like over her head. Across the table from them, Jack was reading a letter from the hospital.

'Your appointment with the Registrar's at four.' Without looking up he added, 'And then there's your second course of chemotherapy.'

'Will I have to stay in hospital?'

'That's up to the Registrar.'

'Meaning you're not going to tell us.'

Hearing the anger in James's voice, Jack looked up. 'I honestly don't know, James. One step at a time, eh?'

'But we'll find out how well I'm doing?' said Chloe.

'They should have your latest cell count, yes.'

Chloe and James looked at each other. This diffident, almost embarrassed approach was the last thing they expected from Jack.

'What are you trying to tell me?' Chloe asked quietly.

Jack studied the pained expression on his friends' faces and sighed. 'It can take a while to . . . to find the right type of chemotherapy. I think they might want to change the protocol.'

It was Chloe who eventually broke the silence, a silence heavy with dread. 'I'm not getting better, am I?'

'It's very early days. You need to keep fighting.'

'Just say it, Jack.'

'No. I'm sorry, love. You're not.'

'Such anger in one so young!' Beth, full of the joys of life, joined Jack at the bar as he savagely ripped open a packet of cheese and onion crisps. Then she noticed the expression on his face and realized this wasn't the time for flippancy.

Jack looked bleakly at her. 'They're changing Chloe's protocol.'

'Oh, Jack . . .'

'Which means that the great cure just isn't working.' He gestured towards his pint. 'Drink?'

'Mmm. Please. Orange juice. I'm on call.'

Jack beckoned to the barmaid. 'Orange juice – and the same again for me, please.'

Beth contemplated Jack's obviously liquid lunch. 'Hope you're not driving.'

'Nope. I'm on foot. I met this nice doctor and he said that a couple of good stiff drinks would do me no harm at all. Still, what the hell does he know?'

Beth patted his arm affectionately. 'It's too soon to tell, Jack. The great cure may not be working – yet – but there's every chance that it might.'

'Yeah.' But Jack sounded unconvinced.

And then, as Beth took the first sip of her orange juice, her bleeper went off. 'Oh, God. Just as well that wasn't champagne, eh?' Leaving the orange juice on the bar, she gave Jack a swift peck on the cheek and picked up her handbag. 'Sorry about the drink. Another time.'

'Yeah. Another time.' Jack stared moodily into his pint. What was it, he reflected, with him and women? He and Beth were finished. Their affair was over – and Beth seemed to be handling it well. She had adapted to 'just being friends', yet Jack couldn't get her out of his system. Was he, he wondered, a prat, or a sucker – or even both? Because as he stared into the amber liquid in front of him he was thinking, not just of Beth, but of the first woman who had got under his skin. That had been fifteen years ago. Jack hadn't given her so much as a thought since his arrival in Cardale – or at least a conscious thought. But now he realized that even after years in London, in Africa, and now in Derbyshire – even during his genuine, passionate pursuit of Beth – Karen had been with him all along. Was that, subconsciously, why he had failed with Beth? God knows he had wanted to marry her. He still did. But somewhere within him a little voice was still reminding him of Karen – the woman who had nearly ruined his life.

And she was still trying to. For the letter about Chloe had not been the only bad news that morning. Karen had written. After two years of total silence she had written. And that meant the whole ghastly business would begin again.

Beth, driving to her call high up on the outskirts of Cardale, was humming to herself – blissfully unaware of the tortures Jack was putting himself through back at the pub. She was also unaware of the existence of anyone called Karen. When she and Jack had been going out, there had been little mention of previous lovers except Alex, who didn't last very long once Jack had settled in Cardale. Beth had deliberately fought shy of the subject – partly because she knew that Jack's love life had been far more eventful than her own. Sure, she had had flings when she was younger – even a couple of long-term boyfriends. But she had never lived with anyone. She had wanted to – desperately and with all her heart – but it had been impossible. Michael Drummond, the one great love of her life, had been married all the way through their relationship. And Beth (had she really been so naive?) had believed his repeated protestations that he was going to leave his wife – when the time was right. Beth smiled ruefully at the memory. Seven years ago he had indeed decided the time was right – to leave Beth. And he had done it so cruelly, so painfully, that Beth had been convinced she would never recover.

Driving through the Dales, fully in control of her life – enjoying it – Beth saw things differently now. Perhaps he hadn't been so cruel after all. Perhaps Michael – older, wiser, the survivor of more knocks than she – had been doing her a kindness. At the time she had felt wounded, bereaved, even crippled – but she had survived. And so, too, had Michael. Seven years, she thought, and not a word. And then, two days ago, a phone call. Despite herself, she had felt a frisson of excitement at the sound of his gravelly, sensuous voice. But she was no longer the trusting, naive Beth that he had known. She was a strong, capable woman who ran her own life by her own rules. Still, she thought with a grin, she couldn't wait to tell Isabel. 'Imagine!' she heard herself saying. 'Not a squeak for seven years and then an invitation to dinner!'

Sarah didn't notice Will hurriedly covering over what he was reading as she entered the kitchen. She was too busy thinking how impressed Will would be when she told him. As he looked up she opened the bag she was carrying and casually threw a large box of expensive chocolates in his direction.

'Hey!' said Will, catching them. 'What's this?'

'A celebration.' Sarah was a picture of happiness – and gleeful wickedness – as she extracted a bottle of champagne from the bag.

Will was puzzled. 'A celebration? What's there to celebrate? Another bloody awful day?'

'Oh, Will!' Sarah, emotion suddenly overcoming her, rushed to his side and tenderly stroked his cheek. I still love him, she thought. I can't help it. After all we've been through. I want it to work.

Will looked at her. As their eyes met he felt a sudden surge of excitement. The spark, he realized with relief, was still there. And then the perfect moment was spoiled.

'I've been offered a job.'

'Oh.' Will tensed slightly. 'But—'

'But nothing.' Sarah put a hand gently to her husband's mouth. 'It's what I want, Will. Don't spoil it.'

119

'Doing what?'

Sarah paused for a moment. 'Conference organizer.'

'*Conference* organizer?'

Sarah looked at Will, amused. 'Yes. Why not? If I can organize you and the boys – this house – a conference should be a doddle.' She saw that Will was about to voice an objection. 'Please,' she whispered. 'You know I need a chance to prove myself. It'll work out. Promise.'

'Well, if it's what you want . . .'

'It is.' Suddenly Sarah noticed the ivory binder of the folder that Will had covered up with a newspaper. 'What's this?'

'Nothing.' Embarrassed, Will tried to push it away.

'Show me.'

'It's nothing!'

Sarah looked at Will with a mixture of alarm and amusement. What the hell was he being so coy about? Suddenly she lunged forward and grabbed the folder.

'Don't!' yelled Will.

But it was too late. As the newspaper fell away, Sarah realized in astonishment that, open in front of her, was their wedding album. In silence, she looked from it to Will; and then started giggling as she noticed Will's expression. He was, without a doubt, blushing. He was also trying, and failing, to look macho.

'Oh, Will,' said Sarah, stroking his hair. 'How . . . how *sweet*.' Beside her, Will squirmed in embarrassment. 'How about', continued Sarah, 'we open the champagne now?'

Ten minutes later they were sprawled in front of the sitting-room fire, guzzling chocolates and sipping champagne. Sarah was screaming with laughter at some of the outfits of nearly twelve years ago.

'Look!' She pointed to a photograph of Will's Aunt Elizabeth, sporting a prolific herbaceous border on her head. 'D'you remember Rob trying to water her hat when he got pissed? What a hoot!'

Will grinned at the memory. But he was also grinning

at the thought of how life comes full circle. There they were, all those years ago, flushed by the excitement, deliriously happy with each other as they launched into a lifetime of togetherness. And, now, here they were again, lying together in the floor of their house, their bodies touching casually, familiarly. It was, reflected Will, exactly how it should be.

Sarah turned the page. 'He's still got those trousers!' she squeaked. 'Imagine!' Then she paused, pointing at another photograph, and lowered her voice. 'D'you remember what happened after that?'

'Er . . . yes. I got very emotional. Made a slightly embarrassing speech and got rather drunk.'

'I mean after that.'

'Everyone stood in a circle singing "You'll Never Walk Alone"?'

'After that.' Sarah was whispering now.

'Mmm. I believe I do remember.'

'And d'you remember if you enjoyed it or not?' Sarah reached over and started unbuttoning Will's shirt.

Will pretended to give this one serious contemplation. 'Well, actually, Mrs Preston, now that you come to mention it, I do believe I rather enjoyed myself.'

'Oh, good.'

'But since you ask, d'you think we could do it again? Just so's I can make sure.'

'Oh, yes, doctor. Oh, yes, please.'

'Why the hell didn't you tell me it was Doland?' Will's voice was chilly, his face an inscrutable mask as he turned from the phone to face Sarah.

Sarah didn't reply at first. Her face was a picture of misery as she contemplated the room – the room where last night they had made proper, passionate love for the first time in weeks. It seemed like years ago now. 'I . . . I was going to tell you . . .' She could almost sense Will

121

trying to suppress a spasm of violent anger. 'It's just a few hours a week, Will—'

'No, it isn't.'

'I'm—'

'There is no job, Sarah.' He gestured to the phone. 'That was Doland – press-up Pete, as we call him. He said he'd "spoken too soon" and his guv'nor couldn't give you a position. But knowing Pete Doland, I doubt there ever was a job.'

Disbelief flooded Sarah's face. 'Why don't you call his mobile?' continued Will. 'You've got the number apparently.'

The words cut into Sarah like a knife. 'I binned it,' she squeaked, 'I'll show you—'

'Oh, don't bother.' Will stalked past her into the hall.

Sarah bit her lip. Damn. Damn. Damn. It was Doland, in a funny way, who had brought them together. His clumsy pass at her – and then his subsequent phone call, telling her his boss wanted to see her tomorrow. Sarah had been elated. Peter Doland had shown her how lucky she was to have Will. And at the same time, he was going to give her back some professional pride. And now she realized she'd been completely duped.

'Will!' She ran after him. 'Just listen to me! I was going to tell you, but I didn't want to spoil things . . . I mean, after last night.' She paused, seeing that she had his attention. 'Look. I wasn't born yesterday. I know what he's like. I know he didn't want me for my shorthand, but I thought I could handle his "I'm irresistible to women" act. In fact,' she added, 'I find him eminently resistible.'

Will frowned. He felt somehow used, yet wanting to give Sarah the benefit of the doubt. 'You don't know him like I do.'

'Oh, yes, I do, believe me.' Suddenly, Sarah grinned. 'Is that really what they call him?'

'What?'

'Press-up Pete?'

A smile hovered on Will's lips. 'Yeah.'

'Suits him.'

'I still want to know what happened, Sarah.'

Sarah went up to him and tugged affectionately at the lapels of his coat. 'I'll tell you – but there's nothing to know.' She looked up at Will. 'Really. Nothing. I can look after myself. There's only one thing to know about Pete Doland – and that's that he's a complete and utter and total jerk. And I can't believe', she added, 'that you could be so concerned about him.'

Will smiled. 'Well . . .'

'Well, you'll be late for work if you stand about gossiping with your wife. Got your car keys?' she added wickedly.

Will tapped his coat and smiled back. 'In my pocket.'

Chloe was looking and feeling worse than ever before. The hospital had changed her chemotherapy protocol and had warned her that the side effects could be different. But she had never expected anything like this. Nausea and some disorientation, the Senior Registrar had said. And then they would find the right anti-emetics. But by that time, she was convinced, she would be dead.

As she lay in bed, moaning, pouring with sweat, and desperately fighting the need to vomit yet again, James hovered by her side. Sometimes she hated James – for no other reason than for the fact that he was healthy. And sometimes she couldn't bear for him to touch her because he was clean and she was dirty, poisoned – and dying. And sometimes she just knew she couldn't go on.

This was one of those times. In too much pain even to attempt to speak, she was barely aware that Jack had joined James at her bedside.

'It's all right, love.' James stroked her arm. 'Jack's here. Jack, they changed her chemo . . .'

'I know. I spoke to the Registrar.' He looked, appalled,

at Chloe and wondered, not for the first time, just how a human body could withstand so much. 'All right, Chloe?' he asked unnecessarily.

Chloe shook her head but didn't – couldn't – speak. 'She's been like this since lunch time,' said James desperately.

'Did they change her anti-emetics?'

'They did but she can't keep them down.'

'Hmm.' Jack, bending to examine Chloe, knew what he had to do. The Manor was no place for her in this condition. He took the mobile phone from his pocket. 'We need to get some fluids into her, James, and I'm not sure . . . I really don't think this is the best place for her.' He sighed, knowing the effect his words would have. 'I think we should get her to hospital . . .'

'Oh, Jack! Oh, no, please.' James was frantic. The one thing that kept Chloe going was to be in a familiar environment; to have James and Sarah Jane near her in her own home. When she was feeling up it was as though nothing had changed. And when she was down, it made things bearable. Just. But if she went into hospital she knew she would never come out.

'They'll take good care of her,' said Jack. He got up from the bed and faced James. 'Look, I know how you feel, but just because she's going into hospital it doesn't mean she's not going to come out. It doesn't mean we're losing the battle, James.' They looked at each other. 'It'll be all right. I promise.'

And then after dialling the number, he made the connection. 'Hello? Yes. It's Dr Kerruish from The Beeches. I want to admit a female oncology patient needing fluids.'

James stared down at his wife. He'd spent so long desperately trying to be bright, cheerful and supportive. But it had been to no avail. He couldn't imagine Chloe's pain, but his own was very real; a sharp, physical sensation as the last ray of hope disappeared.

CHAPTER 9

There was an air of excitement at The Beeches as they all sat down to a makeshift working lunch of bread and cheese.

'Ooh! Grapes as well,' said Kim. 'If I'd known, I'd have brought some of my dad's home-made wine.'

Will grinned and made a face. 'That stuff's lethal, and some of us have work to do this afternoon.'

'And the rest of us', said Beth happily, 'have horse riding to master. You need to be stone cold sober for that, Kim. Believe me.' She allowed her thoughts to slip away for a moment to the great outdoors and her favourite pastime. Riding. She loved it. Ever since she had been old enough to walk, she had been fascinated by horses, and her mother, a highly accomplished horsewoman and joint master of the local hunt, had encouraged her in her passion. There was nothing, Beth felt, to beat the exhilaration of galloping through the countryside, leaping over the dry stone walls and hedges, trusting implicitly in the powerful creature whose hooves thundered over the rough terrain. Since she had come back to Cardale and The Beeches, Beth had had no time to keep a horse of her own, but at every opportunity she had rushed to the riding stables near Matlock to spend as long as she could letting the worries of the world disappear with every graceful stride of her favourite horse. Maria, who owned the stables, waived all her rules for Beth, and let her ride Dancer on her own for as long as she wanted, to go as far as she could. Maria had known Beth since she was a toddler stumbling confidently and fearlessly around the stables. And even at that age, when one angry equine kick could have crushed her to death, Beth had had an intuitive understanding of horses. And they, even the great beasts of seventeen hands and more, had made a point of bending down to nuzzle the little girl.

But, Beth reminded herself, there wouldn't be too much wild galloping this afternoon. After lunch she was taking Kim to the stables for her first ever riding lesson. Beth had to concede that she had made the offer to Kim – who had always wanted, but never had the chance, to ride – as part of the new spirit of togetherness that Will had somehow engendered at The Beeches. Beth was still not convinced about the merits of fundholding, but she was aware of the effect that Will's enthusiasm for it had had on Kim and Ellie. They, in turn, had become more enthusiastic about their jobs.

'Penny for them?' asked Will, jogging Beth out of her reverie.

'A penny? My thoughts are far more expensive than that!'

Will grinned and then looked impatiently at his watch. 'Where's Jack?'

'Some sort of special delivery letter came for him,' said Ellie. 'Looked a bit glum when he saw it.'

'Probably a bailiff's order.'

'Oh!' Kim looked up. 'Does that mean you think we're all underpaid and are going to get a massive salary hike?'

'No,' laughed Beth. 'It doesn't.'

Just then Jack burst in, smiling apologetically. 'Sorry. Here I am.'

'Good.' Beth gathered her papers around her. 'Let's begin then. Fundholding: it's time to put an end to the rumours . . . Will?'

'Right. We've an interview with the health authority in ten days and that's when we'll either apply to fundhold, or say "thanks but no thanks".'

'Ten days!' Ellie hadn't expected that.

'Yeah, and even if we go for it,' said Jack, 'there's a period of accounts and data collection before we sign up.'

Kim looked at Ellie. 'Is this meant to make us feel better?'

Ellie, evidently thinking along the same lines, chipped in with 'Who's going to be doing all this "data collection"?'

'All of us,' said Beth firmly. 'You'll get any help you need, and anyway, there are induction courses for everyone.'

'Will they be compulsory?' asked Ellie. 'We've both got children, after all, and if they're residential . . .'

Will and Beth looked at each other. What, the look implied, had suddenly happened to the spirit of togetherness?

'No, they're not residential,' replied Will. 'We're not expecting you to abandon your families. But we all need as much help as we can get with this.'

'All I'm saying,' continued Ellie, 'is that I've got enough to do without all this fundholding stuff.'

Kim shifted uncomfortably in her seat.

'We won't know if it's right for us,' explained Will, 'until we start getting in all the paperwork. And then, if it's looking good, we'll get extra staff. A business manager for a start.'

'I thought—' began Kim.

'You'd be practice manager, Kim,' interjected Beth. 'Same job, same seniority . . .'

'No one said.' Kim looked mutinous.

Will turned to her, trying to placate her. 'The business manager has to do the accounts. Liaise with the health authorities, Kim . . . be responsible for half a million pounds a year.'

Kim just stared at him.

'So you change Kim's job description,' said Ellie, 'just like that.' She turned to Jack. 'You're always on about workers' rights and democracy. Am I being unreasonable?'

'At the moment, yes. A bit.'

Ellie looked stunned. She had, at least, expected an ally in Jack. Then, realizing she was getting nowhere, she got to her feet. 'Well, thanks.' She looked pointedly at her watch. 'I'd better get ready for clinic.'

'Have something to eat.' Beth pointed to the as yet untouched bread and cheese.

'Not hungry.' She went to the door. 'Vaccinations today.'

Then, as Kim also got to her feet, the three doctors looked helplessly at each other. They had expected a discussion – not a mutiny.

'Kim, aren't you having any lunch either?'

'No, thanks, Beth. I'll get the notes put away. Shout for me when you're ready to go to the stables.'

Kim shut the door behind her – rather too loudly. It was a rueful Jack who broke the ensuing silence. 'Right. That's the staff happy and raring to go. Let's get on with it.'

Two hours later, Beth was revelling in the perfect antidote to a morning of hassle. Dancer had obviously not been fully exercised of late, and he had whinnied with joy at the sight of Beth, who he knew was game for a proper gallop. He was fed up with the tame hacking that had been his so-called exercise for the week. So he and Beth enjoyed a full hour on their own, at first walking and trotting through the lush woods, and then galloping along the ridge that ran for a full three miles across some of the most beautiful countryside in Derbyshire. Both were in their element. Going through the woods, Beth had a rare moment for contemplation, and during that moment she contemplated her social life. She decided to make more of an effort. A dinner party, she decided, was long overdue. Mentally assembling a guest list, she then frowned in irritation as she realized she was a man short. Typical. Bloody men.

Jack, of course, was the obvious choice – but she was wary of inviting him. It was debatable whether or not she really had 'used' him as a lover – but it would be pretty obvious if she used him as a spare man. No, she thought, she would have to find someone else. And then she remembered – Michael. Could they now, she thought, be 'just good friends'? Surely enough time had passed for them to be civilized dinner companions? Well, she would find out next week. If dinner alone together worked, dinner in company could be a great success. After all, Michael was a highly entertaining companion. Then she dismissed all thoughts of dinner parties as the trees thinned out, revealing the ridge ahead of them and the open vista beyond. Dancer lifted his head and gave a little buck of joy. He sensed a gallop coming on.

Half an hour later, almost laughing with joy and exhilaration, Beth reined Dancer in and decided that, much as she would like to continue, she ought to go back to find out how Kim was doing. Patting her horse's flank, she turned and directed him back towards the riding stables.

Kim, back in the paddock, wasn't getting on very well.

Maria – always a fan of the 'cruel to be kind' school of teaching – had put her on the back of a tired old mare who had no interest in moving, let alone galloping. Her main aim in life was to eat as much grass as possible, and in this she was succeeding admirably. Kim sat motionless on her back. Her knuckles, clinging desperately to the horse's mane, were white with strain and her eyes were closed.

'Kim, what *are* you doing?'

Rigid with terror, Kim started chanting, 'Help me . . . help me . . .'

Beth, battling between amusement and concern, went up to her. 'Where's Maria?'

Kim opened her eyes fractionally. 'Watching me from back there . . . she said to keep moving, get used to the feel of her.'

'Well,' Beth smiled, 'go on, then . . .'

'Don't tell me! Tell her!' Kim gestured to her still-munching horse, happily oblivious of the conversation around her. 'She just put her head down and that was it. One minute I had her head in front of me and the next there was . . . nothing.' Her voice rose to a desperate wail. 'I was, like, at the edge of this cliff!'

Beth, suppressing a grin, dismounted and tied Dancer's reins to the paddock fence. 'I'll lead you round, Kim. You'll soon get the knack.'

'Tell them I want something a bit calmer!'

'What, like an old armchair? Come on, Kim, you can do it.'

And, after a fashion, Kim could do it. Half an hour later, as Maria led the horses back to their loose boxes, Kim went up to the mare. All traces of her earlier fear had evaporated. Maria looked on in amusement as Kim nuzzled the placid horse. 'You're a wonderful old lady.' She reached into her pocket. 'OK, one more kiss, one more Polo and then it's goodbye. Till tomorrow.'

'You're coming back?' Beth was amazed – and pleased.

'You bet I am. If I can get my sister to baby-sit Robbie again.'

As they walked to Beth's car, Kim gestured back to the stables. 'Maria reckons', she said proudly, 'that I've got a natural seat.'

Back at The Beeches, Jack was busy with his last appointment of the day. And he could think of no better patient to salvage what had been the nastiest day for months – or even years. It had been, if he wanted to be precise, the nastiest day for two years.

'You're looking a bit glum.' Her voice was cheerful, confident.

Jack looked up. What the hell, he realized, had he to be glum about? Compared to what she had been through. He smiled at Chloe. 'And you're looking positively gleeful, love.'

'Mustn't grumble,' said Chloe, sitting down. Gone was the pained expression, the sickly pallor and the listless voice. Chloe had spent two nights in hospital. And she had come out again. Finally, the new chemotherapy and anti-emetics were working.

Ellie came into the room, syringe at the ready. Chloe proffered her arm. 'Another bruise,' she joked.

'Another battle scar,' said Ellie, deftly inserting the needle. She smiled warmly at Chloe – but not at Jack. She was still miffed by what she considered his betrayal.

'At least you can find the vein straight away.' Chloe looked at Jack from under her lashes. 'Unlike some I could mention.'

Jack grinned. 'You can always tell when the patients are feeling better. The level of abuse soars.'

'Oh, I haven't even begun yet,' joked Chloe.

But before she could begin, the intercom buzzed on Jack's desk.

'Yep?'

'Urgent call for you,' said Eve.

Jack frowned. 'Who is it?'

'Holborn Hospital.'

'Oh.' So it had happened again. Jack sighed. 'I'll . . . er . . . I'll take it in Beth's room. Give me a second to get there.' He moved towards the door. 'Sorry, Chloe, won't be long.'

Chloe and Ellie exchanged glances. 'What's up? Woman trouble?'

'Dunno,' said Ellie. 'He's been a bit withdrawn of late. Not like our Jack at all.'

'Woman trouble definitely,' said Chloe confidently.

The next morning Jack and Ellie arrived at The Beeches at the same time. Neither was in the best of moods. Ellie had been mulling over the proposed changes at the practice if they became fundholders – and even after some gratifyingly sympathetic attention from her husband, she was no happier about it. Jack, for his part, had spent the night worrying about yesterday's letter and the phone call from London – and had come to a decision. He was exhausted.

Ellie propped her bicycle against the wall as Jack killed his car engine. 'Morning!' he yelled, slamming the door.

'Morning.' Ellie was curt.

'Ellie . . . er . . . care to tell me what's wrong?'

Ellie looked coolly at him for a moment. 'Well, since you ask, Jack, yes. I've worked here for six years, you know. You invest a lot of yourself in a place like this. Even if you're not a partner . . .'

Jack sighed. 'We do appreciate you, Ellie. It may not always seem that we do—'

'But no matter how much time and effort I put in, I'll always just be on the staff. Salaried. I'll never have a say in what happens.'

Jack shrugged helplessly. 'I don't know what to say to that, Ellie. It's true – as far as it goes—'

'And it's true I'm being bulldozed into something I'm very unhappy about.'

'Fundholding?'

'Yes.' She considered for a moment. 'My whole life's here, Jack, so I can't just leave The Beeches . . .'

'Ellie!'

'So I guess I'll just have to hold my tongue if we start turning away some patients because they cost too much to manage . . .'

'Oh, come on, you know us better than that . . .'

'It's possible. If all you see when you meet a new patient is what they're going to cost your precious budget—'

'No doctor's going to put finance first.'

'I may be kind to small children, animals and doctors, Jack, but I don't think the latter are saints. In fact, I think most of you are arrogant sods.'

132

Jack wasn't sure if she was joking or not. 'But not me, eh?'

But Ellie wasn't going to be won over that easily. 'What happened to all your arguments against a two-tier health system?'

Jack shrugged. 'The vast majority of local practices are fundholding now. Over seventy per cent in the South Derbyshire region at the moment. *I* wouldn't have invented fundholding, Ellie, but – face facts – it's been thrust upon us. And if there's a two-tier system then we're in the bottom one, and our patients deserve better.' He sensed that, at last, his point was beginning to hit home.

'Hmm. I'll give you a tough time on this for as long as I think you deserve one.' She paused and then added, 'Sean's doing an Irish curry with chips tonight. You'd be very welcome.'

'Oh. Good, is it?' Jack thought it sounded ghastly.

'Horrible. It comes with squabbling kids, moulting dog and my foul temper.'

Jack grinned. 'I'd love to come.' Then he clapped his hand to his forehead. He'd quite forgotten his own troubles. 'Oh God, I can't! Damn. Sorry, Ellie. I've got to go to London.'

'London?'

'Yes. London.'

'London?' Beth had been incredulous. 'Now? Won't it wait till after surgery?'

'I . . . er . . . I was hoping you'd finish for me.'

Beth looked at him for a moment. This, even considering Jack's recent behaviour, was most peculiar. 'Well . . . if you really have to.' Jack's expression said he really had to. 'No chance of telling us what it's all about, I suppose?'

'Sorry. No. It's nothing that affects the practice, though.'

So me finishing surgery for you doesn't affect the

practice, thought Beth waspishly. 'Well,' she had said, turning on her heel. 'I just hope she's worth it, that's all.'

If only, thought Jack, she knew. Oh, years ago he'd thought Karen was worth any price he'd care to name. He had treasured her; they were going to get married, have children, be the most successful pair of doctors in the country. Fifteen years ago, at medical school, it had all seemed possible. They had been the brightest students in their year. And Karen had been one of the most beautiful. And then Karen had started to go mad. No, not mad. Jack checked himself as he negotiated the slip-road on to the motorway. He should know better than that. She'd started to evince the first signs of paranoid schizophrenia. At first it had been just the odd, strange action, like scribbling words that didn't exist when they were in lectures. And then, gradually, it had got worse. Karen became unreliable. She had to leave medical school. She had to be looked after. Jack, initially, had tried to do the looking after. And then it became increasingly clear that Karen, far from working in a hospital, belonged in one as an in-patient. And Karen's parents, who had been looking forward to welcoming Jack as a son-in-law, told him, gently but firmly, to leave, to go away; to forget the increasingly abusive Karen, to get on with his own life and leave them to take care of their daughter during her periods of release and lucidity.

For more than ten years Jack had been doing just that. Yet Karen's brief flashes of sanity also coincided with her demands for Jack. When she was ill, she hated him. When she was well, she alternated between demanding his presence and abusing him. It was, in a word, horrible. David and Mary, her parents, had always refused to let Jack give them his address, yet somehow she had always found it out. And the recent spate of letters culminating in her sending him the key to her flat indicated that she was on to him in Cardale. Jack hadn't replied to any of them.

And then came the phone call. Karen had been found by the police at three in the morning on the Embankment in a state of acute distress. Jack Kerruish, the psychiatric nurse had apologetically explained, had been the only name Karen would utter. Would he, perhaps, come to her?

How could he refuse, thought Jack. How could he, a man whose profession was to look after others, refuse to acknowledge the existence of a woman who used to have everything, and now had nothing – except her jumbled memories of her life with Jack? God help her, he thought as he accelerated on to the motorway. Because I can't. Not any more.

Jack had been to the Carlisle unit before. The admissions and assessment unit of Holborn Hospital, it took in patients in an acute state of need. Depressives, schizophrenics, psychotics; it catered for everyone in need, keeping them for as short a period as possible before referring them on to some other specialized unit. The place was unmistakably institutional, yet tried bravely to look welcoming and homely.

Jack walked into the day room with Liz Walker, the psychiatric nurse who had phoned him the day before. 'Over there,' she said, indicating what Jack took to be a pile of blankets in the corner of the room.

Jack looked at her. 'You mean . . .?'

'Yes, under the blankets.'

As he approached, Jack saw that the blankets were rocking gently back and forth. 'Karen?' he asked gently. 'It's me, Jack.' Slowly and carefully, he began to move the blankets aside. Before he could do so, a hand shot out from underneath and grabbed his, holding tight. Jack looked at it for a moment. He remembered that hand. Now, of course, it was different. Where once it had been smooth and soft, it was now rough, almost scaly in places.

The nails were unkempt, ragged, and dirty. In a reassuring, almost loving gesture, Jack rubbed the hand with his thumb. 'That's right,' he said. 'You hold tight.'

Then, with his other hand, he lifted the blanket off Karen's head. 'Hello, love. Having a bad time, are you?'

Karen didn't reply. She just looked at Jack, wide-eyed. Jack flinched at the sight before him. The remnants of Karen's beauty were just that – remnants. The fine bone structure was still there, but now it lent her face gauntness rather than grace. Her cheeks were sunken and her large grey eyes stared out vacantly from beneath the unkempt hair that was falling over her forehead. And her once-smooth complexion was blotchy and sallow.

'Here I am,' continued Jack. He looked at the crocheted blanket, trying to infuse a note of normality into the situation. 'We used to have one like that, remember?'

At last Karen spoke. 'They took my purse. I'm hiding.'

'No need any more. You're safe.'

Encouraged by Karen's uncertain smile, Jack stroked the hair out of her eyes. 'There. I can see you now.'

'Jack the lad.' Karen stared at him, in admiration, awe and, still, love. Then, with no warning at all, she pushed violently at him, scrabbled at the blankets and pulled them back over her head. 'You're not him!' she screamed. 'You're a liar! A liar!'

'Karen . . . love . . . it is me. Don't hide from me.' He tried to pull the blanket away again.

'Don't touch me! Go away!' Suddenly Karen jumped to her feet and, with her head still bowed under the blanket, ran screaming towards the doorway.

Liz blocked her way. 'It's all right, Karen.' She held the screaming, moaning form. 'No one's going to hurt you. It's OK.'

Gradually Karen's screams of 'Not him! It's not *him*!' subsided and she let herself be led away.

The male nurse who had been watching the proceedings came up to Jack. 'She was going to be a doctor, you know.'

136

Jack stared into space. 'I know.'

'And now she can't even manage to take a tablet every day. Bloody tragic, isn't it?'

Jack didn't answer. He couldn't.

An hour later Jack pulled up outside Karen's flat. He looked in disgust at the tatty building in a run-down part of Muswell Hill. This, he thought sadly, is what it had come to. A tatty, faceless building in bed-sit land. Killing the engine and reaching into the glove compartment, he pulled out the buff envelope that Beth had joked was a bailiff's summons and turned it upside down. The key, attached to a name tag by a red ribbon, fell into his hand. *Flat 7a, 46 Northwood Road*, he read in Karen's jumbled handwriting. *Come*. Well, he thought, he had come. He hadn't wanted to, he hadn't meant to, but he had come.

Except now, of course, Karen wasn't there. It was her long-suffering parents he had arranged to meet. He climbed the dingy staircase. Loud, heavy metal music boomed out from somewhere above him. Below him, a furious slanging match started up and ended, abruptly, with the slamming of a door. Jack shook his head sadly. This place would be enough to drive any sane person mad – let alone someone already suffering acute mental anguish.

The door to number 7a was open. He knocked and walked in. 'Hello, David.'

The elderly, weary-looking man, sweeping empty packets, dirty plastic plates and overflowing ashtrays into a black bin-liner, broke from his task and smiled warmly. 'Jack!'

Jack shook hands and then approached the neat little woman coming out of the kitchenette. He smiled and kissed her. 'Mary.' They looked at each other, memories flooding back. Jack was the son Mary Eastman had always wanted.

'The hospital had no business calling you,' said David.

Jack shrugged. 'Mine was the only name she would give. I went as soon as I could.' He noted a look of faint hope on both their faces. He shook his head. The hope vanished.

'They do their best . . .' began Mary.

'Yes.'

'Will you come back with us,' she continued, 'for lunch?'

Sensing how much this meant to her, Jack accepted the invitation. 'Thanks. And then I'll have to go. I'm sorry.'

'Of course you must,' said David. 'We know that.'

'I'm on call this weekend but I'll try to get a few days off next week.'

'You really don't have to. We're used to it.' David attempted a smile. 'The odd blip.'

But Jack, taking in the scene, felt anger mounting. Why, he thought, should two old people who had worked so hard all their lives, have to cope – alone – with so much? 'It's not a blip, David. It's Karen in distress . . . and . . . and both of you.' He paused for a moment. 'How often does this happen?'

'Christmas was the last time,' said Mary. 'When she takes her medication she gets on quite well. But then . . .' She faltered and gestured at the room, the mess, the squalor, the hopelessness of it all.

But Jack was remembering something. 'Yesterday should have been our fifteenth anniversary. It can't be a coincidence, can it?'

'Whether it is or not,' replied David, 'there's nothing any of us can do about it.'

'"Care in the community"!' Jack mocked his own words. 'They said she'd get all the help she needed from her support team.'

'She wouldn't let anyone in,' said Mary. 'There was nothing they could do.'

'We'd have her home, but it doesn't work.'

'I know, David.' Jack let his anger subside. 'You mustn't think of taking her home when she's like this.' He stopped, wanting to change the subject, not wanting to continue, as they had so many times before, on the endless, useless merry-go-round of Karen's health. He surveyed the room. It was the room of someone who had given up on outward appearances. Nothing matched, nothing was clean or tidy except, in the far corner, for a little oasis of calm that was Karen's desk. The medical textbooks were neatly stacked; pencils and pens were lined up, ready to take notes, annotate texts, ready to inform Karen of the mysteries and wonders of medical science. The sight of the desk saddened Jack more than anything else. How, he wondered, could fate be so cruel? Why did Karen feel driven, in her lucid moments, to pursue her medical studies? Once she had told him that she had decided to become a doctor when she was ten. She was thirty-five now. Jack shook his head. Karen could easily live to be seventy-five or more. Who would look after her then?

Suddenly he needed to do something. Noticing the filthy net curtains over the equally dirty window, he stepped towards them. 'Shall I take these down?' Without waiting for a reply, he started unpinning them.

David and Mary looked at each other. 'No one expects you to feel responsible – tie yourself to her for ever,' said Mary.

'I try not to.' Jack was silent for a moment. 'And then I hear her voice. Or she writes. And I just can't cut myself free.' Sensing the eyes on his back, he turned to face Mary. 'Don't look at me like I'm a saint,' he said. 'I hate her for it.'

The next morning Kim and Will met at The Beeches' front door. Will looked at her in some amusement. 'You're going the wrong way, Kim.'

Kim didn't smile back. Instead she sneezed and replied, in a voice thick with cold, 'Beth's sent me home. I've got ever such a rotten cold . . .'

'Poor old thing. You get yourself straight to bed.' Then, full of concern, he added, 'Who's got Robbie today?'

'Mum, thank God. I really don't feel up to an active six-year-old today. And good job it's Saturday – no clinic this afternoon.' She smiled apologetically. 'So I'm not letting you down too badly.'

Will patted her on the shoulder. 'Don't even think about work, Kim. Go home and get to bed.' Then, as she clambered on to her bike, he added, 'Have you got some aspirin?'

'Yes, doctor.' Kim waved at him. 'I've got an entire medicine cabinet stuffed to the gunwales. I'll be OK.'

But, pedalling wearily down the hill, Kim really didn't feel OK. She couldn't decide what was making her feel worse: the sudden, virulent cold or the fact that because of it she would have to cancel her riding that afternoon. Riding. Even the word brought a smile to her face.

Kim, if ever she cared to think about it, had not had an easy life. Yet, cheerful and resilient by nature, she had never stopped to feel sorry for herself. Unmarried and pregnant at eighteen, an abandoned single mother at nineteen, she had had responsibility thrust upon her at an early age. And she had coped. Roddy Flint, as her parents kept reminding her, was a loser from the word go, would have been a useless husband, a hopeless father and was, for all they knew, now making his mark as a highly incompetent merchant seaman. Kim, they insisted, was better off without him. Kim herself felt the same way, yet she worried that Robbie might be suffering from the lack of a father. Still, she had to concede, her own father more than made amends for that. Both her parents doted on their grandchild.

While Kim was eternally grateful to her parents for being so supportive, she was also mindful that it had been

Beth Glover who had given her another purpose in life. Wrinkling her brow as she rode into the biting wind, Kim remembered that it had been three years ago when her life had begun to change again. She had called Dr Glover out to see Robbie, struck down by one of the endless and alarming childhood ailments that so frightened her. Beth, quickly and correctly diagnosing – of all things – severe constipation, had soon put Kim's mind at rest. Then, accepting Kim's offer of a cup of tea, she had sat down to chat. Kim, at the time, had been flattered, thinking that she had been singled out for attention. Now she knew differently. Beth's interest in her life had been genuine – but she had not singled her out. Every one of Beth's patients got the same treatment. She was that kind of doctor.

It hadn't taken Beth long to realize that Kim was bored. With Robbie at nursery she had more time on her hands, but nothing constructive to do with that time. And then Beth had mentioned the receptionist's job. Part-time to start with, she had said, and then they would see.

Well, thought Kim, they had obviously liked what they had seen. She had been full-time for two years, very much part of The Beeches team and very much – or so she had thought until that awful meeting the other day – appreciated. She would have to tackle Will on his own about this fundholding lark. She wasn't going to be pushed aside that easily.

By the time she reached her road she was panting, sweating and, she thought, slightly feverish. And she was no longer peeved at the thought of having to cancel her riding lesson. She wanted to be in bed, not on the back of a horse. Next week, she said to herself. Next week she would have her third session. She smiled as she remembered the horrors of that first lesson. Yesterday, when she went without Beth, had been different. She had managed to walk Lady round the paddock – on her own. Next week she was determined to tackle trotting. But now her only thought was for sleep. Wearily climbing the stairs with a glass of water and two aspirin, she shrugged off her clothes and tumbled into bed. Oblivion welcomed her immediately.

Two hours later she was woken by a persistent banging on the front door. Stumbling out of bed and down the stairs, she groaned as she saw her son silhouetted behind the glass door. She loved her son dearly. But not just now. She opened the door and let in the walking disaster area that was Robbie. He had chocolate smeared all over his face, a dirty branch – why? she wondered – under one arm and a football under the other.

''Lo,' said Robbie.

'Where's Grandad?' Surely Robbie hadn't walked here on his own?

'In the car.' Robbie indicated the vehicle now speeding down the road. 'We knew you were home. Saw your bike.'

Kim raised her eyes. 'Great.'

Robbie ambled into the sitting-room, dropped his football and kicked it against the wall.

'Robbie!' Kim clutched her head in agony. 'Do something nice and quiet. *Please*.'

'Like what?'

'Anything.' Kim grabbed the banisters for support and began to climb the stairs. 'Watch a video. Read a book. You could always', she added, managing a grin, 'go mad and have a wash.'

'I'm afraid', said Jack, 'I need a few days off.'

'*Again*? You've just had a day off.' Beth looked at Jack in outraged disapproval.

Will frowned. 'You're on call from midday. The whole weekend.'

'That's fine,' said Jack. 'I just want Monday to Thursday.'

'"Just"?'

Jack turned to Beth. 'I'm sorry. I wouldn't ask if it wasn't important.'

Will, looking at the appointment book, missed the look that passed between them. 'I'm off Monday afternoon and Thursday. I'll fill in for you.'

'Thanks, Will. Thanks.'

Beth sighed. 'And I'm off Wednesday . . . oh, go on then, I'll come in.'

Jack was visibly relieved. 'Thanks. That's really—'

'You owe me a day and a half.' Will looked regally at Jack. 'It will not be forgotten.' With an impish smile, he turned and left the room.

'You'll end up covering for him for three weeks in the summer.' But Beth, despite her words, was not in a jocular mood. Nor, judging by his expression, was Jack. 'Is it very bad?' she asked.

Jack shrugged.

'Look.' Beth took a deep breath. 'I'm sorry I made that dig yesterday. I was being silly . . . flippant. I don't know what's going on in your life, Jack, but if you want to talk about it . . .'

'It'll blow over.'

'An old friend?' tried Beth.

'A bit more than that.'

'A woman?'

Jack nodded.

'Oh, Jack. Why do you do these things?'

'What things?' Jack was taken aback.

'I don't know. You tell me.'

Jack, anxious to dismiss the subject, gave her a weak smile. 'You won't be happy until I've got a label round my neck for the whole world to see, will you? "Womanizer, philanderer, Blue Beard."'

'Oh, Jack, that's not what—'

'But on with the day!' Jack didn't want to hear any more. He looked at his notes, at the name of his first

143

patient. 'Kathy Fielder. Hmm. Get ready for a good ear bashing.' With that he turned on his heel, heading for his own room. Beth, worried suddenly about the growing gulf between them, stared at his back.

Jack's first call that weekend came immediately after his arrival home after morning surgery. No sooner had he put his mobile phone back on the recharging unit then it rang.

'Jack Kerruish.'

'Kim!' he added, surprised. 'What's up?' Then after a moment, he started reassuring her. 'No, don't apologize, I'll be right there.' Frowning, he pocketed his phone and left the house.

'Wotcher, Robbie. All right?'

But Robbie wasn't interested in greeting Jack. He had better things to do. Sitting in front of the television, he was in his element. His Lego – all of it – was spread out in front of him. So was every video in the flat, all the rest of his toys, and an untidy pile of magazines. Jack picked his way tentatively through the debris. Kim, wiping tears from her eyes, seemed only vaguely aware of it.

'I don't usually let him watch until the evening,' she said by way of apology. 'He thinks it's Christmas.'

'Can't he go to your mum's?'

Kim shook her head miserably. 'Away for the afternoon. S'pose he could go to my sister, but she's not on the phone.'

'OK,' said Jack, closing the kitchen door behind them. 'What's the problem?' Kim, he thought, looked terrible. She was also on the verge of tears again.

'I know it's only a cold but I feel *awful*. My throat,' she gestured, 'and I've got the worst headache I've ever had in my life.'

'Hmm.' Jack took his thermometer out of his bag. 'And Beth saw you this morning?'

'Yes, she took one look at me and sent me home. Will said to take some aspirin.'

'And you have?' Jack popped the thermometer into her mouth.

Kim nodded.

'Sore neck?' Kim shook her head.

'Any rash or spots?' Again she shook her head.

'OK. Hang on.' Jack, wincing at the noise from the television, decided there was at least one thing he could do for Kim. He opened the door and addressed Robbie. 'Robbie! Turn that row off.' Robbie just looked at him. 'Now!' he added. Robbie, sensing that Jack was in no mood for messing about, switched off the TV. 'There's a boy. Now go and get dressed. You're going to stay with your aunty.' Robbie looked doubtful about that one. 'If you're sharpish,' added Jack, 'we can stop off and get one of your comics.' At that, Robbie brightened and trotted off to his own room.

'Bribery', said Jack, returning to the kitchen, 'is a wonderful thing.' Kim smiled as he took the thermometer out. 'Well, it's highish, but not terrible.'

'Aren't you going to look at my throat?'

'If you insist . . . Hmm. Inflamed.' He reached into his bag. 'I'll give you some antibiotics and then you can have a nice coolish bath, pop into bed and wait for the virus to pass.'

'Antibiotics don't have any effect on viruses.'

Jack grinned. 'OK, clever clogs. But you've got a very bad dose and they help to fight off any complications. Allergic to anything?' he added.

'Aniseed.'

'Oh, well, I'll try not to prescribe gob stoppers, then.' He took a bottle from his bag. 'Tetracycline. One tablet three times a day. Starting now. And I don't want to hear a word from you for three days.'

'Robbie . . .'

'Robbie'll be fine with your sister. And his comics. Now be quiet. All you need is sleep, sleep and more sleep.'

Twenty-four hours later Jack staggered into The Manor. 'A pint,' he croaked. 'My kingdom for a pint!'

'Not a very fair exchange,' said Chloe. 'I'll have your money first, Dr Kerruish, and then you can have a pint.'

Jack grinned and settled on to a bar stool. 'Well, at least someone around here's feeling good. I've had one hell of a weekend.'

'Ooh! Lots of smutty gossip for me then?' Chloe wasn't entirely joking. She was still convinced that Jack was having 'woman trouble' and was miffed at being kept in the dark.

'Oh, very smutty, I've been called out countless times, had a row with Mr Simpson . . .'

'And him with his poorly bronchials! Really, Jack, rubbing your patients up the wrong way again!'

Jack reached gratefully for the pint she had just poured. 'It's true. You're a beast, Chloe. You're really horrible to me when you're feeling good.'

'Want me to be sick again?'

'No, love. We've had enough of that.'

'More than enough.' James joined his wife behind the bar. 'Reckon we're winning, Jack?'

But Jack wasn't going to make any definitive statements. 'Let's just keep on hoping,' he said. Then, after downing nearly half his pint in one go, he cocked the glass at James and Chloe. 'Here's to no more calls today. I need an early night. Off to London first thing.'

'Oh? Why?'

But Jack was already regretting his words. 'I wish I knew, Chloe. I wish I knew.'

*

It was barely light when Jack left Cardale the next morning. Ellie, also making an early start, drove past him in the nearly deserted High Street. She waved cheerfully and then grinned as Jack, totally oblivious to her, shot past. She supposed it wasn't surprising that everyone always noticed Jack – and not vice versa. Not everyone had a thumping great silver antique for a car. Vulgar, Ellie had once jokingly called it, nearly inciting Jack to violence. He didn't take kindly to jokes about his car.

Still smiling, Ellie turned into Kim's street. Kim, she felt, would welcome a visit. Never let it be said, thought Ellie, that The Beeches didn't look after their own.

But Kim obviously wasn't up. The flat was in darkness. Ellie shrugged. It was now or never. Today was a busy day. She knocked loudly on the glass door. 'Kim! Kim! It's me . . . Ellie.' No response. She knocked again, louder, and yelled through the letter box. 'Kim . . .!'

Still no response. Kim must be dead to the world. With a little frown, Ellie turned away. She could hardly, she felt, stay on the doorstep, shouting and banging for ever. She would, instead, phone Kim later from the surgery. And then, suddenly, the door opened.

Ellie turned round, a welcoming smile on her face. But at the sight of Kim, the smile vanished and she gasped with horror. 'Kim! What the . . .?'

Kim looked worse than Ellie could have believed possible. Sweating, dishevelled, she was obviously in pain, and stumbling from dizziness. And her face, Ellie noted with alarm, was completely covered in a violent rash.

'Kim!' Ellie stepped forwards. She was only just in time.

Kim fell, in a dead faint, into her arms.

Mary Eastman was incredulous. 'Surely not so soon? She's still very ill.'

The doctor was sympathetic, but firm. 'I'm sorry, but

she really does have to go. We'll make sure there's support out there . . .'

'But that's why she's in here now! Because your support isn't working.' Mary gestured to the quiet of the ward. 'The ward's damn nearly empty. Why are you throwing her out?'

'It's the way the system works.' As soon as he said the words, the doctor realized how feeble they sounded. It really wasn't much of a system, he reflected, that threw the mentally ill out on to the streets to fend for themselves. And Karen was one of the lucky ones. She had parents to look after her – even if they were tired, both nearing seventy and ill-equipped to cope.

Mary actually wrung her hands in frustration. 'And if she refuses to let anyone in and doesn't take her medication . . .'

'We can't', pointed out the doctor reasonably, 'lock her up for ever just to make sure she takes a tablet every day.'

'Until she's well again . . . that's all we ask,' beseeched Mary. 'Surely she deserves to be looked after until she's well again?'

'Of course she does. She'll have her own GP, the community living unit, a psychiatric nurse . . .'

'And she'll be alone all night, every night.' Mary looked miserably at the floor. 'Oh, God . . . I'm just too old to cope with this.'

'And so', said Mary, 'I had no option but to return to collect her this morning.'

Jack raised his head. He was exhausted. He'd driven hell-for-leather to London – to find this. 'And she wasn't there.'

'No.' Mary looked at him, incredulous as she remembered the behaviour of the hospital staff. 'I mean, how *could* they? How *could* they have been so stupid?'

'What exactly did they say?'

'That she'd gone to the hospital kiosk – by the main gate.'

'They couldn't exactly stop her, Mary. It's not as if she's sectioned or anything.'

'That's what they said.' Mary looked challengingly at Jack. 'But they could have sent somebody with her, couldn't they?' Her voice rose to a wail. 'And now she's gone. Gone. Wandering the streets of London. In her slippers.'

Jack stood up. Karen's dingy bed-sit wasn't the best place to be discussing this. 'Come on, Mary. She's obviously not coming back here. Let's get you home and call the police.'

Half an hour later Mary was once again pleading with someone in authority. One policeman had remained in the car outside the Eastmans' house, the other was listening sympathetically to Mary and David.

'. . . She gets terrified and lost and it just gets worse and worse . . .'

'And when she can't bear it any more . . .' David faltered, remembering the last time.

'She tries to kill herself,' Jack interrupted quietly. 'She's tried twice before.'

The policeman looked at Jack. 'But you didn't section her, doctor?'

'I'm not her doctor.'

'But you *are* a doctor?'

Jack nodded. 'I'm a GP, yes.'

'Jack's a friend,' said Mary.

'And are you going to look for her, officer?' Jack couldn't help the sarcasm.

'We're already looking for her. My colleague put out a description of her as soon as we received it.' He turned to Mary.

'Have you got a photo we could have?'

'Er . . . yes . . . hang on.' As Mary left the room and went upstairs, the other policeman came into the hall.

Seeing his colleague in the sitting-room, he beckoned to him, and after a brief discussion, handed him a note.

'Oh, God! It's bad news,' began David.

Jack checked him. 'Wait and see.'

'A coach driver', said the officer, referring to the note, 'has just phoned in. A woman asked him to take her to Derbyshire. She was wearing slippers – a couple of miles from the hospital. It appears that a ticket collector found her on the Sheffield train. They'd just stopped at Luton; she hadn't got a ticket, screamed at him' – the officer looked up – 'so he called the railway police.'

'Thank God!' said David.

'But she ran off before they arrived.'

There was a brief, disbelieving silence. 'But she's still in Luton?' asked Jack.

'She's on her way to Derby, sir. By hook or by crook.'

Beth was surprised at how much Ellie's words had upset her. They'd been discussing Jack's sudden – and second – dash to London. They all knew that Jack had no family, so it had to be a friend. 'And to rush down like that,' Ellie had concluded, 'it must be a very good friend.'

Beth had remained resolutely silent during the discussion. She could, she knew, be justifiably annoyed about Jack upsetting the routine at The Beeches – but that wasn't it. She wasn't annoyed – she was jealous. Where had this woman sprung from? This woman who so patently had Jack wound round her little finger; at her beck and call at a moment's notice? Beth had told herself she was being irrational: Jack's private life had nothing to do with her any more. He could do what he wanted, with whom he wanted, and when he wanted – couldn't he?

Beth sighed to herself as she entered the dimly lit treatment room at The Beeches. Perhaps it would just take longer then she had anticipated to get Jack completely out of her system. And it was something she had to do. After all, he had obviously succeeded in relegating her to the position of business partner – and nothing else. As she tidied away her stethoscope and the pile of notes she had brought from her room, she forced herself to think of something else. Kim immediately sprang to mind. Poor old Kim, she thought. Ellie had done the right thing by calling an ambulance and rushing her to hospital that morning – but nobody had been able to figure out what was wrong with her. And then Will, good old Will, had remembered the horses and come up with 'Streptococcus Zoo Epidemicus'. Beth, Ellie and even the hospital nurse had looked blankly at him. It was hardly the sort of condition that sprang easily to mind. Yet, after Kim's blood culture results came through, Will was found to be right: Kim was allergic to horses.

And Jack, Beth remembered, had treated her with tetracycline – to which Zoo Epidemicus was resistant. Somehow that made her feel better. She smiled ruefully. So much for Jack the knight in shining armour. She conveniently forgot that both she and Will had originally missed the symptoms as well, and that she had been sympathetic about Will recommending aspirin. Some people were easier to forgive than others.

Beth filed the last of her notes, sighing as she did so. She really must stop doing this. What was Kim here for – and Eve – if not to do the filing when they had time? It was hardly the sort of thing Beth was paid to do. And, Beth reflected, it wasn't a healthy thing for her to be doing – staying late at the end of the day, creeping about the building at night: anyone would think she didn't have a home to go to. Then she clicked her tongue in irritation. She'd left some important notes on her desk.

She was almost at the door of the treatment room when she heard the noise. She paused and looked out of the window. Nothing, except pitch black. Shrugging, she continued on her way. Unidentifiable night noises were, after all, part and parcel of living in the countryside.

Then, as she was about to turn the handle of her office door, she heard the splintering of breaking glass from within. Her hand shot to her mouth. This was no harmless creature of the night. Then, hearing the unmistakable sound of someone climbing through the window, she turned and fled, on tiptoe, out of the building. As she passed reception she grabbed her mobile phone and rushed out into the safety of the night.

She ran over the road and, half-hidden by the overhanging trees, dialled the police. Shaking slightly, she nevertheless felt more like her old self again: cool, calm and in control. Then she retracted the aerial of her phone and sat down on the wall to wait. Two minutes, they had said.

She was more than a little surprised when, less than thirty seconds later, a car appeared and started to turn into The Beeches' driveway. As Beth emerged from the shadows of the trees, she stopped, taken aback. This wasn't a police car. It was a silver, handmade Bristol dating – so she had been endlessly told – from 1955. She ran up to the driver's window.

'Jack! What the hell are you doing here? You're supposed to be in London?'

Jack smiled at her through the open window. 'I could well ask the same of you. What d'you think *you're* doing, flitting about the night like the wild woman of the woods?'

Beth thought, incongruously, how glad she was to see him. 'We've got burglars.' She gestured towards the building. 'We've been broken into.'

Jack, suddenly serious, got out of the car. He looked up at The Beeches – and as he did so the light in his own room went on. 'Putting lights on as they strip the place?' He was silent for a moment. Then he looked strangely at Beth. 'It's not burglars.'

But Beth hadn't heard him. 'I've called the police.'

'Damn!' said Jack through gritted teeth. 'It's not burglars. I know who it is.' He started to move away from the car. 'Don't let the police in, Beth.'

'Are you sure? Who is it?'

'Just don't let them in. And stay clear yourself.'

'Why?' Beth was becoming increasingly puzzled. 'Is it dangerous?'

'Just stay here.' With that, he ran into the building.

His own room, by the time he reached it, was empty. He moved on into Beth's. That too was empty. And then he saw the broken window-pane – and the blood. He swore under his breath and, with a renewed sense of urgency, hurried into the treatment room.

She was there. She had her back to him, and was calmly looking through the medical cabinet, as if to choose an instrument.

Jack took a deep breath. 'Hello there. This is a nice surprise.'

At his words Karen turned to face him. She had a stethoscope round her neck, Beth's name-badge on – and Beth's notes in her hand.

Jack walked slowly towards her. 'How did you get here? You had us so worried, love . . .'

'I've come to work with you.' Karen's voice was bright and businesslike. 'Just like we always said.'

'We did, didn't we?'

'Why has it taken so long?' Then, sensing something in Jack's gaze, she looked down at the badge on her lapel. 'But this is wrong. They put the wrong name on it.'

'That's someone else's name,' said Jack gently.

'Well, they'll have to change it, won't they?' She looked at Jack again. Something was wrong. 'Are we married?' she asked suddenly. 'I can't remember.'

'No, love, we're not.'

Karen's moment of doubt passed. Brightly, almost playfully, she held the end of the stethoscope to her own chest. 'Very strong systolic. You've not broken it yet, then.'

Jack couldn't take any more. He rushed towards her and pulled her into his arms. 'No, love, not yet I haven't. Not yet.' He was nearly in tears.

They stood like that for nearly a minute. Then Jack pulled away and smiled at her. 'Shall we go now?'

'Yes.' Karen smiled. 'That would be nice.'

Outside, two police cars were parked in the road. Jack, with one arm round Karen, walked down the driveway, pausing for a brief word with one of the policemen. Then he went up to Beth.

'Karen,' he said, 'this is Beth, my partner. Beth, this is Karen, my first ever sweetheart.'

Whatever Beth had been expecting, it certainly wasn't this. She looked at the peculiar woman Jack was almost holding up. She was wearing the oddest assortment of clothes Beth had ever seen, finished off, she noticed, with a pair of bedroom slippers. Beth had never felt quite so nonplussed in her life.

'Hello, Karen,' she said.

Karen looked happily at her. 'We're partners. I'm moving in. This is our surgery.'

'Oh . . . how . . .'

'She's frozen,' said Jack, as if that explained everything.

Beth, still stunned, looked at him. 'What now?'

'Dunno.' He gestured towards the policemen, now inside The Beeches. 'I've told them we're not pressing charges. It's only a window.'

'Of course.'

Jack patted Karen's shoulder. 'Karen's agreed to take her medicine tonight and if we're a good girl and can manage a good night's sleep as well . . .'

Beth had by now taken some measure of the situation. Karen, whatever else she needed, should at least be under medical supervision tonight. 'Why don't you go back to my place?' she offered. 'I'll stay until the window's boarded up and then Karen can have my room . . .' She saw Jack's puzzled look. 'I'll be across the landing in case she needs anything in the night. And', she looked at Jack, 'you can sleep downstairs on the sofa.'

Jack breathed a sigh of relief. He could have kissed

Beth. The last thing he needed was to be alone with Karen this evening. He smiled in gratitude and turned to Karen. 'That's a brilliant idea, isn't it, love? Shall we spend the night with Beth?'

'Will we be safe?'

'Safe as houses.'

Jack cradled his wine glass and stared into the fire. Beth, curled up on the sofa, was listening intently.

'. . . And then she began these small strange hatreds of people. People she hardly knew. She then accused me of having an affair. And then another.' Jack looked at Beth. She smiled back encouragingly. 'But she seemed to come out of it and we were both overworked hospital doctors, y'know, eighty hours a week and so tired we couldn't think straight . . . Anyway—' he gulped his wine and smiled, almost apologetically, 'anyway, it was the grand romance. We were the magic couple. Everything going for us. And then, quite quickly, it got worse. She'd come to lectures late, wearing bizarre clothes, her hair full of old ribbons and bits of rubbish. She couldn't concentrate. She submitted papers that were just gibberish.'

Beth looked at him, seeing how painful this was for him. She felt inadequate. 'I'm sorry,' she said quietly. 'This is too hard for you.'

But Jack barely heard her. 'She sat up all night covering page after page in scribbles. I'd watch her, beg her to come to bed. She was sent home, query schizophrenia, but by that time . . . by that time we all knew. She kept coming back to the hospital, looking for me, thinking she was still in our group. I couldn't bear it. I wouldn't speak to her. I was very cruel,' he added, almost in a whisper.

'You were very young.'

'And then they sectioned her. And for five years I slept around, drank too much,' he smiled ironically at Beth, 'was dazzlingly successful at medicine, of course, and played at being a bastard for all I was worth. And then . . . and then, when I was sick of being a heartless young sod, I went to see her in hospital.' He shuddered. 'Whatever's wrong with care in the community, it's better than what we had then.' He stopped and gazed into the flickering fire, letting it take him back to painful memories.

Beth finished her wine and got up from the sofa. 'Thanks for telling me, Jack. I'm going to bed now.' She looked at him, suddenly swamped by memories – recent ones – of her own. She grinned. 'Sorry you've got the sofa.'

Jack returned her smile. 'Ah, but I've also got the fire.' On impulse, Beth went to him and gave him a warm, sisterly hug. 'I'm ashamed of the way I feel about her,' he mumbled into her shoulder.

'You still love her.'

Jack stiffened. 'No. Most of the time I wish she was dead or locked up or just plain silent. Every time I think it's over and I'm free, something like this happens. And when she comes out of it – realizes she's been ill again – she loathes herself. Tries suicide. She nearly succeeded a couple of times. So,' he added bleakly, 'even if you wanted to be a bastard and walk away, you daren't.'

Beth perched on the edge of Jack's chair. Somehow she didn't want to leave him yet, and somehow she sensed that he still didn't want to be alone. Funny, she thought, how this of all things could bring them closer than they'd been for months.

'Before she became ill, what did you see for your-selves?'

'Oh, we had it all worked out. She was going to specialize in neurosurgery. I'd have a general practice in the inner city, she'd be at one of the big London hospitals. Dead easy.' He snorted. 'Dead corny.'

'No.'

'Marriage, y'know. Two or three kids. Big old Victorian terraced house. Happy families.'

'And that's why you never settled down with anyone else?'

'Well . . . I s'pose. If it could go wrong for us, it could go wrong for anyone.' He looked at Beth. 'And then, fifteen years later, I met you . . .'

'I wish you'd told me all this months ago.'

'Would it have made a difference?'

Beth looked into the fire. 'We'll never know now, will we?'

Jack took Karen to the hospital the next morning. As he left her with the ward sister, she became sullen and withdrawn, like a recalcitrant child.

'Your parents are coming this evening.' Jack bent down to her. 'You'll be OK now, won't you? You do understand why I'm leaving you here?'

Karen nodded. 'Because I'm ill again.'

'But getting better.' He patted her shoulder. 'I'll come down to see you as soon as I can.'

'Don't.' She spoke the word with sharp vehemence.

'Don't?'

Clumsily, Karen took Jack's face in her hands. 'You look older.'

'It's been over two years, love.'

But Karen just stared at him, as if willing herself to say something painful. Then she said it. 'Don't come back.'

'What?'

Karen's words were lucid, her expression normal. 'I don't think I'll ever ask for you again, but if I do – whatever I say – just ignore me.'

'I don't think I can do that.'

'You can.' Her hands started trembling. 'Make this the last time.'

'I'll . . . I'll write, then.'

'No. You mustn't. And if I write, don't read it. Rip it up.'

Jack stared, open-mouthed. 'I can't . . .'

But Karen was now staring straight ahead. Her words came loudly, forcefully. 'This is as good as I'll ever get so listen to me. You've been good at pretending, but you're not as good as you were.'

'Oh, God . . . I'm sorry.'

'No. I *want* you to go away. For my sake. I don't want you looking at me like that any more. I never wanted pity.' Jack tried to say something but couldn't find the words. Karen, visibly upset, tried to reach out for Jack – but couldn't see him through her tears. He held his arms out to her – but she turned away. 'Go away,' she choked. 'Go away, please. And don't come back. Ever.'

CHAPTER 10

'So that', said Beth, 'was probably the reason for his peculiar behaviour all along.'

'*His* peculiar behaviour?' This was a new one on Isabel. 'I thought you were the one always wittering on about not wanting your wings clipped.'

Beth glared at her. 'I don't mean his peculiar behaviour in relation to *me*. Although', she added loftily, 'there's been plenty of that lately. I mean his always rushing around, desperately being indispensable. You know.'

Isabel looked at her. 'No, Beth, I don't know. I think you're being unfair on Jack. The poor man's obviously had a really bad time with that woman. And', she added, 'I think it speaks volumes for his character that he came rushing back to you, declaring undying love. Again. He's always known you're the one.'

'Well,' Beth was indignant, 'we *are* going out again.'

'Oh, good.' Isabel's tone dripped sarcasm. 'And just how long's it going to last this time? Until you decide he's cramping your style? Again. Until you decide you want more breathing space? Or until you go off with Michael Drummond and decide that's what you want.'

'Isabel! I'm only having lunch with him!'

'I thought it was dinner?'

'No. I . . . er . . . changed it to lunch.'

'Oh, I see. Less lust over lunch, I suppose.'

'Oh, for God's sake, Isabel! I really don't see why I should sit here and listen to this.' She sighed, trying to regain a measure of composure. 'Look, Isabel . . . I'd never do anything to hurt Jack, you know that. That's why I haven't told him.'

'Then why go?'

'Curiosity, if you must know. It's been seven years and I thought if Michael wants to see me . . . well, why not? It'll help me lay a ghost, Isabel.'

'As long as that's the only thing you lay, my dear.'

Will and Jack also had a lunch appointment, at The Manor. Miracles, as Jack had said, sometimes did happen – and this one had come in the form of the Cardale Town F.C. winning its first ever league match. The celebratory lunch was therefore going to be lengthy – and largely liquid.

'Busiest day for months and some prat orders a dry martini,' said James as he came through from the bar to the kitchen.

Chloe, looking full of life, clicked her tongue in irritation.

'Sssh! I'm counting.' She went back to the starters arranged in front of her.

'We had two jars of green olives.'

'We used them in the starters.'

'Oh. So we did.' Then he looked in concern at his wife. 'I wish you'd rest up, Chloe. You know how much the treatment takes it out of you. If you get tired just say so and me 'n' Sue'll cover.'

Chloe turned to him. 'If you make me count these pâtés again, I'm going to divorce you.'

'They're not pâtés, they're terrines.' Then, seeing the look on Chloe's face, he shot back into the bar. It was being propped up by Will and Jack. He looked beyond them to the footballers, already raucous after several pints. 'Next year they'll be knocked out in the first round, with any luck. Anyway,' he looked accusingly at the doctors, 'What're you two doing here?'

'Team doctors,' said Jack. 'Got to be with them at all times.'

'Oh, aye. That'll be right. What're you having, then?'

'A pint of best and . . .' He looked at Will.

'Orange juice and soda.'

'Manning the fort, eh?'

Will grimaced. 'Worst luck. Still, someone's got to stay sober to keep an eye on those who're planning to get completely blotto.'

'So, what've you done with your lady doctor?' asked James.

'Beth?'

'I believe that's her name.'

Jack grinned. 'Oh, she's gone to have lunch with some old pal from school. Hasn't seen her for years. Daresay it'll be all head girls and what they got up to in the dorm.' He took a deep draught of his pint. 'How's Chloe?'

'Oh . . . tired, y'know. Working too hard . . .' He leaned forward. 'But I've learned my lesson. The less you say, the better. And, of course, I keep telling her I love her.'

'See?' said Will, nudging Jack in the ribs. 'Told you.'

'What?' asked James.

'I keep telling him he's got to say that to Beth all the time. Works a dream. You've got to tell them you love them at least once a month. Otherwise they think you're taking them for granted.'

James's sharp look went undetected by Will. Who was he, thought James, to preach about love? Chloe had succinctly summed-up Will and Sarah's relationship as 'a marriage made in hell'.

'You've been reading those magazines we litter our waiting room with,' laughed Jack.

'Believe me,' replied Will. 'I know everything there is to know about true love. Ask Sarah.' Then he rolled his eyes and thankfully they all laughed.

Beth made no small effort with her appearance. She agonized over the jacket, discarding one after the other in search of the perfect smart-but-casual compromise. In the

161

end, she was highly satisfied with the way she looked. Country living, she decided, suited her. She looked no older – and far more relaxed – than she had when Michael had last seen her. Shame, she thought, about the weather. Grabbing her raincoat as she went downstairs, she put it over her head, paused to switch on her answering machine, and ran through the driving rain to her car.

Three-quarters of an hour later she arrived at The Cavendish Hotel, the grand country house hotel that Michael had chosen as the venue for lunch. She had to hand it to him: without asking, he'd booked lunch in a place far enough from Cardale to spare Beth the embarrassment of bumping into anyone she knew. Furthermore, The Cavendish was wildly expensive. Sweeping up the front drive, she reversed into a space as near to the porte-cochère as possible and killed the engine. She was ten minutes early. Still in the privacy of her car, she closed her eyes and took several deep breaths. Then, relaxed, she smiled to herself. She had driven here far too quickly: on one sharp corner she had all but skidded into the dyke. She was behaving, she told herself, like a teenage girl on her first date.

After she had touched up her make-up in the mirror, she glanced at her surroundings. The Cavendish was perched high on the moors, directly to the north of Cardale. In summer, she remembered, the place could be wonderful. Years ago, she had come here with her father, and after lunch they had tramped through the moors for a good two hours, before repairing to the warmth of the hotel for tea. Now, rain-drenched, everything looked bleak – even the Hall. The grey stone of the rambling Victorian building, streaked greyer by the lashing rain, gave the hotel a brooding appearance. Almost merging with the low-hanging clouds, it looked positively Gothic.

Inside everything was different. Suddenly her spirits lifted. Whoever owned this place knew exactly how to make people feel welcome. The roaring log fire in the

162

grand hallway, the casually scattered magazines, the inviting armchairs and the discreetly hovering butler conspired
to give an impression of all-embracing warmth. Seeing that
Michael hadn't arrived yet, she smiled at the approaching
butler, the words 'gin and tonic' already forming on her
lips.

Half an hour later she was feeling decidedly edgy. She
had flicked through several copies of *Country Life*, sipped
her drink, gazed into the fire, studiously avoided the
interested smiles of two men drinking alone – and still no
Michael. She was still feeling warm – but not towards him.
Then, finishing her drink, she decided enough was
enough. She stood up, marched towards the front door –
and ran straight into Michael.

'Beth!' Suddenly she was transported back seven years.
Here he was, this man who had once dominated her life,
standing before her. He hadn't really changed and seemed
to have lost none of his power and vitality. Standing before
him – almost beneath him – she smiled shyly.

'Michael. I thought you'd forgotten.'

'Oh, Beth.' He put a hand on her arm. Hardly a
passionate gesture, he somehow managed to infuse it with
an air of almost indecent intimacy. Beth felt a tiny tremor
race through her whole body. 'I'm *so* sorry,' he said. 'The
traffic was awful. I phoned from the car when I knew I
was going to be late . . . but you must have left. I left a
message on your answer phone.'

'Not much use to me there, is it?' laughed Beth, getting
a grip on herself. She looked at him. 'Let's start again.
Hello, Michael.'

'Hello, Beth. How are you?'

'Hungry.'

Their eyes met and lingered for a moment. Then
Michael laughed. 'Well, that's one situation we can definitely remedy. Come on.'

I'd forgotten, thought Beth, how easy he is to be with.
She had been secretly terrified that, after all that had

passed between them and the passage of so much time since, they would be reduced to small-talk. Not a bit of it.

Toying with the remainder of her pan-fried fillets of lamb, wondering if she'd have any room for pudding, she mused: 'I never thought I'd get used to living in the country. Running a rural practice.' She looked up and smiled. 'But I did, remarkably quickly. There's almost nothing about city life that I miss.'

'Does that mean you've forgiven me?'

Careful, thought Beth. She looked at him again – without smiling. 'Michael. You had me fired. From a job I loved.'

'Yes.' He put down his knife and fork. 'Yes. I did. I was very selfish.'

'I wouldn't argue with that.'

'More selfish than you knew, Beth. I told you I wanted to protect my wife's feelings, remember? It wasn't true. I was protecting my own. I arranged for you to be . . . relocated . . . because I loved you.'

This was not what Beth had expected to hear. She looked at him, stunned.

'After you and I split up . . .'

'After you finished it.' Beth wasn't going to let him get away with that.

'OK, after I finished it I . . . I couldn't face the prospect of working with you, of seeing you every day. It would have hurt too much. So I did what I did and I've regretted it ever since.' He lowered his voice. 'If seven years isn't too long to wait for an apology . . . I'm sorry.'

'To be without a job hurt more,' Beth said quietly.

'So, am I forgiven?'

Beth was cool. 'I'm here, aren't I?'

And there she stayed, despite her good intentions, for pudding, a thimble of Beaumes de Venise, and coffee. It was a full hour later when Michael raised his glass in a toast.

'To . . . to what?' He grinned.

'I don't know.' Beth frowned. 'To . . . successful partnerships.'

Michael looked at her. 'Such as?'

'The Beeches. Despite our hiccoughs, we're doing fine.'

'To The Beeches then.' They tilted their glasses.

'And to you and Antonia.'

'We . . . er . . . we separated.'

'Oh. I'm sorry.'

'Don't be. We aren't. You look shocked. Are you surprised?'

Beth considered for a moment. 'No, I suppose not. Alarmed, perhaps. Was it long ago?'

'No, it was recently.' He was silent for a moment. 'Why alarmed?'

'Because . . . because that would make you available and I'm not sure I want you available.'

'Is there another partnership to drink to, then? Beth Glover and . . . who?'

But Beth didn't meet his eyes. She looked round for the waiter. 'I'd like some more coffee now, please.'

With the coffee came the bill – a subtle hint from the head waiter that they would quite like their dining-room back to prepare for the evening. The hint was lost on Michael. He signed it by giving his room number.

Beth idly twirled her teaspoon in her cup. 'Can I ask you something?'

'Go on.'

'If this conference in Manchester wasn't taking place, would you have contacted me?'

'If this conference wasn't taking place, I'd have invented it.'

Silence.

'My turn for a question.'

'Go on.' But Beth refused to look at him.

'How angry would you be if I suggested you came up to my room? And do you mind me asking?'

'That's a supplementary question. You're not allowed a supplementary.' Beth still refused to meet his eye.

'Beth . . .?'

It was after four by the time the football lunch at The Manor finished. Will was stone cold sober and Jack, while not exactly drunk, was in ebullient mood. They were making for Will's car when Jack suddenly stopped.

'I've changed my mind. No need to give me a lift. You go on home.'

Will turned up the collar of his Barbour against the rain, now almost torrential. 'You're not walking back in this weather?'

Jack grinned. 'I'll pop into Beth's. Tell her I love her.' Will laughed. 'Good on you, mate.'

Remembering to respect the fact that this was Beth's house even though he had a key, Jack rang the doorbell. No reply. He frowned and looked at his watch. It was four-thirty. There must have been a lot of goings-on in the girls' dorm, he mused as he let himself in. Yawning, he switched on the television and flopped down on the sofa. Ten minutes later he was sound asleep.

He woke up at nine o'clock, feeling slightly groggy, not sure where he was – and completely unaware of the time. It was only when he was halfway through a restorative cup of coffee that he realized how late it was. He looked at his watch, puzzled. Perhaps she had come in and gone straight upstairs for a rest.

'Beth?' he called. 'Be-eth!' There was, as he suspected, no reply. Beth wasn't the sort of person to have a nap in the middle of the day and, even if she had come home, she would have been highly unlikely to leave him alone, sprawling in an ungainly fashion in front of the television.

Worried now, he went over to the telephone and punched out a familiar number.

'Isabel? Isabel . . . It's Jack here. Look, I'm sorry to bother you but I'm over at Beth's and she's not back yet. You don't know if she was planning to stop over with this friend of hers, do you?'

Isabel was glad Jack couldn't see her face as she replied, 'It's hardly late, Jack. I'm sure there's nothing to worry about.'

'She said she was only going for lunch. And it's been such filthy weather, I was getting anxious.'

Isabel looked out her own window at the lashing rain. 'Maybe she's waiting for the weather to clear before she drives back.'

'Hmm. Maybe.'

'Don't worry, really. Why don't you go home? No point in staying there, fretting.'

'Well, for one thing, I don't have my car here and—'

'I'll come and drive you home, then. For all we know she could have decided to stay the night.'

'Oh . . . I don't—'

'Good, that's settled then. See you in a minute. Bye!' But Isabel's face belied her cheerful manner as she replaced the receiver. She looked thunderous.

Jack was on the phone to the police when she arrived. '. . . And you've not had any reports of any accidents at all. Well, I'm pleased to hear it. Thanks very much for your help.' He looked thoughtfully at the receiver in his hands and punched out another number.

'Who're you calling now?' asked Isabel, returning from the kitchen with two cups of coffee.

'Beth's mobile.'

'Jack! She doesn't need a minder, you know! I'm sure she's—' She stopped in full flow as Jack replaced the receiver.

'Jack,' she began again, more gently this time, 'you are naughty. You ought to give her the freedom to stay out with a friend without panicking.'

Jack turned to her, his face strained. 'It's just so unlike her not to let her movements be known. And why wasn't she answering her mobile?'

Isabel sighed. 'Why don't you let me drive you home?'

'You're not trying to get rid of me for some reason, are you?' There was something in Isabel's manner that puzzled him.

'Course I am. When Beth arrives back at three in the morning or whenever, I don't think you should be there, wearing out the carpet. Very bad for a relationship, that kind of thing.'

'Yes, Auntie.'

Isabel, without prompting, took the coffee cups back into the kitchen and Jack, still worried but resigned to Isabel's bullying, shrugged into his coat. He looked at his watch. It was now ten-thirty.

'Come on.'

'You don't think,' he said, 'I should phone the hospitals?'

'No, I do not.'

'I'm worried, Isabel, I can't help it. I'm afraid something's happened to her.'

Isabel stroked his arm affectionately. 'We'd know, Jack. The police would have phoned. Now, why don't you get some sleep. It's late.'

Reluctantly, Jack nodded and turned to switch off the lights. As he was doing so he noticed the telephone answering machine bleeping. 'There's a message on here.'

'So?'

'Perhaps we should listen to it.'

'Jack, really.'

'May be important.'

'Oh, for heaven's sake, come on! I'm tired.'

But Jack couldn't resist. He pressed the 'message' button and immediately the machine crackled into life.

'Beth, it's Michael. I'm still on the motorway and the traffic's dreadful. I'm going to be at least half an hour late,

I'm afraid . . . But it looks like I've missed you anyway. Sorry!'

For the second time that evening, Isabel was glad Jack wasn't looking at her.

'What was all that about?' he asked.

'An old message probably. Come on.'

Jack turned round to face her. 'Who's Michael?'

'I don't know. Jack . . .'

'What's going on, Isabel? You're a rotten liar.'

'Nothing's going on!'

But Jack was desperately trying to remember something. 'Michael.' He frowned. 'She used to go out with a Michael, didn't she? The consultant. D'you think that's him?'

'I don't know. Now do you want a lift home or not?'

But Jack was no longer interested in lifts. 'It *is* him, isn't it? She's not seeing a girlfriend at all. That was a blind, wasn't it?'

Suddenly Isabel sat down. 'Oh, Jack . . . she's a very stupid girl.'

Jack glared at her. 'So, where are they?'

'At some hotel in the country, I'm not sure where.'

'A hotel.' Jack snorted. 'That's original. How long's this been going on?'

'It hasn't. Today was the first time they've met up in years. They only arranged to have lunch.'

'But it's nearly eleven o'clock!'

Isabel looked at him. For once, she was at a loss for words.

'Well,' Jack returned her look as the truth dawned on him, 'at least we know she hasn't wrapped her car round a tree.'

CH**A**PTER 11

Isabel was right – Beth was a very stupid girl. It was something she kept telling herself as she drove, in tears, away from the hotel. Why did I do it? she wondered. Why did I deliberately set myself up to be seduced? Why – when I knew I wouldn't be able to resist? She stamped on the accelerator, heedless of the appalling conditions in which she was driving, torturing herself about why she had been with Michael. Did her relationship with Jack lack some excitement? No: she found Jack's company endlessly stimulating. Did she want to make him jealous? That couldn't be it – he could hardly be jealous about something he would never be aware of. The answer was, she told herself, that she was plain stupid; that she had thought – as she had said to Isabel – she could simply lay an old ghost without hurting herself. Well she *had* hurt herself. She had, she acknowledged, been within a hair's breadth of going to bed with Michael, but some hidden sense of self-preservation had made her pull away at the last minute.

But, she thought, I'm still not particularly proud of myself. Then she cursed loudly, her attention suddenly diverted by the enormous puddle she had just shot through without noticing. The wipers, working overtime, could barely cope with the deluge and, for a second, she nearly lost control of the car. 'Get a grip, girl,' she said to herself. If self-preservation could stop her misbehaving, it jolly well ought to stop her dying in a car crash. Changing down to second gear, she peered through the gloom, trying to figure out where she was. The road ahead rose at a steep gradient, winding ever higher to the top of a ridge.

Then she remembered. She was still a good fifteen miles from Cardale, and was about to drive through the highest, most desolate part of Derbyshire. She shuddered and looked at her watch. Five-thirty. She had a sudden, intense desire to be at home. Now. In front of a fire, with Jack. Soon, she told herself, I'll be home soon. Then, more carefully than before, she pressed on.

Five minutes later, as she rounded a sharp bend, she was forced to screech to a halt. Standing before her, in the middle of the road, was a young man. Although he was quite expensively dressed, he looked a little dishevelled. He was also gesticulating feebly back down the ridge. Beth paused to steady her heart-beat. There was nothing for it but to get out of the car.

'Help her,' said the man, again gesturing. 'Help her.' Beth looked at the direction in which he was pointing and gasped in horror. Not fifty feet away from them was another car – on its roof. And, hanging upside-down inside it was the barely discernible figure of a girl. Beth, in control now, leaned back into her car and grabbed her phone. She switched it on and waited for the signal. There wasn't one.

'Dammit!' she said. 'Shit! No signal.' She looked around her. Without pausing, she delved into the boot, retrieved her doctor's bag, and hurried over to the man. On closer inspection, he was younger than she'd first thought – probably not much more than a teenager. He was also clearly in some distress. Seeing blood on his sleeve, she reached towards him.

'I'm all right,' he said. Beth looked at him again. Clearly he was in better shape than his friend was going to be.

'Go and sit in my car then. Get warm.' She smiled. 'What's your name?'

'Sean?'

'What's your friend's name, Sean?'

'Lisa.'

Beth nodded. 'Lisa. Right.' She patted his shoulder and pointed to her car. 'Go on, go on. Get in.'

Beth looked down at the other car. She was hardly dressed for clambering down rocky slopes in the rain. Yet she had precious little choice. Frowning in concentration, she made her way towards the car. As she neared it, she tried to figure out what had happened. The car, she reckoned, must have veered off the road at some speed. It looked as if it had crashed against the rocks on the passenger side and then turned over.

Peering through the open window, she grimaced. Lisa was barely conscious and, she reckoned, in a bad state. There was a deep gash on her leg and the inside of the car was covered in blood.

'Lisa, can you hear me, love?'

Lisa opened her eyes.

'I'm just going up to my car for a minute. You're going to be all right.' Then, with an encouraging smile, she left her bag by the crashed car and clambered back to the roadside.

Sean was sitting in the passenger seat of her Saab. He looked terrified.

Beth jumped into the driver's side, glad to be out of the rain for a moment. 'She needs help,' she said, 'but I don't want to leave her.' She looked closely at Sean. 'Are you well enough to drive, Sean?'

Sean stared at her, wide-eyed. 'Is she going to die?'

'She . . . she needs urgent attention. Very urgent. Will you take my car, drive until you reach a phonebox or a farmhouse or somewhere. Ring 999 and tell them where we are. Are you up to that, Sean?'

Sean looked even more terrified now. 'There's nowhere for miles around here!'

'Just keep going till you find somewhere.' She tried to look encouraging. 'Don't be frightened. We're all going to be fine.' With that she got out of the car. Sean hesitated, then slid across to the driver's side.

'Lights.' Beth pointed. 'Wipers. And, for God's sake,

don't belt it, will you?' She tried a smile. 'I want this back in one piece.'

Sean put on a brave face and started the engine. As he pulled away Beth gave a cheerful wave. And as her car disappeared into the night she headed back down the slope, her face now furrowed with anxiety.

'My name's Beth. I'm a doctor.'

Lisa didn't reply. Beth paused for a moment, assessing the damage. First things first, she thought, and began to free the girl from the confines of her seat belt and lower her on to the roof of the car. With only the dim interior light for illumination, it was a struggle. Eventually, and with a lot of effort, she managed to get Lisa down. Gently, she arranged her as comfortably as possible on her back, half inside and half out of the car. Then she fished around in her doctor's bag for her 'space blanket' and draped it as best she could round the shivering girl. Taking out a hypodermic, she filled it with ten milligrams of morphine.

'This'll take the pain away, Lisa. And then we're going to do something about the bleeding. There.'

Next she looked at Lisa's wounded leg. It was worse than she had first suspected. Sighing, she cleaned and dressed it as best she could, all the time talking to Lisa.

'I think some improvising is called for here . . .'

Lisa merely groaned.

'You're not really supposed to do this . . .' she said, taking a length of rubber tubing from her bag and fashioning a makeshift tourniquet. 'Be brave, love . . . you're doing great.'

Then, as she was taking Lisa's blood pressure, she became aware of a steady sound of dripping above the noise of the rain. She looked towards the back of the car, soon confirming her worst suspicions. The petrol tank was leaking.

'I'm going to have to move you, Lisa. I'll try not to hurt

you.' It was just as well, she thought, that Lisa seemed hardly aware of what was going on. Half dragging, half carrying the girl, she managed to get her clear of the car. Brushing her sodden hair out of her eyes, she looked desperately around her. There was nowhere that could pass, even remotely, for 'shelter'. Only the nearby clump of bracken looked as if it might provide some sort of comfortable resting place. Renewing her efforts, she manoeuvred Lisa on to it.

'There,' she said, panting. 'Are you OK?' Lisa nodded weakly. 'Sean'll be back soon,' she continued. 'And then the ambulance'll be here and we can get you into a nice warm bed.' She crouched down beside Lisa and smiled. 'Boyfriend, is he?'

Again Lisa nodded.

'Is there anyone at home, expecting you back?'

Lisa shook her head.

'Does anyone know where you've been this evening?'

Again a shake of the head.

'Sean'll have found a phone by now, I expect.' Beth shivered, both with the cold and a twinge of unease. It was all up to Sean now.

By seven o'clock Beth was frantic. Even though the rain had stopped, the temperature was dropping by the minute. She had done everything she could to keep both herself and the girl warm. She had built a small fire with bits of damp bracken and wood, using Lisa's lighter and the petrol from Sean's petrol-can for fuel. What heat it provided was negligible – but sorely needed. Beth prayed that it would last them until help came.

She looked again at Lisa's tourniquet. 'I'm just going to loosen this for a few seconds, Lisa. Can't stop the flow of blood altogether, can we?'

She concentrated on her task for a few minutes. 'Where do you live, Lisa?' she asked, examining the wound again.

Lisa winced. 'Buxton.'

'I love Buxton. Such a pretty town. I haven't been there for ages. Now, I'm tightening this up again. Don't worry.'

She stood up and looked around. Was it possible, she wondered, that the ambulance was already looking for them, but unable to find them? Turning back to Lisa, she smiled. 'I'm going to wait up on the road for a while, Lisa. Don't want them driving right past and missing us. Back soon.'

Huddling into her flimsy coat, she climbed back to the road. The rain was starting again, this time as a miserable, thin drizzle. And the wind was increasing. Once on the road, she looked around. The visibility was poor although that, thought Beth, didn't really matter. There was nothing to see. A new pang of fear hit her as she realized the gravity of their situation. Sean had been right – there was nothing for miles around in this inhospitable landscape. If something had happened to him, she and Lisa were on their own.

And Beth had lived in Derbyshire long enough to know that even the most experienced and properly clad hiker would have to be insane – or suicidal – to contemplate spending the night on this moor in conditions like these.

The minute Sean pulled away from the scene of the accident, he knew what he was going to do. He wasn't terribly bright, but he was smart enough to know what happened to joy-riders who crashed stolen cars, injuring people in the process. They got into a lot of trouble.

Still slightly fuzzy in the head, he sped through the countryside towards Cardale – passing several phone-boxes on the way. His only thought was to dump the car and get home as soon as possible.

As the Little Chef on the outskirts of Cardale came into view, he made a decision. Pulling into a lay-by, he killed the engine and got out, leaving the vehicle in darkness. As an afterthought, he locked it. Then he threw the keys over a nearby hedge. And as he did so, he was aware of the faint sound of Beth's mobile ringing. He ignored it.

Twenty minutes later he reached the dilapidated farmhouse that he and his brother Damien called home. Entering the hallway, he saw that the door to the lounge was open and that Damien and his girlfriend were, as usual, entwined together on the sofa. There was a half-empty bottle of vodka on the table in front of them.

'That you, kid?' Damien pulled away from the embrace.

'Yeah.' Sean stayed in the darkened hallway. 'I'm . . . I'm going up. I'm knackered.'

'You all right?'

'Yeah.'

'Sure?'

'Sure.'

'Oh, leave him alone, Damien! If he says he's all right, he's all right.' Susie had better things to think about than Damien's little brother.

It wasn't until nearly midnight that Susie and Damien went up themselves. Giggling drunkenly, they tried to climb the stairs arm-in-arm. On the tiny landing, Damien put a finger to his lips.

'Sshh! Sean'll be sleeping.'

'Sean'll be unconscious. Pissed as a fart, that boy.'

'You reckon?' Damien frowned. 'Maybe I'd better go and . . .'

'Yes, you just go off and play daddy, why don't you?' Susie stalked into Damien's bedroom. Susie was jealous of how much Damien, despite his macho protestations, cared for – and worried for – his little brother.

But Sean was lying wide awake in bed, still fully dressed. The scene of the accident was playing round and round in his head.

Seeing the glistening sweat on Sean's forehead, Damien grinned. 'You're pissed as a rat, aren't you?' Then, stepping closer, he took in the clothes – and the bloodstain on the jacket sleeve. His grin was replaced by a frown. 'What's happened to you?' He sat on the bed. 'You've cut yourself. You've been in an accident, haven't you?'

Before Sean could reply, Susie put her head round the door. 'Oh, come *on*, Damien!'

He turned to her. His face was full of concern. 'Susie, go and get some hot water. There's a bowl under the sink. And a clean towel from the bathroom.'

Susie, biting back a reply, did as she was told.

'You've nicked some wheels and folded them, haven't you, you stupid prat?'

Sean just shook his head.

Damien considered for a moment. 'Well, it's not as if I'm going to tell your probation officer, is it? Were you on your own?'

But Sean didn't reply.

Beth had quickly dismissed any thoughts of trying to walk to get help. It would take her hours, and on the high exposed road, she knew she could die from hypothermia.

Back with Lisa, now more alert as the morphine wore off, she tried to make conversation again. 'It's just you and your mum, is it?'

'She's gone off for a few days. Leeds, I think.'

'What about Sean? Where does he live?'

'Dunno.'

Beth looked closely at the injured girl. A new and nasty thought had just occurred to her. 'Does he live on his own or . . .'

'With a brother. So he said.'

Beth tried to sound light-hearted. 'None of my business, I know, but I'm a nosey old cow, me. You only met Sean this afternoon, didn't you?'

'Yes.' The word came in a whisper.

'What were you doing out there in the middle of nowhere?'

'He likes driving up here, he said. No one's ever about.'

Beth groaned silently. 'I'm not going to sneak on you, Lisa, I promise, but . . . the car's stolen, isn't it?'

Lisa stared up at Beth. Her long hair, now damp and matted, clung to her head emphasizing the sharp contours of her strained face. She nodded.

'Oh, well.' Beth was almost maniacally cheerful. 'Sean'll still have phoned for an ambulance.'

'He won't have,' whispered Lisa. 'He won't want to get into trouble, will he?'

Beth didn't reply. This was the worst possible scenario – and somehow she knew it was true. For what seemed like hours, she sat in silence, gently stroking Lisa's head. Eventually she asked, 'Are you in pain, love?'

At Lisa's nod, Beth rummaged in her doctor's bag and took out an ampoule of morphine. It was her last one. 'Beautiful moonlit night now.' She tried to comfort the girl as she administered the drug. 'Beautiful, but bloody freezing. Far too cold,' she added to herself, 'for either of us.'

As Lisa drifted into semi-consciousness, Beth went back to the car. With difficulty she opened the boot. Digging around in the darkness, she found what appeared to be an old tarpaulin sheet. She dragged it out and, heading back to the barely alight fire, draped it round Lisa.

'That's almost Vivienne Westwood, that,' she joked. Lisa didn't reply. Bending close to her, Beth stroked the hair off the girl's face and spoke gently. 'Can you hear me, Lisa?' Lisa nodded. 'I'm afraid you were right about Sean. He isn't coming back. So . . . so I'm going off to find some help.' She stood up and looked at her watch. It was nearly midnight. Fighting a wave of panic, she looked around her. The road, she knew now, offered no hope. So, slowly and steadily, she made her way down the slope towards the clump of trees below her.

Yet only now did she become aware that to reach the trees she had to leave the relative shelter of the rocks behind the bracken. Suddenly the full force of the wind hit

178

her, nearly knocking her off her feet. It was icy-cold, and bit right through her few layers of thin clothing. Beth knew she wouldn't survive long exposed to its full force. Almost in tears, she turned again and headed sideways, towards a small stream at the bottom of the valley. Yet what had seemed like a good idea quickly turned into a nightmare. The stream was bordered by thick clumps of brambles which snagged at her clothes and hands. Angrily, she swiped at them – and lost her footing. Suddenly she had one foot in the freezing water of the stream. Moaning with cold, terror and shock, she hauled herself out, hurting her hands again on the brambles. Breathing hard, unnerved by the fall, she looked ahead and then cocked her head, listening intently. She was right; she could hear the sound of a car. Running through the thick undergrowth, she made for the headlights now approaching in the distance.

'Help us!' she screamed. 'Help us! Oh, God, *please* help us!' Then she fell to her knees as the lights disappeared. She shook her head in frustration as the tears started to flow. It had been futile anyway. The car had been miles away. Resisting the temptation to sit where she was, to give up and give in to her tears, she wiped her eyes and began the slow, careful climb back to Lisa.

The girl looked even worse than before. Hearing Beth approaching, she turned her head and smiled hopefully. 'Did you find anybody?'

'Yup.' Beth, shivering with cold and fear, knelt beside Lisa and took her in her arms. 'A farmhouse. They phoned for an ambulance. Won't be long, love. Won't be long.'

A huge smile broke over Lisa's pained face. Then she closed her eyes and nestled against Beth. Beth held her tighter. No, she thought, it won't be long. You can't last much longer and I doubt if I will either.

She didn't know how much later it was when she started talking about Michael. She had dressed Lisa's wound again, worried about how cold the girl's limbs were. Yet there was nothing she could do. The fire had long gone out and there was no petrol left in the can. All Beth could do was hold Lisa close, pray – and chat.

'. . . Maybe I was only ever infatuated with him. He was older and wiser and he seemed to know so much more about life. He was also my boss which made things very difficult, I can tell you, when things went wrong.' She paused and smiled. 'I never thought I'd love another man. That's when I moved back to this neck of the woods where I remained single and content enough without a fellah. And then I met Jack – and now I'm all confused again.' She looked at Lisa and grinned. 'We never seem to learn, us girls, do we?'

At ten past three Damien called the doctor. Susie had found Sean wandering through the house, dazed, bleeding and uncomprehending. He was obviously in shock.

As he let Will Preston in half an hour later, Damien figured he could get away without telling the doctor about the accident. The cut on Sean's arm could have been caused by any number of things and, more importantly, there was the probation officer to think about.

'How did it happen?' asked Will as he bent to examine the invalid.

Damien shrugged. 'We were larking about, y'know. He fell.'

Will looked unconvinced. Still, he thought, what business was it of his what they had been up to? 'And he's been sick just the once?'

'I think so. We were all drinking.'

Will nodded. 'That explains his vagueness. Alcohol and slight shock. You did right to phone, Damien.' Finishing the dressing on Sean's arm, he stood up and turned to Damien. 'He'll be fine. But keep an eye on him and if you're worried about anything at all, call me again, please.' He grinned ruefully. 'My night's sleep's ruined already.'

Damien looked guiltily back. Seeing his expression, Will put a hand on his arm. 'No, no. Not by you. Someone else.'

Will's grin vanished as he walked towards his car. The someone else had been Sarah. She had told him, in no uncertain terms, to sleep on the sofa when he came back. It had been that sort of night.

And it continued to be that sort of night. No sooner had Will started the engine than his mobile bleeped. Will grimaced. Another poxy farmhouse in the middle of nowhere, he thought uncharitably.

But it wasn't a patient calling, it was the police.

'Dr Preston? It's Cardale police here. PC Warner speaking. Nothing to be alarmed about, doctor, but we've found Dr Glover's unattended car – in a lay-by. There's no report of it stolen but she's not answering her phone.'

'I'll call by,' replied Will. 'She's probably only fast asleep.'

'Get back to us if you're at all concerned, won't you?'

'Of course.'

'Thanks. Sorry to have troubled you.'

'Not at all. Good night.' Funny, thought Will as he replaced the handset. Very unlike the meticulous Beth to leave her car somewhere other than outside her own house. He grinned. Must've got pissed with her girlfriend. Then, relieved not to have to go back to his own house immediately, he headed for Beth's.

Jack, fully clothed, answered the door.

'You're up early,' said Will.

'Not been to sleep.'

'Oh. And Beth?'

'What about Beth?'

'She asleep?'

'No. She's not here, why?'

Jack, thought Will, was being uncharacteristically antagonistic. 'Oh.' He shrugged. 'It's just that the police called. They found her car in a lay-by outside the village. They

181

say it hasn't been crashed or stolen but . . .' He faltered, sensing Jack's anger. 'Where is she, Jack?'

'She obviously met him there,' said Jack stonily, 'so no one in the village would see them together. Then they went off in his car.'

Will was completely baffled. 'Who did she meet? What *are* you talking about, Jack?'

'An ex-lover called Michael.' Jack's shoulders drooped. 'I was so hoping I was wrong. Why did the police have to find the bloody car? Now Beth can't even lie about where she spent the night.'

Will, sensing Jack's distress, yet not fully understanding, put a friendly arm round his shoulders. 'Look, why don't you come back to my place? We can . . . we can talk about it. No point in you staying here.'

'I've got mud on my shoes,' said Jack as he traipsed into Will's kitchen. 'Sorry.'

Will either didn't hear or didn't care. He went straight to the drinks cupboard and poured Jack a stiff whisky. He looked at the kitchen clock as he was pouring it. It was five-thirty in the morning. He shrugged and sloshed in a bit more. Jack really looked as if he needed it.

He smiled ruefully as he handed Jack the drink. 'Hurts, doesn't it? Betrayal.'

'But *how* do you forgive?' snapped Jack. 'How did you forgive Sarah?'

Will pondered that one for a moment. 'Y'know, I don't think I ever did. I didn't mean to, of course, but I think I made her feel as if somehow she owed me.' He shrugged. 'Maybe that's been our problem.'

'I've always found it easy to be the understanding man,' said Jack, 'the guy who could never be jealous. You know why? 'Cos secretly I've always thought that no woman would ever dare be unfaithful to me. I mean, how arrogant can you get?'

'Well . . . I guess you can look back on tonight as a learning experience, then.' Will had been through too much himself to offer trite sympathies.

'I feel like driving out to that hotel, if I knew where it was, and punching Michael's lights out.'

Will was silent for a moment and then smiled ruefully. 'It's funny how we always want to blame the men, isn't it? If you or I were in Michael's position, we'd do exactly the same thing.'

'Yeah, probably.'

At that moment a bleary-eyed Sarah appeared. She looked, thought Jack, as if she were ready to do battle with Will. Then she saw Jack and brightened. 'Oh! It's you. Anything the matter?'

Jack sighed. 'A massive, maybe fatal dose of hubris.'

Sarah looked at him sympathetically. 'You pissed?'

'Not nearly enough, Sarah.'

Then, for the second time that morning, the phone rang. Will wearily reached for it. 'Dr Preston, yes? . . . oh! Yes, I see.' He listened to the agitated voice for a moment. 'No, that's no problem, I'll be right over.' He replaced the receiver and looked at Jack. 'Care to come on a call with me?'

'I'll be dead soon, won't I?'

'Sssh. You have to hold on, Lisa. It'll be daylight in a couple of hours and then somebody'll find us.'

Lisa lay thinking for a moment. 'Bad luck all this. For you, I mean.'

Beth grinned. 'You may find this hard to believe, but I'd rather be here with you than where I might have been tonight.'

Lisa did find that hard to believe. 'How come?'

'Because . . . because I was nearly prepared to risk the most important thing in my life for a one-night stand. For the adrenalin rush, for the thrill. Perhaps for the memory. God, I was so tempted!'

'Fellahs.' Lisa sighed. 'I've not been too lucky, me.'

Beth looked at her, almost motherly in her concern. 'When you find someone to love, Lisa, and you settle down with them, try not to give in to fantasies about other fellahs. Because that's all they are – fantasies. And they're not worth the candle to what you'll lose back home.'

Lisa thought about that one for a moment. Would she, she wondered, ever have the opportunity to test Beth's words? 'I don't want to die,' she said in a quiet voice.

Beth couldn't think of anything to say to that. Instead, she hugged Lisa closer. I have to close my eyes, she thought, just for a second.

She awoke with a jolt. For a moment she was in a blind panic, her heart racing, her eyes not focusing in the gloom. Then she remembered. Shivering, she looked at her watch. It was nearly seven o'clock. Then she felt for Lisa's pulse. It was dangerously weak.

'Lisa. Help me stay awake, love, please.'

'I'm cold. I'm tired. I can't.'

'Yes, I know. I'm cold too. Come on.' She forced a positive note into her voice. 'Let's play that game. Y'know, the one where you have to name a seaside town for every letter of the alphabet.' She thought for a moment. 'Aberystwyth. Blackpool. One with "C", Lisa. Come on. You can do it.'

But Lisa couldn't.

'Clacton,' prompted Beth. A note of desperation crept into her voice. '"D", Lisa. What starts with "D"?'

'Derby.' The word came in a faint whisper.

'Derby. Yes. Derby.' Beth nearly cried. 'That's great.'

'Two of you?'

'This is Dr Kerruish, a colleague. He's an insomniac.'

Damien looked at Will and Jack. Odd lot, doctors.

'So, how is he?' asked Will, climbing the stairs behind Damien and Susie.

'Right peculiar. He's been wandering around, moaning a bit, but not saying anything and not replying. Like he's deaf or something.'

Will strode into Sean's bedroom. The boy was still fully dressed, still lying wide-eyed on the bed. Apart from the bandaged arm, he looked exactly as he had on Will's first visit.

'Sean, how many fingers can you see?' Will held up three fingers.

'Four.'

'Hmm.' Will turned to the anxious faces of Damien and Susie. 'I'm afraid he's got mild concussion. I didn't realize before. I'd put his vomiting down to the drinking. We'll have to get him to hospital.'

'For a bang on the head?'

'Only for observation. He'll probably be out in twenty-four hours.'

'But . . . but will they ask questions? Y'know, like how it happened?'

'So? What's the problem? How did it happen anyway?'

'Fell off the shed roof.'

Susie, hitherto silent, suddenly spoke. The words came out in a rush. 'No, he didn't, doctor. He had a car crash.'

'Susie! Shut up!'

Susie rounded on him. 'They have to know, Damien. He's injured and he's your brother, for Christ's sake!'

'But . . .?'

'Where was the crash?' Will was now alarmed. And annoyed. 'Was there anybody else involved?'

'No. Nobody else,' said Damien. 'I don't know exactly where it was, but somewhere on the Buxton–Flagg road, up by Stanton Moor.'

Will raised his eyes. That was miles away. 'How did he get home, then?'

'He hitched a ride in a lorry.'

'And you're sure nobody else was involved?'

'Yeah, sure.'

Susie, now intent on coming clean, turned on Damien again. 'How do we know nobody else was involved? You told me he always goes twoccing with mates or girls.'

'Shut your mouth, will you?'

Will, leaving them to bicker, rummaged in his doctor's bag for his mobile phone. As he began dialling for an ambulance, Jack moved closer to Sean. The boy was trying to speak.

'What's that you're saying, Sean?'

'Lisa,' he whispered.

'Lisa? Who's Lisa?'

'In the car.'

'Shit!' Jack looked at his watch. It was nearly seven-thirty. If the girl was still there . . . It didn't bear thinking about. He turned to Will. 'Better alert the emergency services while you're at it.' Addressing Sean again, he added, 'Do you know exactly where you crashed?'

Sean shook his head.

'Damn.'

Five minutes later Will switched off his mobile. 'I've spoken to the police. No one's seen the crashed car and reported it, so they're sending out a couple of squad cars to search and they're keeping an ambulance on stand-by.'

'What about Sean?' Damien gestured towards his brother.

'There's an ambulance on its way for him.' Will was tight-lipped as he added, 'Why didn't you tell us any of this before?' He glared at Damien and Susie. 'Do you realize there could be an injured girl out on the moor – all night?'

'We didn't—' began Susie.

'No, you didn't, did you?'

Jack put a restraining hand on Will's arm. 'Cool it, Will. It's a bit late for all that now.'

'Yeah.' Will ran a weary hand through his hair. 'I s'pose so.'

'What about helicopters?' asked Jack, referring back to the phone call.

'They'll send them at first light if the car still hasn't been found.'

Jack stroked his chin pensively. 'It's a wide area, Will. They might not find the girl for hours. And in this weather, how long's she going to last?'

They caught each other's eye. 'We have to wait for the ambulance . . .' began Will.

'And then we'll go and help them search.'

'"S" is easy. Come on. "S" stands for Scarborough, doesn't it? What does it stand for? Tell me, Lisa. What did I just say?'

'Scarborough.' Lisa's voice was barely audible.

'Good. Well done. Where else begins with "S"?'

Lisa didn't reply.

'Southsea. Southsea begins with "S". Southsea. Have you ever been to Southsea, Lisa?' Beth was aware that she wasn't far off becoming hysterical.

'No.'

Beth battled on for another fifteen minutes. Her befuddled brain, straining at the end of the alphabet, managed Torquay, Winchelsea and Yarmouth. With the mention of each town, she quizzed Lisa relentlessly about it. The smallest acknowledgement from the girl spurred Beth to renew her efforts. Yet she didn't know how much longer she herself could go on. She knew she was beginning to suffer very badly from hypothermia. Surely to God, she thought, someone would come with the dawn?

'There aren't any "Z"s, I don't think. I'll let you off that one.' She stopped, desperate to find a way to keep Lisa awake. 'Tell me about your mum, Lisa,' she said suddenly. 'What's she like?'

Lisa didn't answer.

'Your mum, Lisa. Tell me about her.' As Beth touched

187

Lisa's face, a prickle of fear ran down her spine. 'Come on, love, don't die on me now. Not after the night we've had together.' Gently, she slapped Lisa's face. 'Wake up, wake up!'

But Lisa didn't wake up. She couldn't.

Beth craned her neck up towards the sky as the tears started to flow silently down her face. She felt she herself was up there in the heavens, looking down at the small figure, cradling a dead body, all alone on the wild, dark moor.

As dawn was beginning to break Will and Jack arrived at a fork in the road. Will lifted his hands off the steering wheel in a 'where now?' gesture. Jack pointed to the fork that led upwards. It was the road that, hours earlier, Beth had taken.

'Call the police,' said Will, 'and tell them we're covering the B6001 from the junction with the Buxton road.'

Jack fiddled with the mobile. 'Shit. No signal.'

'Christ. We really are up in the middle of nowhere.' Will turned to Jack and smiled. 'Must say, I'm jolly glad you're with me.'

'Yeah, well, takes my mind off other things, doesn't it?'

Two minutes later they drove past the scene of Sean's accident. Jack, scanning both left and right, suddenly touched Will's shoulder. 'Pull up! I saw something. Looks like skid-marks on the road.'

Now, with the coming of dawn, the scene of the accident was visible. Reversing, Will stopped by the weaving, blackened marks that spoke of a desperate attempt to control a car. They got out of the Range Rover and followed the direction of the skids. And then, some way down the slope, they saw the car. They stared at each other.

'Let's just hope the girl managed to walk away from this,' said Jack. He shuddered and looked around him. 'This place is grim enough even in summer.'

A minute later they discovered that Lisa hadn't managed to walk away; that she had only managed to walk a few yards, to light a long-dead fire, wrap herself in a tarpaulin sheet – and die.

Jack knelt beside her body and felt in vain for her neck pulse. He looked up at Will and shook his head.

'Poor lamb,' said Will, looking at the desolate landscape. 'She hadn't a hope in hell.'

'Poor kid,' said Jack very quietly, almost to himself. He stood up. 'Look, why don't you get back into the car and keep driving until you get through on the mobile. Tell them where we are. I'll stay here.'

'Sure?'

'Sure.'

'I'll try not to be too long, then.' Will turned gratefully away from the lonely scene of death and climbed back to the road. Jack shivered and pulled his coat tighter against the bitter wind. He moved away from Lisa towards the wrecked car, kicking savagely at the undergrowth as he went.

And then he saw the ampoule, glistening in the first feeble rays of sun. Frowning, he bent down to pick it up. He twisted it around in his fingers. An ampoule. New-looking. What, he wondered, was an ampoule doing here?

Somewhere in the back of his mind, an alarm bell began to ring. Starting back towards the car, he tripped on something. Jack stared down at the ground for a moment. The brown bag was lying there. Then he knew. He ran. He didn't know why, but he ran downhill, towards the trees, and as he ran he screamed at the top of his voice. 'Beth! BETH! BE-ETH!'

Frantically scanning the landscape as he stumbled along the uneven terrain, he wondered, briefly, if he was going mad; if the long night had been a bad dream culminating in this unreal, ghastly nightmare.

Shouting for Beth, he plunged down the slope. Something in the distance caught his eye, and as he approached it, he felt a sickening tightness across his chest. Huddled against a large rock, wrapped in a space blanket, and for all the world at peace, was Beth. Jack scrambled down towards her and pulled her cold, limp body into his arms.

'Beth! Wake up! Beth! BETH!' With tears pricking at his eyes, he shook her, stroked her face and pleaded with her. 'Please, God, wake up! Beth! Speak to me, Beth!' He felt for a pulse. It was there, weak but steady.

'Lisa.' The word came slowly, and in a whisper.

Jack instinctively clutched Beth tighter. He fought back the lump in his throat and whispered back, 'I've found her. Don't worry.' He saw Beth's eyelids flicker and her lips begin to move. 'Don't talk.' He added, 'It's all all right.'

'I had to leave her.' Beth opened her eyes and stared, puzzled, straight at Jack. 'How far did I get?'

Jack grinned down at her. Suddenly he knew it *was* going to be all right. 'About fifty yards.'

Half an hour later the hillside was no longer bleak and deserted. Crawling with police and rescue teams, it was the scene of frenetic activity. Will, having tactfully left Jack and Beth alone in the back of his car, looked stonily on as the stretcher bearing Lisa's covered body was carried up to the waiting ambulance. What a bloody waste, he thought. What an utter, bloody, hopeless tragedy.

Beth, in the warmth of the Range Rover, sat huddled in a blanket, clutching a cup of scalding, steaming tea. Jack, beside her, couldn't trust himself to speak.

Suddenly Beth turned to him and smiled. 'I must look a sight.'

'You've looked prettier.'

'Poor kid,' added Beth, remembering.

'Yes. But you did your best. Don't ever forget that, Beth.'

There was a pronounced, almost embarrassing silence.

'I let you down,' whispered Beth.

'I let you down too. I never gave you the benefit of the doubt.'

'I never deserved it.'

'Then we're quits.'

Again Beth was silent.

'Jack?' she said eventually.

'Mmm?'

She turned to face him. 'Will you marry me?'

'What?'

'You heard.' Beth's grubby face broke into a huge smile. 'I believe there are only two answers to that question.'

'Oh, you do, do you?'

'Yes.'

Jack cupped her tousled head in his hands. 'You took the word right out of my mouth.'

CHAPTER 12

Beth, being Beth, tried to keep things as low-key as possible. She should have known, in such a tight-knit community, that it was impossible. The *Cardale Chronicle*, recently starved of local tragedies, made a huge drama of her lonely vigil on Stanton Moor and transformed Beth, overnight, into a cross between Florence Nightingale and Mother Theresa. Beth was hugely embarrassed by the attention she received and her only public statement was, typically, a plea that it was Lisa's mother, not Beth, who deserved sympathy. This, naturally, only served to enhance Beth's status as a heroine.

Two weeks after the event, Beth started wearing the engagement ring she and Jack had chosen. If she was hoping that nobody beyond her immediate circle would notice, she was again very much mistaken. On the first day, and while she was twirling the ring around, still unused to the sensation of wearing it, Alice North's beady eye fell on it. Beth might as well have taken out a full-page announcement in the *Chronicle*. And sure enough, shortly after that, the headline screamed 'Local Doctor to Wed her Saviour.'

Beth threw the paper at Jack. 'They make it sound like I'm marrying the Messiah.'

'And aren't you?' Jack looked put out.

Beth grinned and looked for something else to throw at him. 'No. I'm marrying an ordinary bloke,' she noted his expression and added, 'who I happen to quite like. Anyway,' she sighed and sat down beside him, 'I suppose "Local Doctor to Wed Local Doctor" doesn't make much of a headline, does it?'

'No. It'd be better if you were a nurse.' He grinned at her. 'Y'know . . . falling for my masterful, manly way with—'

'Enough!' Beth laughed. 'It would actually be better if you were a painter and decorator.' She looked around the room. 'I'm dying to witness your masterful manly ways with a paintbrush.'

'Ah. Well . . . the thing is . . .' he faltered, not, in fact, very sure what the thing was.

It seemed to Beth that events in both her personal and professional life were suddenly moving very quickly. Such as marriage. And fundholding. Will, roaring ahead with almost alarming confidence, had finally amassed all the data he needed to submit in order for The Beeches to become a fundholding practice. In a few weeks the South Derbyshire Health Authority would be ready to present them with a projection of what their first year's fund would be. But, much to the annoyance of Will's golfing acquaintance, Greg Miller, the two other doctors were still prevaricating. Beth was still convinced that fundholding was but the first step to total privatization of the health service – something she found abhorrent.

'What're you thinking about?' Jack secretly hoped it was the wallpaper.

'Fundholding.'

'Oh, God.' Jack looked as if he were about to make some sort of joke. Then, a thought occurring to him, he turned and looked earnestly at his fiancée. 'Beth. Can't we leave all that for when we're at work? I . . . I don't care.' He paused and corrected himself, 'No. I *do* care, I care very much about how we treat our patients. I care very much about the whole issue.' He looked Beth straight in the eye. 'But I care much more that when we're at home we're not just two off-duty doctors but that we're . . . us. You and me.'

Beth looked at him. He was right. She smiled and slid across to his side of the sofa. Then she giggled. She was still getting used to the idea that, for the first time in years, there was more to life than being a doctor.

Will, however, was thinking just the opposite. He was thinking that he spent his days being a doctor, his nights, when not on call, preparing to be a fundholder, and his weekends – when he had the time – being a father. He had almost completely given up on the idea of being a husband.

What, he wondered for the umpteenth time, had gone wrong? For the last few weeks, Sarah had been increasingly bad-tempered when she was at home which, he reflected, was seldom. She seemed suddenly to have found a great deal to occupy her outside the house. Was she maybe having another affair? Will was shocked to find that he didn't much care any more. He didn't care any more what Sarah got up to unless it hurt the boys.

And that had been the cause of the latest episode of serious friction between them. Last weekend, Tony had arrived from school with a letter – another letter – from the headmaster complaining about his behaviour. Sarah had immediately flown off the handle. Tony, fearing for a moment that his mother was about to hit him, had darted through the kitchen, slipped on the tiles, and cracked his head against the work-surface. Thankfully, the wound hadn't been serious, yet Sarah had been alarmed enough to call Will from The Beeches. Will, tight-lipped, had dressed the wound in silence and Sarah, looking on in silent agony, had reflected – yet again – that she had failed as a mother. And since then she had persistently refused to talk to Will about her relationship with Tony.

It was that relationship that Will was now steeling himself to tackle. Laying his fundholding papers aside, he admitted to himself, for perhaps the first time, how he really felt about his wife. He no longer loved her. He wondered if he ever had – if he had mistaken love for lust in the first place. He didn't respect her; she was too selfish, too ready to fly into a rage if she didn't get her own way. And it was those rages that determined the feelings Will now had for Sarah – the feelings of fear. Will was ashamed of himself. In some ways Sarah had been right all along. He *was* spineless – where she was concerned. He was afraid of confronting her, so he avoided confrontation. But not, he swore, any more.

'Sarah?' He heard what he had been waiting for, the slamming of the front door. 'Sarah! We need to talk.'

'Talk, then. Don't yell.' Sarah stalked into the sitting-room, still wearing her coat. 'What is it? I'm tired. I want to go to bed.'

'And I want to talk about Tony.'

Sarah rolled her eyes. 'Oh. That again. The boy's out of control.'

'He is not out of control! He's angry. Angry with us.' Will's smile was self-mocking. 'Which is hardly surprising, when you think about it. My God, Sarah, what kind of example do you think we set our children?'

Sarah glared at him. 'All Tony needs is a father who'll exercise some bloody discipline over him instead of giving in to him all the time.'

'D'you really think it's that simple?' Will glared back. 'But you're right in one thing. I *do* give in too easily. But not to him. To you, as a matter of fact. But that's going to change.'

Sarah stared at him, completely taken aback. 'What *are* you on about?'

Will was now pacing up and down, steeling himself for the fight. 'I am sick and tired of the way you talk to me. I am sick and tired of the way you behave in this house. I'm not referring to last weekend – that was an accident. I mean the tedious tantrums you throw when the tiniest things don't go your way.'

Sarah stood up and turned back towards the door. 'I don't have to listen to this!'

Will's reply stunned her with its vehemence. 'Oh, yes, you bloody well do!' And as Sarah looked back at Will she saw something in his face that she had never seen before. She couldn't think what it was – but it sent a chill down her spine. 'You're going to change your ways, Sarah,' he continued. 'You're going to start caring more.' Seeing her shocked expression, he relented and added, 'OK, so I admit I'm not perfect either. I'll start caring more as well. Caring more about us. Caring about the effect we're having on the boys. But, Sarah, you've got to admit that things have got to change. We can't go on as we are, can we?'

Sarah continued to stare. Then, appearing to come to some sort of decision, she smiled at her husband. But it was a brittle, humourless smile.

'No,' she said. 'We can't, can we?'

The next morning Jack, feeling at one with the world, whistled merrily as he drove through a particularly scenic part of the countryside. This, he thought, beat the hell out of working in some practice in some godforsaken inner city. How many doctors, he wondered, were lucky enough to be called out to attend to a minor injury on the banks of one of the most beautiful rivers in Britain? Very few.

Negotiating the final bend that led down to Harepath River, Jack looked around him with interest. He had never been here before. He was not allowed. The clipped tones of the voice on the phone had been at pains to emphasize that the accident had occurred on the 'private stretch' of the river. The man, remembered Jack, had given detailed directions, assuming that a mere doctor wouldn't have a clue how to find Cardale Fishing Club. Doctors, the pompous tones had implied, were a lesser species, neither important enough nor rich enough to be allowed to join.

If the golf club was the social barometer of Cardale, the fishing club went one better. It was the province of those who fancied themselves as the 'county set' or, as Beth called them dismissively, the local Mafia. Jack, months ago, had listened with fascinated amusement as Beth had described the intricacies of the local social system. The fishing club crowd, she had explained, regarded themselves as the local aristocracy and, to an untrained eye, could pass themselves off successfully as such. But their clothes let them down. They were too new, too expensive and too clean – a sure sign that the occupants of them were, in fact, *nouveau riche*. The real aristocracy, Beth had said, couldn't give a damn about what they wore – especially outdoors.

Why, thought Jack, had Beth taken pains to warn him not to antagonize them? The fishing club, she had said, may be full of 'pompous sounding gits', but it was also full of movers and shakers, high-powered businessmen who had influence with a capital 'I'. Was this an oblique reference to the possibility that she was about to become more than just a doctor; that, as senior partner in a fundholding practice, maybe she would be joining the ranks of local business people?

But would she ever want to join *this* place? Jack mused as he parked beneath a large, pristine sign. 'PRIVATE. NO PUBLIC FOOTPATH.' He doubted it. It was rather more the sort of thing Sarah Preston aspired to.

Opening the gate, Jack walked briskly along the path. The grass, beautifully mown, looked more like a country house lawn than a river bank. All very stylish, he thought. The man who was waiting for him a hundred yards on was also very stylish. Mr Walsh, as he had announced himself on the phone, was wearing a spanking new waxed jacket, thigh-high waders, anti-glare glasses, and a spaghetti western hat. In one hand he held a landing net: in the other he clutched his mobile phone. Jack was amused by the latter. Fishing, he thought, was supposed to be a relaxing way of 'getting away from it all'. Still, if Walsh had been without the phone, he wouldn't have reached Jack so quickly.

'Ah. Good.' Walsh eyed Jack without interest. 'Thought I'd better call you people.' Evidently feeling this was explanation enough, he turned on his heel and, assuming Jack would follow, proceeded along the river bank.

Jack, irritated, drew abreast with him. 'So what's wrong?'

'The keeper. Hurt himself. Leg. He went in to clear the feeder stream.'

Jack bit back a rude reply. Walsh might as well have been speaking Swedish for all the information he had imparted.

'Just along here.' Walsh gestured with his phone.

As they rounded a bend in the river, they could see the injured man, lying half in and half out of the water. His grimace of pain turned into a relieved smile as he saw Jack with his doctor's bag.

'Here we are.' Jack scrambled down the bank, soaking himself in the process. The 'we' was a misnomer. Walsh, despite his waders, stayed on the bank, looking bored.

Jack then noticed the vicious-looking scythe, lying abandoned and entwined with water weeds. He winced in sympathy as he noticed the slash across the legs of the man's waders.

'Ouch. Cut yourself with that, did you?'

'Yes.' The man gestured painfully. 'Just here.'

'OK.' Jack bent down for a closer examination. 'I'm Jack Kerruish. Don't believe we've met before.'

'No. Tom Makin. I'm the river bailiff.'

'Lucky you. Beautiful place to work.' Jack put his arms round Tom and tried to haul him out of the water. 'Can you try and ease yourself out?'

'Yeah . . . ow!' Tom grunted as he used his good leg to help Jack lever him clear of the water.

'That's fine,' said Jack, panting with exertion. He looked angrily at Walsh. The man was making no attempt to help. He was now, Jack noticed with incredulity, making a phone call.

'I'll need to cut these off.' Jack indicated the waders. As he did so, he saw the wound more clearly. 'Hmm. You've been lucky. These waders have saved you. But I'll need to clean you up. Stitch the wound.'

'. . . Yuh. Yuh. Is there a transcript of that?' Walsh was talking loudly into the phone.

'Is that your cottage back there?'

Tom nodded.

'If you lean on me, d'you think you could manage to stand up?'

'. . . So tell him I want it on my desk in the morning . . .'

'Ouch!' Tom yelped as he leaned against Jack. Jack grunted as he tried to support him.

'Yah. That's what I said. First thing . . . OK . . . *ciao*.' Walsh retracted the aeriel and pocketed the phone. Then he looked, only mildly interested, at the two struggling men.

'D'you think', said Jack, 'you could possible give us a hand?'

Walsh, completely oblivious to Jack's sarcasm, looked at him in surprise. 'Oh!' He looked at his watch. 'Well, I suppose so.'

As soon as they got to Tom's cottage, Tim Walsh marched off, sighing and looking at his watch again. Clearly, he felt he had been greatly inconvenienced.

At Jack's knock, a young woman opened the door. She was wearing an apron and a pair of rubber gloves. Her expression indicated that she was not best pleased at being interrupted in her household chores.

Then she saw Tom. 'What's wrong?' She looked in alarm at the cut-off wader and rolled-up trouser leg. Then at the gaping wound.

Tom smiled reassuringly. 'Nothing to worry about, love.'

Jack also smiled. 'Mrs Makin?'

'Yes. Sandra Makin.'

'Dr Kerruish.'

But Sandra was still looking at the wet, muddy waders and the blood dripping down her husband's leg. 'You can't come inside like that,' she said.

This was not what Jack had expected. He looked at her in surprise.

Tom, at once apologetic and pleading, sighed patiently. 'Please, love. Don't make a fuss.'

'But you can't!' Then, after a moment's hesitation, she added, 'Wait here.'

A minute later, she reappeared with a pile of newspapers and a towel. Spreading the papers on the floor, she ushered the men forward, mopping up after them with a towel.

In the kitchen, Sandra indicated a chair. 'Here,' she said. 'Sit here.'

As she busied herself with yet more newspapers, Jack looked around the gleaming, pristine room. There was no clutter, no mess. The windows shone, the cooker top was fitted with clean tin foil, and there were plastic runners on top of the quarry tiles.

Tom noticed Jack's expression. 'Bit house proud, Sandra,' he whispered.

Jack smiled back. Obsessively so, he thought. Then, reaching into his bag, he prepared to clean and dress the wound.

'Do you happen to know', he asked after a few minutes, 'if you're covered for tetanus?'

'Yes. I am.'

'Good.' Jack finished stitching and put his suture pack back in his bag. Then, standing up, he added, 'Well, stitching the wound on a site like this is hardly favourable. I'd better drop by again tomorrow to take a look at it.'

Tom frowned. 'What about work?'

'You'd be advised to rest for a couple of days.'

Tom frowned. 'I can't promise that, doctor. Not with this job. My bosses want the river looking at its best at all times. That's how they make money.'

'Well, light duties, then. You don't want to pull the stitches out.'

At that moment Sandra re-entered the room. She looked anxiously at Jack. 'How is he?'

'He'll be fine.'

'Good.' Then she looked around her with distaste. 'All this mess.' Heading for the duster and can of polish on the work surface, she began to peel off her gloves. As she did so, Jack noticed her hands. They were red, almost scarred, and there were traces of blood around her fingernails.

'What's wrong with your hands, Mrs Makin?'

Sandra instinctively hid them behind her back. 'Nothing.' Then, seeing Jack's expression, she added, 'I've just got sensitive skin, that's all.'

'Oh.'

Ten minutes later, Jack pulled out of the carpark and turned left along the narrow road. Just before he reached the first bend, two vehicles came screaming round it from the other direction. Seemingly oblivious to the narrowness of the road, they showed no signs of slowing down as they approached him. The first vehicle, a Shogun, shot past Jack with inches to spare. The second, a Discovery, was wider and actually forced Jack into the grass. And the occupants of both vehicles were laughing and blaring their horns as they sped past. Jack, shaking with anger and disbelief, turned in his seat. The Shogun, tyres squealing, turned sharply into the fishing club. The second vehicle, which, Jack now noticed with distaste, had a fox's brush dangling from the aeriel of its car phone, abruptly followed suit. God help us, he thought, if these are the 'movers and shakers' we're supposed to look up to.

*

That same morning Sarah brought Will a cup of tea in bed. It was the first time she had done so in twelve years of marriage. Will opened one bleary eye and then, noticing the cup and saucer, was instantly wide awake. 'A cup of tea in bed?' He smiled and pulled himself up against the pillows. 'You *never* bring me tea in bed.'

Sarah too smiled. 'And *you* never sleep in. It's nearly seven-twenty, Will.'

'Oh, God, is it?' He looked at the alarm clock and frowned. 'Well, I'll hurry in a minute. I want to wallow here first and enjoy this new luxury.'

Sarah handed him the tea. 'It's to celebrate,' she said.

'Eh? Celebrate what?'

'It's your big day, isn't it? Don't you get your fundholding money today?'

'No. The notification of the budget proposal from the Regional Health Authority gets posted today. The big day's tomorrow, or maybe the day after tomorrow, when I receive it.' He sighed and sipped his tea. 'After all the hard work I've put in, I won't be giving three cheers until I've got that notification safely in my hand. Anyway,' he added irrelevantly, 'what're you doing up and dressed so early?' He grinned. 'That's not at all like you.'

'I know. I got my timing wrong.'

'To my benefit.' He indicated the tea. 'Thanks, Sarah, it was a nice thought.'

'No problem.' As Sarah turned to leave the room the smile vanished from her face. It was replaced by a frown of irritation as she looked anxiously at her watch.

'I thought', said Will as he came downstairs five minutes later, 'that I'd get in touch with James. See if I can organize some kind of surprise party at The Manor for when we get the cheque. Can you come?'

Sarah, bending over the sink, was non-committal. 'I'll see.'

'Oh,' continued Will, 'and perhaps we could do something with the boys this weekend. Take them out. Just the four of us.'

This time Sarah turned to him and smiled. 'That's a nice idea.'

Encouraged by her expression, Will grabbed the initiative. 'In fact,' he said, 'I should have much more free time from now on . . . what with the fundholding plans being finished. Maybe . . . well, maybe we could try to make things work again.' Leaving a question mark hanging in the air, he opened the back door and left the house.

Sarah called him back. 'Will?'

'Mmm?'

'Things *are* going to be better for both of us from now on. I know it. No matter what happens.' Smiling, she moved towards him and, much to his surprise, planted a kiss on his cheek.

Trying not to look astonished, Will laughed. 'First tea in bed. Now a kiss.' He grinned broadly. 'What comes next?'

Without replying, Sarah returned his grin.

'Oh, don't forget,' said Will as he turned once again towards the Range Rover. 'That do at The Manor. It's a surprise.'

'Don't worry,' replied Sarah, 'I'm good at surprises.'

Renowned she may have been for her unpredictability, but this time Sarah was as good as her word. Had Will been able to witness the frenetic activity that overcame her as soon as he had driven away, he would have admitted that, yes, his wife was an expert at surprises.

On a high, Will drove to The Beeches thinking of the future. At last, all the hard work he had invested in preparing the practice for fundholding looked like paying off. The only fly in the ointment was Beth. As senior partner, her signature on the agreement was vital – and so far she had refused to give it. Her excuse of 'thinking it over' was, Will reckoned, beginning to wear a little thin. Still, Sarah had started the day with an unspoken wish to improve their marriage; perhaps Beth would adopt the trend and improve their partnership.

It was unfortunate, however, that Will kept his first patient waiting while he phoned James to organize the surprise dinner – and that Beth noticed him, feet up on his desk, engaged in what looked like a private conversation. Keeping patients waiting was, as far as she was concerned, a cardinal sin. But it wasn't until the morning's surgery was over that she had a chance to tackle him about that sin.

'Will?' She put her head round his door. 'Can we have a word?'

'Yes, boss.'

Beth walked in. 'I couldn't help noticing that you kept Mr Prentice waiting for about ten minutes this morning while you chatted on the phone. What on earth are you playing at?'

Will glared at her. 'I'm not a child, Beth. I don't need constant supervision. And I don't like being spied upon.'

'I wasn't . . .'

'If you must know, I had a pressing budget problem to deal with. And Mr Prentice', he added scathingly, 'comes to see me every week and there's never anything wrong with him. He must like it here.'

'Hmm.' Beth was distracted by the hated word 'budget'. 'I thought all your budget problems had been solved.'

'They will be when I've got your formal approval.'

'Yes . . . well, I'm still thinking about that.'

'But what is there to think about? We're being offered a generous budget. And everyone else has given the go-ahead.'

Beth exhaled loudly. She'd come here to give *him* a lecture. 'I said,' she spoke the words as if to a child, 'I'm still thinking about it. In the meantime, perhaps you could deal with all your non-medical phone calls in your spare time.'

'Spare time?' Suddenly Will smiled. 'What spare time?' But Beth, having said her piece, chose not to reply. Will shook his head in resignation as she left the room. It was too much, he supposed, to expect two miracles in one day.

Tom Makin looked out of his cottage window and shook his head in disgust. When the young drivers of the Shogun and the Discovery had descended on the club with their girlfriends, their champagne and their high spirits, they had churned up the immaculate grass, left an empty bottle and plastic cups lying around, all but destroyed two of the fishing platforms and, worst of all, made so much noise that they had disturbed the fish. They hadn't much cared. As friends of Miles Holt, the owner of the fishing club, they had merely come to inspect it, to see if it would suit their purposes as yet another venue for their endless pursuit of fun. They hadn't given a thought to who might have to clear up after them – or who might be blamed for the mess. Miles Holt, reflected Makin, would blame him. Just as he had on previous occasions when his 'friends' had wreaked havoc on his hallowed fishing ground.

Makin reckoned he'd just have to leave the grass until he'd had his stitches out. Bloody yuppies, it was all right for them, he thought. Plenty of money, plenty of time, and plenty of friends. He glanced in annoyance towards the sitting-room where the vacuum cleaner had been humming incessantly for the past half hour. Yeah. Plenty of all the things I don't have. Then he sighed and applied himself anew to his task. He was sitting at the kitchen table, making artificial flies. He picked up a hook and, the picture of concentration, fixed the delicate ribbing, body and hackle to it. Gradually, both the thought of the yuppies and the sound of the vacuum faded from his mind.

Ten minutes later, Sandra unplugged the machine and surveyed the sitting-room. It would have to do, she thought. Not perfect, but it would have to do. Then, still wearing her rubber gloves, and now armed with a dustpan and brush, she went into the kitchen.

Her husband looked at her as she entered. He smiled. 'Come and sit down, love.' He indicated a chair. 'Come on. Come and talk to me.'

Sandra looked doubtfully at him for a moment. Then, quietly acquiescing, she peeled off the gloves and, keeping her hands in her lap, sat at the table.

Maintaining his gentle, soothing tones, Tom looked down. 'Let me see your hands. Please.'

After a moment, and like a child showing a parent, Sandra held out her hands. They were red, raw and sore-looking. And, as Jack had noticed earlier, there were flakes of dried blood around the nails. Tom sighed.

'It's all right . . .'

'It's *not* all right . . .'

'I'll put some cream on them. My skin's a bit sensitive, that's all.'

'That's what you're always saying.' He looked at Sandra, irritation beginning to show through his concern. 'That's what you told Dr Kerruish. He noticed. He seemed worried about you.'

But Sandra, glancing around her while Tom was talking, had now found other things to discuss. 'I hope you're going to tidy that lot up after you,' she said, indicating the flies.

'Sandra, for heaven's sake! No one has to clean a house day and night, seven days a week.'

'It's an old house.' Sandra was defiant. 'It's dirty.'

'I can live with it.'

'Well, I can't!' With that Sandra got to her feet.

Tom was desperate to stop her embarking on yet another round of cleaning. 'Look,' he suggested, 'just forget the house for once. Let's go out.'

'Where?'

'Anywhere. To the pub. Have a meal.'

'No.'

'But, Sandra! We never go out together. Not any more. We don't see people.' He gestured towards the window and the beautiful river beyond. 'You don't even bother to come down and work with me on the river these days.'

'That's because it's muddy.'

'Of course it's bloody muddy! What the hell d'you expect? It's a bloody river, isn't it?'

Sandra, unused to her husband losing his temper, just stared.

'Sandra.' This time he was gentle, pleading. 'This is crazy. I need you around. I need your support. Please.'

'No.' And with that Sandra left the room. As Tom hurled the artificial flies to the ground in frustration, she quietly went into the bathroom. Shutting and locking the door behind her, she went to the basin and turned on the hot tap. Wincing with pain, she reached for the soap and nail brush. And then she began to scrub.

That evening, Jack suggested to Beth that they go out for a drink. Unlike Sandra Makin, Beth accepted with alacrity. After 'one of those days', she felt she needed a spot of sustenance. And she also wanted to see how Chloe was coping.

'Y'know,' said Jack as he opened the door to The Manor, 'you wouldn't believe the inside of that keeper's cottage.'

Beth rolled her eyes. Jack had been wittering on about Harepath River all day. He'd decided that he wanted to be a river bailiff when he grew up. Beth, he'd offered generously, could be Mrs Bailiff. Jack knew how to sweet-talk a girl.

'What wouldn't I believe about it?'

'How tidy it is.'

'Is that some sort of hint?'

Jack laughed. 'No. Anything but. You know me, I like my mess. Not', he added hastily, 'that you're the messy

207

one.' As they walked towards the bar, he continued. 'No. It's ghastly. Spotless. Coverings on everything. It's like a show house – only worse.'

'The Makins don't have children, then?'

'No.'

'Animals?'

Jack turned to her and grinned. 'Only fish.'

'Hmm. But you're worried about this Sandra Makin, aren't you? Her hands.'

'Yup.' Then, as Chloe, sporting a new headscarf, came from behind the bar, he dismissed Sandra Makin from his thoughts.

''Evening, Chloe.'

'Hi, Jack. Beth.'

'How are you, Chloe?' asked Beth.

'Me?' Chloe touched her head and grinned. 'Running out of headscarves. I like to sport something different every hour, on the hour. This', she gestured again, 'is my new Paisley number. Thought I might take up fortune-telling in my spare time.'

Jack and Beth laughed.

'So, what'll you have?' asked Chloe, reverting to barmaid mode.

'Large G and T, please.'

'And a pint.'

Chloe sighed as she reached for the optic. 'But apart from all that, I feel sick most of the time. And tired. Very tired.'

'You will, Chloe. For a while. We've explained that to you.'

'Yes, Jack. I know.' For a moment Chloe looked weary, defeated. Then she brightened again. 'Anyhow, my poor husband. I've told you I absolutely refuse to wear a wig.'

James, coming in from the kitchen, heard her. 'But that, my love, is the least of our problems. Would you believe,' he turned to Jack and Beth, 'that we could be bought out, along with the brewery?'

'What? The Manor?' Beth was aghast.

'Yes.' The news had come that morning. Ron, the tenant landlord at the Coach and Horses in Brompton, had phoned to say that the brewery that owned both pubs was about to be taken over. James was trying, unsuccessfully, to hide the fact that he was desperately worried. 'I mean,' he continued, 'where would that leave us as tenants?'

'Well,' said Jack, 'I know the brewery's small, and just about getting by, but I didn't know they were looking for a buyer.'

'Nor did we.'

'So who's trying to bid for it?'

'Dunno.'

Will looked at his watch. Sarah would be pleased, he thought, that he was home early. Perhaps this time, after so many false starts, they would finally be able to get their act together. This time it looked like they were both moving in the same direction at the same time. Perhaps, he reflected, he ought to have lost his temper with Sarah long before now. Last night's outburst – about which he was scarcely feeling guilty – had obviously had an effect.

Humming to himself, he pulled into the driveway and looked at the house. It was in complete darkness. Frowning slightly, Will got out of the car, locked it, and made his way to the front door. Fumbling in the dark for his house keys, he silently cursed Sarah for going out and spoiling his plans for the evening. But to give her her due, he thought, she was unaware of those plans; of his intention to take her out for a romantic dinner.

Inside the hall, he groped for the light switch – and as soon as he switched it on he realized something was wrong. At first he couldn't figure out what it was. Then it dawned on him: the light was too bright. Looking up, he frowned at the naked bulb dangling from the ceiling. What on earth, he wondered, had Sarah been up to? He went into the sitting-room, put that light on – and gasped in disbelief. The shade in that room, too, had gone. And the stark brightness only served to emphasize what else was missing: the three-piece suite, the television, half the books from the shelves, and all the pot plants. Will felt suddenly weak. Reaching out to support himself against the wall, he shuddered as he noticed that most of the pictures had gone as well. Shaking his head, he went back into the hall and then into the kitchen. It was worse in there. The cupboards were all open, or half-open, and most of their contents had gone. Staring mutely for a moment, he then made his way upstairs noticing, as he did so, the empty cardboard box at the foot of the stairs and the forlorn coat stand in the corner. There was only one coat on it. His coat. Hurrying now, he flew up the stairs and burst into the boys' room. And then he felt his legs give away. Slumping against the wall, he stared open-mouthed at what used to be the messiest room in the house. Now there was no mess. There was nothing with which to make any mess. The room was completely empty.

CH**A**PTER 13

The next morning Jack returned from his second visit to the Makins and, in high dudgeon, immediately started regaling Beth with Tom Makin's woes.

'. . . So poor old Makin', he was saying, 'is now worrying himself silly about the mess those ghastly yahoo yobs made of that beautiful sight. They even managed to knock down a tree, would you believe it?'

Beth, busy with her notes, nodded. 'I'm afraid I can believe it. That lot care for nothing except themselves. What does it matter to them if Makin gets into trouble?'

Jack was slightly irritated by Beth's calm acceptance of the situation. 'But the poor man could get sacked if this sort of thing continues, so he said. And it's not even his fault!'

'I know. I know.' Beth, although sympathetic, was just a little tired of the subject. 'How is Makin, anyway?'

'Oh, he'll be all right. As for the wife . . . well, he suggested there was some sort of problem there.'

'But you knew that anyway.' She looked up. 'The handwashing, right?'

'Right. But it goes deeper than that. He asked me to see her, but I can't, of course. She has to make the first move.' He thought for a moment, looking, as he did so, at the basin in the corner. 'Handwashing. It's an objective. A criterion of cleanliness, if you like, that's being striven for.'

'Sure.'

'For most of us, we compare the *actual* state of our hands being clean with the *desired* state. Usually they're the same – so we're happy. Goal achieved.'

'But people like Mrs Makin never reach that goal?'

'No.'

'Mmm.' Beth, intrigued by the analogy, thought for a moment. 'Ah, so that's it,' she said after a moment.

'What?'

'She's probably washing away some past sin. But she can't. So she tries harder and harder and it all just gets worse and worse.'

Jack thought about that one for a minute. 'Nah,' he said. 'Too easy.' With that he turned and headed towards the door.

Beth stuck her tongue out at his retreating back.

'Jack?' Kim put her head round the door before he reached it. 'Sorry, forgot to tell you. There was a message left for you this morning. A Mr Alex Latimer rang.'

'Who?'

Kim looked again at the piece of paper in her hand. 'Alex Latimer. He's invited you for drinks this evening.'

'But I don't know an Alex Latimer.'

'I do.' Kim and Jack turned to Beth. 'One of the local Mafia,' she continued. 'Probably one of the very people you've been talking about.'

'Eh?'

'I'd bet my bottom dollar he's a member of the Cardale Fishing Club.'

'Yes, he must be.' Kim waved the piece of paper at Jack. 'Drinks at the Cardale fishery clubhouse, he said.'

Jack looked dumbfounded.

'The Mafia', laughed Beth, 'are after you.'

At that moment, Will walked in, looking tired, worn and bad tempered.

'Hi, Will,' said Beth brightly. 'Oh!' She turned to Jack. 'Will'll know about Alex Latimer. I seem to remember Sarah talking about him. Will . . .?'

But Will, after a mumbled 'Good morning,' had already disappeared into his room.

Beth turned back to Jack and Kim. 'What on earth's up with him?'

Kim rolled her eyes. 'Don't even ask. I'm not going to. I suspect he got out of bed the wrong side. Or', she added with a wicked grin, 'he was thrown out.'

But there had been nobody to throw Will out of bed that morning. He had been lucky enough, he thought, even to *have* a bed to get out of. Sarah, obviously, had gone to a lot of trouble thinking about what to leave and what to take. She had left, he had soon discovered, the bare minimum for him to get by with. Everything that she and the boys could possibly need had gone.

After the initial shock of discovering what Sarah had done, Will had phoned her mother in Lancashire, and Pauline's guarded tones when she had recognized Will's voice immediately told him what he wanted to know. Sarah was there, and probably with the boys. Pauline had initially tried to deny all knowledge of Sarah's disappearance, but she had been no match for Will's anger. Yes, she had eventually admitted, Sarah and the boys were with her. And no, Sarah didn't want to speak to him. She was, she explained, writing him a letter.

A letter? thought Will as he cradled his head in his hands. Twelve years of marriage and all I'm going to get out of it is a letter. The most appalling thing about it all, he thought, was the *shock*. Sarah had not even given the slightest hint of what she was planning; and she must have been planning it for weeks. The removal men, the lists she must have made, the arrangements – as he had discovered this morning – to leave her job, and to take the boys out of school. And that was the worst of it, he thought bitterly. The boys. Did she think they were just pieces of furniture, to be plucked from one place and deposited in another? Pauline had refused to allow Will to speak to them last night; had claimed they were in bed. Well, perhaps they had been, thought Will, but he was determined to speak to them today. And he was also determined to get them back.

As the day wore on, Will wondered how to tell his

colleagues. How did you announce that your wife had left you, taking your children and most of your joint possessions? The more Will thought about it, the more foolish he felt, and the more extraordinary the whole situation appeared. It seemed more like a dream – or a nightmare – than reality. But by the end of the day he had come to a decision. He wouldn't tell anyone at The Beeches about Sarah's departure – at least not yet. He felt he could only cope with one thing at a time and, until tomorrow, that thing was the budget agreement for fundholding. Tomorrow they would get the notification of a budget for three-quarters of a million pounds and, Beth's approval permitting, they would agree to become fundholders. Then they would have the celebration dinner at The Manor. And then Will would tell them that his marital as well as professional status had changed.

It wasn't until he woke up in the middle of the night that he realized both were changing for the better; that Sarah, for all the astounding suddenness of her flight, had – the boys excepted – done them both a favour.

Despite his being certain that he would have absolutely nothing in common with Alex Latimer, Jack's curiosity overcame him as, later in the day, he prepared to go out.

'Can't think why you're going,' said Beth.

'It's probably the only chance I'll ever get to enter the hallowed portals of their precious clubhouse. And anyway, I'm intrigued. What can Latimer possibly want with me?'

Beth suddenly looked serious. 'It's not what he wants *with* you, Jack. It's what he wants *from* you.'

'Oh, come on . . .'

'No, I'm serious. Believe me, Jack, it's no accident that Alex Latimer and his ilk are members of the fishing club. They're piranhas. They eat people alive.'

Jack was still smiling at Beth's words as he pulled into

the carpark. While he realized that she held no truck with the fishing crowd, he also reckoned she was slightly miffed that it had been himself, not her, whom they had invited. Beth, after all, was no different from anyone else when it came to invitations: it was always preferable to be presented with the opportunity to decline them. And anyway, Jack had another, more important reason for accepting Latimer's invitation.

Thank God, he thought, that he had bowed to what he knew would be the form and donned a smart jacket and tie. There was not a shirt sleeve in sight as he entered the bar. The atmosphere was very subdued, very country club, with the uniformed staff trying their best to look invisible as they moved around the room, dispensing drinks from silver trays.

'Ah! Kerruish.'

Jack looked at the hearty individual approaching him. This, he presumed, was Alex Latimer. Or perhaps just Latimer.

The man smiled warmly and proffered his hand. 'Alex Latimer.' He gestured vaguely around the room with his other arm. 'Amongst other things, I'm the chairman of this rabble.'

Bully for you, thought Jack, looking round. He frowned as he caught sight of the driver who had forced him off the road.

'Now, then,' said Latimer as they approached the bar, 'what do you drink?'

'Scotch, please.'

As he ordered their drinks, Latimer nodded at a man sitting nearby. 'That's Miles Holt. He'd like a word with you later.'

'Who?' Jack was already feeling out of his depth. Appropriate, he thought, looking at the bland pictures of rivers all over the walls.

'Miles Holt. He's the managing director of the club.

Mainly because he owns it.' Latimer laughed uproariously. 'Then again, what doesn't he own around here?' Abruptly, he changed tack. 'So, I hear you're getting married?'

Jack nearly choked on his newly acquired drink. 'Er . . . yes.'

'To one of your colleagues. Now that's good. That means stability, and we need that stability in Cardale.' He smiled at Jack. 'We also like to be sure of who's who and what's what. Anyhow,' he raised his drink, 'congratulations.'

'Cheers.'

'By the way, doctor, do you fish?'

'Me? No. Only a bit when I was a lad. A bit of string and a bent pin job, y'know.'

Latimer's wan smile indicated that he didn't know – and didn't want to.

At that point Miles Holt came up and introduced himself. 'So. The famous Dr Kerruish. You used to work in Zimbabwe, didn't you?'

'Yes.' Jack looked faintly annoyed. 'How did you know?'

'Oh, word gets around, you know, in the business world.'

Jack smiled thinly. 'But I'm not in the business world. I'm a GP.'

'Quite. But your practice is going fundholding, isn't it?'

How the hell did they know that? 'Ye – es. It is.'

'And is that because it has to?'

Jack glared at Holt. 'No. We get by.'

'But getting by is hardly enough, is it? You see, with the people we know, and the companies we're involved with, we could perhaps put some private doctoring your way.'

'Oh, yes. In exchange for what?'

Holt smiled. 'Co-operation. Help when we need it. An understanding, if you like, between businesses. Local ones.' He paused for a moment, then added, 'I'm told you worked for the Red Cross in Zimbabwe?'

216

'Yes.'

'Then you'll know what tribal means.' Holt leered at him, his smug, drinker's face rather too close for comfort. 'We're tribal, you see. Have to be. That way we can protect and help each other.'

Jack was more than wary now. He was completely repulsed. Yet Holt, seemingly oblivious to Jack's distaste, ploughed on. Smiling at Jack, ordering him another drink without prompting, he added conspiratorially, 'Right now, we could actually do with a small amount of assistance ourselves . . .'

Jack had had enough. 'Look, can I just say . . .'

But Holt was now looking at Alex Latimer. 'Medical assistance, right, Alex?'

'Absolutely. At The Manor Hotel.'

Suddenly Jack stiffened. 'The Manor? What about it?'

'We want to buy the brewery that owns it,' said Holt. 'Only there are a few difficulties.' He took a contemplative sip of his drink. 'You see, they're not likely to sell while pubs like the Manor Hotel are making a profit.'

'So? What's that got to do with me?'

'Well, doctor, we think you could help us there. The landlord's wife. Mrs White.' Holt looked slyly at Jack. 'We're told she's sick. Diseased.'

Jack, horrified, stared dumbly at the man.

Holt grimaced at the thought of Chloe. 'Now what kind of hotel and restaurant would allow a sick woman to help prepare and serve food?'

Jack wanted to throttle him. Barely able to keep his composure, he replied through tight lips, 'Chloe White happens to be a patient of mine.'

'We know that,' smiled Latimer. 'So you're aware of how she's endangering—'

'And she also happens to be a friend of mine.' Abruptly, and loudly, Jack deposited his unwanted drink on the bar. 'Goodnight,' he added, turning towards the door. 'Thank you for the drink.'

Stalking furiously across the room, he was aware of Latimer at his heels. Jack swung round. 'And before any more tribal whispers start going around, I didn't come here to gain points from the likes of you, Mr Latimer. I don't need to do that.'

'So why did you accept our invitation?'

'I have two other patients. Tom and Sandra Makin.'

'Oh. The bailiff. Yes?'

'As their GP, I consider their well-being to be of paramount importance. In other words,' he glared contemptuously at Latimer, 'I was anxious to see what kind of crooks they're working for.'

Suddenly Latimer smiled. It was a smile totally without humour. 'Professional curiosity, eh?' He chuckled. 'Don't worry. We have a remedy for that.'

Jack, not understanding, yet unable to bear the man's company any longer, left the room without replying. Later, he would come to regret ever having mentioned the Makins.

'I can't bloody believe it! Those bastards! Those smug, arrogant, conniving bastards!' Jack threw his coat on to the sofa. 'They were trying to use me.'

Beth, her evening's peace dramatically shattered, put her book down with a sigh. 'Well, you did rather ask for it. I did warn you.'

'But even to *contemplate* . . .' For a moment he was speechless with rage. 'Just think.' He swung round. 'Trying to use me to get rid of Chloe and James. They called her *diseased*, Beth.'

At that, Beth shuddered. Even she hadn't thought they would stoop so low.

'And another thing. I heard some prat at the bar talking about Sarah Preston. Seems she's a friend of theirs. In fact,' he paused as a thought occurred to him, 'I bet it was

Sarah and her big mouth who's been feeding those vultures with all sorts of classified information about The Beeches.' He turned to Beth. 'I wonder if Will knows?' And then, with a sigh, he added, 'I wonder if Will knows how much better off he'd be without her?'

Beth looked up in surprise. It was most unlike Jack to criticize anyone openly. Beth had always suspected he wasn't keen on Sarah, but he had always kept his feelings to himself.

'That's unlike you, Jack,' she said mildly.

'I know, I know. I'm just in a rage, that's all.'

Beth smiled up at him. 'Well, before you wind yourself up even further, would you like to hear some relatively good news?'

Jack's look indicated that he didn't believe in such a concept.

'Sandra Makin,' said Beth. 'She's asked to see you. About her hands.'

But in the end Jack had to go and see Sandra. Although she had made an appointment, and even turned up in reception, she bolted before Jack had a chance to call her in. But Jack wasn't going to let her get away with that. As soon as he could, he too bolted – down to the Makins' cottage.

As he drew up outside the house, he noticed Tom Makin, limping slightly, talking to an older man near the scene of the devastation caused by the gang of obnoxious yuppies. Makin was looking worried. The other man, holding a clipboard in front of him, was making notes. Something about the scene made Jack feel uneasy.

Sandra was not in receptive mood. Only after Jack's repeated apologies for keeping her waiting too long in the waiting-room did she begin to unbend.

They sat in awkward silence at the kitchen table. 'Would

219

you like', began Jack gently, 'to talk to me about your hands?' Sandra stared blankly ahead. 'And about why you feel you need to wash them so often?'

'I . . . I expect you're busy, doctor.'

'No. No, I'm not busy. I'm here. Ready to listen to you. Please, Sandra. Tell me.'

Sandra looked miserably at the floor. 'I know . . . I know I'm not well. In my head. And I . . . I get very confused.'

'And do you feel that you need help to cope with this?'

'Yes.'

'If you like, I can refer you to someone. A specialist. Someone who understands—'

'No!' Sandra looked up in fear. 'I want *you* to help me, doctor.'

Jack nodded. 'All right. Sure.'

Then, suddenly, she blurted out, 'My brother died.'

'Your brother?'

'Yes. My baby brother. He died in hospital. It was an infection, they said.' She looked angrily into her lap. 'I expect someone didn't wash their hands.'

Jack watched her silently. She was close to tears. 'And then . . . and then my baby died. My tiny baby.' She fished for a tissue. 'He didn't even have a name.'

'When was this?'

'Oh . . . I don't know.'

Jack frowned. 'Was it stillborn?'

'Yes. I saw it before they took it away. It was lying there all moist.' She flinched at the memory. 'Like a fish. Like a poor dead fish. I expect . . . I'm sure it was because I was dirty. The doctors said no, but I didn't believe them.' She looked out of the window through misty eyes, at her husband, at the river – at her livelihood. 'And now . . . and now I'm pregnant again. I'm going to have another poor baby.'

Silently, she began to cry.

*

'Does her husband know Sandra's pregnant again?'

'No. Not yet.' Jack put his arm through Kim's. 'Poor woman. She's in a real state. So's her husband – I met him on the way out.'

'A state about her?'

'No. He thinks he's going to get the chop.'

'Why?'

''Cos of all those bloody yuppies and the mess they make. It's not even his bloody fault! It's Holt and his cronies.'

'Is that the Mafia Beth was talking about?'

'Yup. She wasn't kidding about those people, you know.'

'Mmm.'

Then Jack brightened up as they approached The Manor. 'Come on. Happy faces on. This is supposed to be a celebration.'

They were celebrating – or supposed to be celebrating – the offer of their first year's fundholding budget. Will, determined that the occasion should not go unmarked, had pressed on regardless with his surprise party. His phone call to James – about which Beth had been both ignorant and disapproving – had reaped its rewards in the shape of champagne to be followed by a three-course dinner. And everyone had been delighted when Will had sprung that surprise on them. Everyone, that is, except Beth. She had smiled thinly and said that she wasn't sure if she would be able to make it. Even Jack, tackling her later on her own, had been unable to persuade her to commit herself. 'Why should I', she had said, 'celebrate something I don't believe in?'

So, in the private function room at The Manor, they drank their champagne without Beth. Smiling, accepting a glass from James, Will turned to the others. 'I'd just like to say,' he announced, 'with feelings of both pride and relief, that we've done it. We have our budget. And this little get-together this evening is my way of saying thanks to you all for all your hard work. I couldn't have done it without you.' With that, he raised his glass of champagne. 'So here's to it. Here's to a brand new era for The Beeches.'

In unison, the others raised their glasses and cheered. 'The Beeches!'

Then, as the cheers died down into the general murmur of conversation, Will sidled up to Jack. 'Jack. Is Beth coming?'

Jack looked embarrassed. 'She, erm . . . she said she hasn't made up her mind yet.'

'Oh.'

Ten minutes later Jack heard Chloe whispering anxiously to James about the food. Looking at his watch, he sighed in exasperation and reluctantly went up to Will. 'She's obviously not going to turn up, Will. So I suppose we should go ahead and eat.'

Will looked at him strangely for a moment. 'And I suppose', he said, 'I should go ahead and tell you all my other news.' And he did. Gathering the little group around him once again, he made another speech. Only this time there was no tone of triumph in his voice. Instead, quietly and matter-of-factly, he told them that Sarah had gone, that their marriage was over.

His announcement was greeted with a stunned silence. Whatever any of them had expected to hear, it certainly wasn't that. Will smiled uneasily, willing someone to say something. Someone did.

'I thought', said Beth as she rushed, breathless, into the room, 'this was supposed to be a celebration?' She looked, puzzled, at the serious faces around her. 'Why all the glum faces?'

Will went up to her and put a hand on her arm. 'It *is* a celebration, Beth. I think it's probably a double celebration, although it doesn't feel like it at the moment.'

'I don't—'

'It's Sarah, Beth. She's left me. Gone. Our marriage is over.'

'Oh, Will! I don't . . . I don't know what to say.' She looked in concern at Will. 'Now, of all times! Just when things were going so well . . .'

'Not really, Beth.' Will smiled and said, almost to himself, 'I think I was fooling myself about my marriage.' He shrugged. 'Life moves on, you know. Changes. And I think I'll come to see this as a change for the better.'

Beth looked back at him. Suddenly she grinned. 'Yes, I think I will too. Have you got a pen?'

'What?'

'A pen, Will? Have you got one?'

'Why?'

'The budget agreement. I want to sign it.'

chAPTER 14

'And you want to invite them to the wedding?'

'They're very old friends of mine, Jack.'

'But I've never met them.'

'So?' Beth looked at Jack, half in annoyance, half in amusement. 'Am I not allowed a previous life?'

Jack was silent as he steered the car round a particularly sharp bend. Then he looked at Beth and grinned. 'Sorry, yes. You are. I s'pose it would be a bit sad if you'd no surprises for me. After all, we're neither of us spring chickens.'

'Oh, thanks. Remind me to polish my zimmer before I walk up the aisle.'

Jack laughed. 'Sure, no problem. And you can oil my Bath chair while you're at it.'

Beth giggled and looked at her fiancé. This is what it's all about, she thought. Silly, companionable banter. Easy silences. Feeling at one with the person you loved. They were lucky, she thought – even if neither of them was in the first flush of youth. Some people never found true love. And others had to watch in helpless frustration as their dreams were shattered before their eyes.

As if reading her mind, Jack glanced at her. 'Will seems to be bearing up well,' he said.

'Mmm.' Beth thought back to the day, nearly a month ago now, when Will had announced that he and Sarah were finished. 'I never thought Sarah'd do it, you know. Walk out like that.'

'It was for the best, Beth.' He paused. 'Y'know, it must have taken some courage on Sarah's part. I mean . . . I know it was a brutal way to end it all, but *something* had to happen. It can't have been an easy decision for Sarah to make – and it's not like she got a great deal out of it.'

'She got most of the furniture,' said Beth drily.

Jack laughed. 'I know. Imagine! But', he added seriously, 'it's not as if she had anything much to go to. I mean, back with her mother and all that. No job.' He shrugged. 'And it's not as if Will's really wealthy or anything. Whatever else you might say about her, it's not as if she's taken the easy option.'

'No, I s'pose not.' Beth looked appraisingly at Jack. How typical, she thought, and how nice of him. Always trying to see the best in everyone. Privately, Beth wondered just how much Sarah had been – however unwittingly – instrumental in the dismissal of the Makins at the fishing club. Frowning at the memory of their abrupt disappearance, Beth hoped that Sandra Makin, wherever she was now, was getting the psychological help that Jack had so strongly advised. Beth also wondered how much Sarah had been responsible for informing her 'friends' about Chloe's state of health and for sewing the seeds of the takeover of The Manor which had, thankfully, come to nothing. Yet Jack appeared to have forgotten about Sarah's possible indiscretions. Then a new thought occurred to her.

'What about the boys? They've got that one sorted out now, haven't they?'

'I think so. Different school now. Weekdays with Sarah. Weekends with Will.'

'Every weekend? What about when he's on call?'

'Dunno.' Suddenly Jack grinned and turned to her. 'Why? Are you going to offer to baby-sit?'

Beth gave him a withering look and, just as she was trying to drum up a crushing retort to go with it, she was dragged back to the present as she noticed a high brick wall on their right. 'It's after the next bend, Jack.'

Jack gestured to the wall. 'Behind that?'

'Yes. Behind that. I told you they were well off.'

'You didn't tell me they were filthy stinking rich. That's Cardale House, isn't it?'

'Yes.' Beth was quiet as they turned off the road and swept past the imposing gateposts.

Jack whistled as he took in the immaculate, winding driveway and the beautiful parkland. At the end was the gracious Georgian façade of Cardale House and, set behind and at right angles to it, a large and well-kept stable block. 'Nice,' he said.

Beth looked sharply at him. 'They're not the idle rich, you know. In fact I don't think they're even that rich. They started off modestly but they've got real talent—'

'For making money.'

' – For breeding champions and winners.' This time there was no mistaking her warning tone as she added, 'They're a hard-working couple, Jack.'

'OK, OK. Point taken. I promise not to behave like a bolshie Geordie with a chip on my shoulder.' Then he grinned at Beth. 'I suppose I'll have to be terribly well behaved, won't I?'

'Certainly.' Beth grinned back. 'They're *terribly* formal. Even on a Sunday.'

They weren't, of course, in the least bit formal. Jack couldn't fault the friendly manner and easy hospitality of Dominic and Annie Kent. Yet he didn't warm to them. He was painfully aware that they belonged to a different world. Theirs was obviously a life of sophisticated drinks parties, of effortless dinner parties, of easy camaraderie with the landed gentry. Beth, Jack knew, fitted happily into that world when the occasion required, and had sometimes criticized him for his inability – or unwilling-ness, as she saw it – to do likewise. Months ago Jack had decided that it was pointless trying to explain the situation to Beth. The supposed classless society was both a myth and a far cry from the world Jack had been raised in. His parents had lived in one of the most deprived areas of Newcastle, his mother had subsequently abandoned the family and his father had abandoned himself to drink. Education was considered something that got in the way of life, and Jack, in his determination to do something more with his own life, had had to fight every inch of the way to 'better' himself. Had he not been clever and a scholarship-winner, he wouldn't have stood a chance.

Yet Jack had to admit that Annie and Dominic weren't the slightest bit affected. When he and Beth had arrived, they had welcomed him with genuine warmth, ushered them both into a beautiful, antique-filled sitting-room, and served both coffee and small talk. The former had been welcome; Jack had always been hopeless at the latter and it was only when Dominic had suggested a game of indoor bowls that Jack had begun to feel at ease. Sport, the great leveller, had always appealed to him, and finally the ice had begun to break. The 'bowling alley' was, however, a bit of a surprise. Jack had imagined something along the lines of an indoor leisure complex, not a formal drawing room with the antiques shoved against the walls and the Persian rugs rolled up. Jack was slightly thrown by that – and by the fact that the 'bowls' were in fact miniature bean bags. Still, he thought, anyone who hurled proper bowling balls across their parquet flooring would have to be mad.

Dominic rolled up his shirt sleeves, eyed the skittles as one would an enemy, and prepared to pitch a bean bag. 'Stand by and watch the master,' he said. They all laughed good-naturedly: his first turn was a total failure. All the skittles were still standing.

Annie turned, smiling, to Jack. 'I apologize for my husband's competitive spirit—'

'Don't,' interjected Beth. 'You haven't seen Jack yet. He treats all games like a war.'

'Well, this is a war which I've just lost,' said Jack ruefully as he watched Dominic's second bean bag knock all the skittles to the ground.

'Yes! Yes! Yes!' Dominic punched the air gleefully.

Beth raised her eyes in amusement and turned to Annie. 'Where's Victoria? She should be here to see her dad demolish the opposition.'

Annie frowned and looked at her watch. 'She'll be having lunch. It's twelve o'clock.'

'You've got a little girl?' Jack couldn't help sounding surprised. They'd been here nearly two hours now, and this was the first mention of children.

Dominic, already flushed from his success with the skittles, smiled even more broadly. 'Yup.' He looked at his wife. 'Just the one. So far. She's nearly two years old.'

There was a brief silence. Then Annie turned to Jack. 'Dominic lends new meaning to the concept of a doting father. Can't see enough of her.'

'I *don't* see enough of her.' Dominic sounded genuinely peeved.

'Oh?' Jack was puzzled. 'Why?'

'Our nanny', sighed Dominic, 'is very mingy about parental access.'

'A nanny?' Jack could well have been referring to a Martian.

'Yes.' Annie's voice was slightly brittle. 'A nanny.' Then, with a bright smile, she changed the subject. 'Who's on for a swim before lunch?'

Oh, God, thought Jack. A swimming pool. They would.

Dominic ushered them out of the drawing room. 'Great idea. And then you can open your wedding present.'

Beth looked alarmed. 'Not yet! We've got nearly two weeks to go.'

'Ah,' Dominic smiled mysteriously, 'but if you opened it on the day, you'd be very cross indeed.'

Beth and Jack looked at each other; the former with an amused, questioning smile on her lips; Jack with the beginnings of a frown. He had the feeling he was being bought – and he didn't like it.

The indoor swimming pool did nothing to lessen Jack's feelings of alienation. It was everything the brochures claimed a swimming pool should be. Located in a glass extension, with wide doors opening on to a terrace and the garden beyond, it was also fully equipped with all the requisite paraphernalia in the shape of changing rooms, a sauna, and a little cluster of tables and chairs beside the pool. Jack's good humour, however, had been restored by a swim and he was chatting animatedly to Dominic when he noticed Annie, beside him at the poolside table, handing an envelope to Beth.

Beth opened it, examined the letter inside, and then turned to Jack in delight. 'Oh . . . Jack! Look.' She handed the letter to Jack and turned, smiling, to Annie and Dominic. 'I don't know what to say. That's just . . . it's just fabulous!'

'When you said you weren't getting a honeymoon—' began Annie.

'Where's Barnholt House?' interrupted Jack.

Beth turned to him, slightly irritated by his tone. 'About an hour away. It's the country seat of the Holt family.'

Dominic grinned. 'I'm sure it'll meet with your approval, Jack. It's a stunning place and we thought you'd prefer that to a normal wedding present. Wedding night in a four poster,' he continued, 'oyster supper, buffet breakfast in the great hall, a morning hack across the parkland of Derbyshire . . .'

'We were panicking in case you'd got something else fixed up.'

'No.' Jack gave Annie an odd little smile. 'Nothing. Thank you. That's great.'

Dominic, seeing Jack's expression, couldn't help laughing. 'You're appalled, Jack. Come on, it's not exactly as if we're buying you a stately home.' He shrugged. 'It's only one night in a country house hotel.'

Beth, however, determined not to let Jack's ungracious acceptance of the offer spoil the atmosphere, snatched back the envelope. 'He'll love it,' she laughed. 'We'll both absolutely adore it. Thank you both so much.' Then, as if on cue, the nanny walked in. Beth, out of the corner of her eye, saw the little girl, smiling shyly and clinging tightly to her nanny's hand. 'Victoria! Hello there!'

The adults turned to greet the new arrivals. All of them smiled instinctively – except Annie. 'This is Sarah,' she began, 'our indispensable nanny . . .'

'And this,' said Dominic, opening his arms in delight, 'is our first born. Come here, you beautiful creature.' He bent to fondle her hair as she rushed into his arms. 'What have you been doing today, little thing?'

But it was Sarah, not Victoria, who answered. In the clipped tones that spoke of a good public school, an even better training establishment for nannies, and the confident expectation of being, in time, a wealthy mother like Annie, she reeled off Victoria's activities of the morning. Beth, evidently much taken by the little girl, had eyes for nobody else, and it was only Jack who noticed the strange expression that clouded Annie's face as she looked at her daughter.

Then, abruptly, Annie got to her feet, announcing that she was off to look out a suitable horse for Jack, the only learner, for their afternoon's ride.

As she left, Dominic hugged his daughter and looked at Beth. 'Sometimes I just kidnap her from the nursery and we go off together for the day, don't we, Vicky? One day we'll have a clutch of kids and they'll follow me around like puppies . . .'

'I hope you have a clutch of nannies in mind as well,' laughed Sarah.

'None at all,' said Dominic. Then, reluctantly relinquishing Vicky to Sarah and her afternoon nap, he indicated the seat vacated by his wife. 'Annie', he said to Jack and Beth, 'will be much more relaxed with the next one. It's just the first one they're over-anxious about, isn't it?' He nodded to himself. 'She'll be OK with the next. And the next.'

Beth laughed. 'Do I detect a heavy hint?'

Dominic looked affronted. 'Certainly not. I've promised Annie that I won't hint anything to anyone.' Then he winked and continued in a whisper, 'She's two months gone. Not a word to anyone or I'll be in the dog house.'

'I can't think why they want more kids if they just exclude them from everything,' said Jack on the way home.

Beth glared at him. 'Oh, for God's sake, Jack, don't be so judgemental. And don't be so . . . so *prejudiced*. You really were irritating me, you know. You decided not to like them before you even met them. Just because they're rich.'

'I thought you said they weren't rich.'

'Oh, for heaven's sake! You know what I mean. They're comfortable. Nice house. Pool. Stables. Nanny . . .'

'Exactly.' Jack snorted. 'A nanny. Poor child hardly appeared to recognize her mother.'

'Oh, don't be so ridiculous. Anyway, she seemed happy enough, didn't she?'

'Yeah. OK. She did. But *they*'re not.'

'Annie and Dominic?' Beth looked at him in genuine surprise. 'Of course they are. Married seven years and as happy as day one.'

'He may be happy. But she's anything but.'

Beth was so surprised she couldn't reply immediately. Then, in a quiet voice, she asked, 'What makes you say that?'

Jack shrugged. 'Tense. Neurotic. Defensive. Just look a bit deeper than the happy families act, Beth.'

'Humph! You try looking under the surface, too. Try seeing the people under the money. They're *nice* people, Jack, doing their best.'

Jack had to admit she was right. But for a moment he

shifted his attention from the road in front of him and turned, grinning, to his passenger. 'OK, OK. But just leave me alone with my prejudice, woman. I'm comfortable with it.' Then, concentrating anew on his driving, he added seriously, 'But I'm right about your pal Annie. I foresee trouble ahead.'

Jack was right. There was trouble not only ahead, but also behind the story of Annie, Dominic and the question of children. From the day, three years ago, that Annie had discovered she was pregnant with Vicky, she had looked forward with a passion to impending motherhood. She and Dominic – whose excitement was, if possible, greater than her own – had read nearly every book on every aspect of parenting, and both of them had agreed that nine months was far, far too long to wait for the happiest day of their lives.

And then, when that day came, it all went horribly wrong for Annie. The pain of childbirth was both interminable and unimaginable: hours of unmitigated agony trying to give birth to a baby who seemingly did not want to be born. Later Annie had decided that the baby must have had some sort of sixth sense; must have somehow known that she was about to enter a world that was almost perfect in every respect – except the most important one. The baby, she felt, knew that her mother would be incapable of loving her; knew that from the moment she was placed in her arms she would be greeted with bewilderment, panic, fear – and even revulsion.

The fear and the distaste had quickly worn off. The doctors had assured Annie and Dominic that post natal depression was not uncommon and never permanent. Dominic had tried valiantly to understand what Annie was going through. From the moment he had set eyes on Vicky he had been besotted – and had remained that way ever since. He had not worried about Annie: he knew that he would be able to give the baby enough love for both of them until Annie was better. And now, two years after Vicky's arrival, he was still doing just that.

Annie had recovered from the birth, regained her composure, learned to care for Vicky – but not to love her. She had tried, but she had failed. And now, every time she looked at her daughter, she felt nothing but shame. How could she not love the beautiful, sweet-tempered, angelic little girl that even strangers stopped to admire? *Why* were her heart-strings seemingly unconnected to Victoria? Every night now, Annie lay awake, full of self-loathing, and torturing herself with thoughts she didn't dare voice, not even to Dominic. Lately she had tried to imagine Vicky lying dead, just to see if she herself would feel any emotion. And she felt nothing. Then she would imagine Vicky growing up, each year becoming increasingly aware that her mother was cold, cruel and callous. She mentioned none of this to Dominic, she even pretended – successfully for the most part – that nothing was wrong. But privately and secretly she tortured herself, elevating her failings into wickedness – and loathing herself all the more. Her feelings for everything around her became increasingly negative; yet there was one thing she was unwaveringly positive about. She would never put another child through that experience.

The day after Jack and Beth's visit to Cardale House, Annie went to see her doctor. Something about the way Jack had looked at her yesterday spurred her on to this decision. It was as if Jack had been able to see right through her; had been able to read her true feelings. And, with a considerable loss of pride, she tried to explain those feelings to Dr John Reginald at the Health Centre.

Tearful and distressed when she went into his consulting room, she was now getting angry. Like many other private patients, she had assumed that because she paid for her treatment she could get anything she wanted.

She looked across the table at John Reginald. 'Then tell

me a clinic I can go to if you're not going to help me yourself.'

Reginald's normally calm, solicitous expression had vanished after the emotional outburst of the woman before him. Frowning, mindful that he had to tread carefully, he leaned towards Annie and clasped his hands in front of him. 'Any clinic', he began, 'will want to speak to you and your husband.' He sighed. 'Annie, you're in a very emotional state . . .'

'Of course I am! I'm having a child I don't want. I've already got one. I've got a business to run—'

'Come in with Dominic and we'll discuss it—'

'No! It's my body, my pregnancy. Where's the woman's right to an abortion gone to?'

'I'm a doctor, Annie, not a butcher. I don't do what the patient demands regardless of my responsibilities . . .'

'But I'm a paying customer!'

Reginald looked stonily back at her. 'The fact that you're a private patient doesn't entitle me to neglect your care.'

'You took me off the pill and now you walk away from the result.'

'You had a thrombosis, Annie. And you agreed . . .'

'You said the other methods were safe,' challenged Annie.

Reginald sighed. Was he to be held directly responsible for her pregnancy? 'These things happen. I'm sorry, but they do. And, Annie, I can't terminate a pregnancy unless I'm sure you understand all the implications.'

'I do. Do I look like I don't know what I'm doing?'

Reginald didn't reply. Distressed she might be, but he had to concede to himself that she seemed in control.

Annie used the brief silence to take stock. Then, in a cold, hard voice, she continued, 'I do not love my child. I feel nothing for her. What sort of a start in life is that? She's not even two yet but she knows. How can I do the same thing all over again to another baby? Stand watching it cry and feel nothing except annoyed.' She stopped, suddenly remembering Jack's face. 'We had a visitor yesterday. He knew. I could tell.'

'That's silly.'

Annie had had enough. She stood up and glared at the doctor. 'I don't need another man telling me I'm silly. What do I need to get an abortion at a private clinic?'

'A referral from your GP.'

'And you won't give me one?'

'At the moment, no.'

Annie turned towards the door. 'I don't want Dominic told about my wish to have a termination. I hope you'll respect my confidence?'

At least, thought Reginald, that was one positive response he could give her. 'Of course I will.' Then, getting to his feet and crossing to open the door for her, he added, 'Can I call you at home later?'

'No. I won't be there.'

Beth smiled at Will as he hurried into reception. 'How was your weekend?'

'Fraught.' He paused, evidently unsure whether or not to joke about it. 'The boys', he continued, with a lop-sided smile, 'are determined to make life as difficult as possible for me.'

Beth made a sympathetic face. 'It'll pass,' she said. 'I don't suppose they're finding this separation any easier than you are.'

Will looked surprised. 'I'm not finding it difficult! It's actually what I've wanted for ages. It's . . . it's . . .' Then he smiled. 'Yes, you're right, it's not particularly easy. But it is *right*.'

Will still had very mixed feelings about the sudden and dramatic break-up of his marriage. Initially, after the shock and anger had worn off, he'd been filled with remorse. Perhaps it had been his fault Sarah was so unhappy? Surely, he had thought, they could have worked things out? And then he remembered how many times they'd trodden that route before. He remembered the pain they were causing Tony and Julian. He remembered Sarah's blatant betrayal of him, her indiscretions and her tantrums. He remembered how many times he'd wished he'd had the strength to 'sort her out'.

But it had been Sarah who'd sorted herself out. As soon as he received her letter, as soon as he learned that she'd left the only way she knew how, that she'd taken the boys because she hadn't wanted them to witness a final, cataclysmic screaming match, he had been able to understand her behaviour. And the strange thing was, they were now getting along quite amicably. Now that neither of them had to endure the strain of pretending all was well, everything had become, oddly enough, substantially better.

And now they were both in accord over what would happen. Their separation would be permanent, followed by a divorce. They had finally reached the end of the road. The boys, they had both naively thought, would be pleased. No more bickering, no more tempers flaring – only two serene and separate parents. With Sarah now ensconced at her mother's in Lancashire, the boys would be able to divide their time between both parents, seeing each at their best. Neither Sarah nor Will had bargained for the fact that Tony and Julian were determined to make life hell for both of them. They felt hurt, and betrayed, and they were determined to apportion blame wherever they could. Will's weekend had been terrible: every suggestion he had made had been met with a derisive snort and snide remarks about how separated parents were supposed to behave with their children. Evidently they were supposed to spoil them rotten and give in to their every whim.

Will, realizing he had been staring vacantly at Beth, smiled suddenly. 'Yeah. You're right, it'll pass.' He sighed, 'I must say I do love those boys but I do wonder why the hell I ever got married.'

'I know why I'm getting married,' said Beth.

Will looked at her, realizing he had been less than tactful. 'So do I,' he said quickly. 'Your reasons are kosher. You're madly in love.'

Beth started to say something, but changed her mind as Kim joined them with a cheery 'Good morning'. Then Beth grinned. 'No,' she said, 'that's not it. We just need a new toaster.'

Will burst our laughing. Kim, hearing the word 'toaster', did likewise.

The Beeches' staff, madly excited by Jack and Beth's impending marriage, had been deeply disapproving about the absence of a wedding list. Kim had been nothing less than horrified. 'You *must* have a list,' she had said. 'How else will we know what to buy you?' Both Jack and Beth had been adamant that they didn't want anything – especially not a toaster. They already had two fully equipped houses and there was nothing either of them needed. Jack had told Ellie that if she was really determined to part with money she could buy him a new silencer for his car. Ellie's reply had been unprintable.

'You'll be getting eighteen toasters at this rate,' said Kim disapprovingly as their laughter subsided.

'Hardly,' said Beth. 'We're not even having eighteen guests.'

Kim snorted. That was another bone of contention. Weddings, in her book, were lavish affairs, and she was aghast at Jack and Beth's plans to have a quick, low-key service in Cardale Parish Church followed by lunch at The Manor. Admittedly it was to be an elaborate, champagne lunch that already had James drooling. But it was not, as far as Kim was concerned, a proper reception. When she heard, later in the day, of Annie and Dominic Kent's gift of a five-star wedding-night, she was slightly mollified.

'Well,' said Beth, 'no time to stand about chatting. I've got calls to make.'

'Rather you than me,' said Will, looking out of the window. 'Another typical tropical morning.'

Beth followed his glance and grimaced. The weather *was* typical for Cardale. Cold, damp, drizzling and windy was about the best that could be said for it.

As she draped her coat over her shoulders, Beth silently reiterated the only wish she had made for her wedding-day – a plea for sunshine. The rest she was quietly confident about. She was going to marry the man she loved. Their union would be blessed in the presence of her closest friends, and toasted in the warm intimacy of The Manor. That last thought brought a smile to her lips as she dashed through the rain towards her car. Jack, that morning, was going to impart some pretty good news to the chatelaine of The Manor.

Jack grinned broadly as, two hours later, Chloe walked into his surgery. 'Make yourself comfortable,' he gestured, 'and get ready to give us a great big smile.'

Chloe smiled uncertainly. 'Really?'

'Really.' Jack bent his head and examined Chloe's notes as she perched uneasily on the seat opposite. The notes in front of him were the results of the six-month tests that Chloe had undergone. Whatever they said would be crucial – and Chloe knew it. 'Your first checks', he continued, 'are everything we could hope for. Your cell count's greatly improved and that's the pointer we're looking for.' He looked up at Chloe. She blinked. 'Shall I show you the figures?'

Chloe sniffed and brushed a hand over her eyes. 'No. They don't mean anything to me anyway.'

Jack paused and then gestured towards the phone. 'Want to call James?'

'I'll tell him when I get home.' She smiled through the tears that, in the end, she was unable to prevent. 'I'm sorry,' she sniffed.

Jack didn't say anything. There was nothing to say.

Allowing her to cry but not remarking on it, he waited until she had regained a measure of composure and continued. 'The cell count shows that we've knocked the disease on the head. Stunned it with the chemotherapy and radiation. Now there's a break from treatment while you go through a series of tests.'

'CAT scan and all that, you mean?'

Jack grinned. 'Little Miss Oncology Expert. Yes, that's right.'

Chloe laughed suddenly. 'I feel like celebrating.'

'Why not? You deserve it. Celebrate every step of the way.' Then Jack too laughed. 'And you do live in a pub . . .'

Chloe's tears started again. Yet through them, she was still laughing. 'Sorry, Jack. I don't know whether I'm laughing or crying.'

'You're doing both, Chloe. And you're doing both just fine.'

After Chloe's departure – again amidst a flurry of tears and laughter – Jack himself gave way to emotion. He could understand Chloe's reaction. So much pent-up fear and frustration; so much hope; so much willpower: so much of everything had happened to Chloe in the last six months that the first piece of positive good news was difficult to cope with, even difficult to believe. Yet there was every chance that Chloe's further scan and blood count would reveal that she was in 'confirmed complete remission'. It would mean that she had beaten Hodgkin's disease.

Jack's next patient, when he had seen her name in the appointment book, had come as a complete surprise. Kim had apologetically explained that the woman had been insistent, both in her wish to register at The Beeches, and in her claim that Jack, as a friend, would agree to see her at short notice. Jack had stared in disbelief. The woman's name was Annie Handscombe.

And now here she was, in the middle of a half-tearful, half-truculent confession. Jack, listening carefully, now regretted his slightly smug 'I foresee trouble ahead' to Beth. Annie was indeed in trouble and she was in danger, Jack suspected, of falling apart at the seams.

'John Reginald cares about us as a couple,' she was saying. 'Beth sees us as a sort of ideal family. But you don't even like us . . .' Seeing that Jack was trying to stammer a denial, she waved his protestations aside and even smiled slightly. 'It's all right. You were terribly polite, but I could see.'

'I'm sorry I gave you that impression,' said Jack evenly. 'You were very welcoming.'

But Annie ignored him. 'So I thought maybe *you*'d made a clinical decision rather than an emotional one.' She stared belligerently at him. 'Well?'

'Easier said than done.'

'If I was single you'd refer me, wouldn't you? No questions asked.'

'No, Annie. I wouldn't. I'd still want to talk to you.'

'Fine. So now you've talked to me.' Her eyes narrowed as she looked at him. 'What you really mean is, you want to talk to Dominic.'

'Annie.' Jack sighed and leaned towards her. 'If you want me to be your doctor, I will. If you want me to be a rubber stamp for any surgical procedure you choose, forget it.'

Annie's voice was almost dangerously quiet as she replied, 'You have no idea what this is doing to me.'

'Then tell me. Please.'

'You're all raping me!' Annie was shouting now. 'Dominic, Reginald, Beth, if she knew, the child, you . . . You've taken over my body, haven't you? It's *my* body! I can't stand living in it any more! I can't stand having this baby in it. I don't *want* this baby! It will have a terrible life. It'll look at me as soon as it's born and it will hate me. And I will hate it.' Her last words made Jack wince slightly. She noticed his reaction and added, 'Are you shocked?'

'Yes.'

'So am I. I never imagined I could be like this, but I am – and now I feel like some Victorian spinster begging permission to take control of her life.' She folded her hands in front of her. 'It's the end of the twentieth century and here I am.'

'Yes.' Jack looked thoughtfully at the distraught woman in front of him. 'Can you tell me anything about Victoria's birth?'

'No.'

'Was it a bad experience?'

Annie gestured dismissively. 'That was then. This is now. This is different. It's not Victoria's fault, it's mine. If I don't get this abortion soon,' she added calmly, 'I'll kill myself.'

'All right then,' said Jack. 'I'll call a clinic and refer you.' Annie just stared in complete surprise as he went on. 'I'll recommend that the operation be performed no sooner than a week from today. What you do with that week is up to you but I advise you to talk to Dominic, to go into this together.'

'Is that it?'

'They'll want to meet you and come to their own decision. But I'll back you up as a medical abortion. I'll also have to tell Dr Reginald what I'm doing.'

'Why?'

'Because you were his patient and with my help you're going against his advice.' With that he reached for his phone and started dialling the clinic. 'I wish you and Dominic weren't giving us our one-night honeymoon, you know. What I'm doing now may just cause Beth some embarrassment.'

CH**A**PTER 15

'Embarrassment?' Beth was gibbering with rage as she rounded on Jack. 'Try anger, Jack! Mixed with incredulity and rage. Try imagining how I felt when Dominic rang me up . . .'

'I didn't know he'd ring you up.'

'No, you didn't, did you? I don't suppose you even thought of the position you were putting me in!'

'Beth . . . Come on. I take new patients every day. Am I supposed to run in and tell you about them all the time?'

'Don't be naive,' snapped Beth. 'Annie's not a run-of-the-mill new patient.' She paused and looked disbelievingly at Jack. 'She's my friend, and you don't even *know* her.'

'But how many of your patients do you really know? We listen to what they tell us and make a clinical judgement. Which is exactly what she asked me to do.'

'But why did you decide there and then? What's the big rush?'

'Because she told me—' Jack stopped, biting back his retort. Then he shrugged in apology. 'She's a patient, Beth, and she spoke to me in confidence. I've said what action I've taken and that's it. I'm sorry.'

'You really are the most infuriating bloody man I've ever met!' shouted Beth. 'I really don't think you've any idea what sort of position you've put everyone in!' Then, as if in afterthought, she added quietly, 'And I don't suppose you've any idea what day the clinic have scheduled her operation?'

'Course I do.' Jack was offended. 'I don't wash my hands of my patients as soon as they walk out of the door you know. She's having the operation on . . . Oh, my

God!' Jack's hand flew to his mouth as he realized the significance of the day.

'Exactly!' Beth stormed over to the door and wrenched it open. 'Our wedding day.'

Beth couldn't decide what upset her most: the fact that Annie was going to have an abortion, or the fact that it had been arranged by Jack and without her knowledge. Her phone conversation and subsequent meeting with Dominic had been, at the very least, highly revelatory. In the few days since Annie's consultation with Jack the Kents' lives had been turned upside down. Yet, curiously, they had not fallen apart.

Beth's prolonged conversation with Dominic had been both sad and satisfying. Dominic admitted that when Annie had told him what she'd done, he had wanted to kill her. Then he had conceded that, in his desperation to extend their family, he had turned a blind eye to Annie's distress, to her problems with Victoria, to her terrors about the new baby. And by the time Beth bade him an affectionate farewell, she was convinced that Dominic now understood his wife better than he had ever done before. Although Annie had moved to a hotel to await the operation, she and Dominic had met every day. With a wry smile, Dominic had said it was like courtship all over again – but a courtship with a cloud hanging over it. Dominic, for all his genuine understanding, for all his reluctant cooperation in the abortion, wasn't sure that he would ever be able to forgive his wife.

Annie, when Beth visited her the day of her confrontation with Jack, was calmer than she had been for weeks. At once sad, fatalistic, depressed and hopeful, she was, Beth noticed, unable to talk about anything else except for Dominic and Vicky. How were they? she asked. Was Dominic coping? Was Vicky missing her? Did Vicky know where she was? And – obviously uppermost in her mind –

would Dominic ever be able to forgive her? Beth had avoided the last question. Nothing could alter the desperately sad situation the Kents had found themselves in. Annie's agonized decision would be with them for the rest of their lives.

Jack turned over in bed as Beth came out of the bathroom. 'Are you still talking to me?'

Beth pretended to consider his question as she turned out the light and threw her dressing gown to the floor. Jack's hair was standing on end. It made her want to giggle. Could one be angry with someone who looked so silly?

'Well,' she said as she snuggled up beside him. 'I've been thinking.'

'Oh?'

'I've been thinking that if we sulk every time we have a disagreement we'd have a very silent marriage.'

'Oh dear. Yes, we would.'

'So, I've forgiven you. In fact,' Beth sounded serious for a moment, 'you were right to refer her. I'd have done the same myself if I'd known. I hadn't realized how distressed she was.'

'Mmm. But I should have told Annie I'd be keeping you informed. I could have handled it better.'

Beth grinned and gently touched his face. 'That wasn't you. That was my bloody junior partner. You're my soon-to-be-husband.'

'The one you're talking to?'

'Actually, it wasn't conversation I had in mind.'

Two days later Beth received two gifts from Jack. The first one made her laugh – it was a toaster. The second, much to her surprise, brought tears to her eyes – it was his hand in marriage. She had vaguely supposed that grown women

244

didn't come over all emotional at their own weddings – but she had been wrong. Walking down the aisle with Jack, she realized that this was the most emotional, and the most wonderful day of her life. She was, she knew, grinning stupidly, and she couldn't help it.

As she walked she noticed the faces of those around her. Will, grinning broadly. Isabel, looking slightly peeved (the photographer had mistaken her for Beth's mother). Chloe, looking radiant. James, giving Jack a thumbs-up sign. And there were the The Beeches' staff, all smiling happily. And further back, Alice North was positively beaming, Trevor and Leanda were looking tired, Rob Clulow was looking forward to a drink, Ken Alton was looking for Isabel and practically the entire population of Cardale was looking at the newly-weds. It had never occurred to Beth that so many people would attend their wedding service. It had never occurred to her that she and Jack were the most popular couple for miles around.

She looked at Jack. He was, like her, grinning stupidly. He raised his eyebrows, as if to say 'I can't help it'. And then, as they stepped outside into the glorious sunshine, Beth thought fleetingly of the Kents. Suddenly she knew that they would be all right. Annie and Dominic may have found themselves in the most appalling situation, but somehow they would weather the storm. They loved each other and love, she knew, conquered all. Her smile broadened as she made a mental note not to tell that to Jack. It would go to his head and he had, she felt, quite enough to be pleased about at the moment.